This is the Moon

fictions by
Michael L. Woodruff

[handwritten inscription] Tina —
Create life!
Thanks
Michael D. Woodruff

OAB
Orange Avenue Books
Lincoln, Nebraska

Acknowledgements

A special thank you goes out to Laura Landress, Cheryl Wheelright and Daryl Brende for the work they put into this book.

Great appreciation goes to Della for putting up with me when I hid behind my office door to write.

The portrait of the little girl on the front cover of this book is Leah Gustafson, the granddaughter of Della and Michael Woodruff.

Credits:

The Pioneer Spirit Lives: Mayetta Centennial in "Smoke"

Cover Artwork: Della Woodruff

Book Layout and cover design: 10000 Cranes Studio

Printing by: Bang Printing

Library of Congress Control Number: 2010940100

ISBN: 978-0-615-41610-6

1st Printing

For Della

THIS IS THE MOON

"I wander the island, inventing it."
- Robert Coover

"It is sophism to imagine that there is any strict dividing line between the waking world and the world of dreams."

- Lawrence Durrell

I start my sleep with nice, sweet narcissistic thoughts that create comfort, a lullaby, like playing in a rock band before a group of my friends, my fingers lambent along steel strings I could never caress until this night. There are stunned reactions in the audience, all white-eyed and confused, and I push myself beyond all the reasons why I should be able to play, but I am all the reasons I need tonight. I manipulate the moments, and after working through my limitless potential, the musical repetition overcoming my thoughts, I begin to imagine, and my thoughts are like water bubbling out the top of a radiator into a reservoir, a strange mixture of desire and curiosity.

I pour out into a void of a thousand possibilities.

These are expanding thoughts, words that fill, finding their form, stumbling into the shuffle of space, wedged between fact and fiction, and a satisfied Descartes slips somewhere between the thin slices of air saying that all images come from something we nearly know. These are ideas conceived through a darkened glass. They have the potential for an ever-cascading illumination. But it's ultimately left to me, in my murky pool of verbiage, to pull the fragmented semantics together like an awkward jigsaw puzzle, and in the end, I lose the continence needed to manipulate the forms; I drift like a clownish wraith in and out of these shades of silent darkness. It takes so much more than mere language to convey an idea. I'm not ashamed to confess that I occasionally misappropriate my thoughts liked a red-eyed sage fumbling absent-mindedly through a stack of dusty books.

So I learn to dwell.

How I dwell melts quickly into a slippery yearning, and this yearning nurtures a myriad of satisfactions, all surprising my ability to control. I always continue to need, to take, and to own what pours out of my head.

My mind empties out all the excesses of the previous day. I'm as light as the air that floats me.

I don't know why I could never ride in a convertible without floating upward, my hands reaching back to grab the steering wheel, going up and growing up, being pulled into the white translucence of the sky. I knew I could never fall far enough to hit the ground because falling is a constant. It is a form of release, letting go, like attempting to ride a rickety bicycle for the first time, collapsing and skinning my knee, and this is okay, because as long as I am always something that falls, then I can never be at rest. As long as I have kinetic potential, I can never cease to be something, and being something is life.

I fall until everything becomes silent and I am propelled into a blinding moment, sustained by the calm that pushes against me.

It is the loudest silence I have ever endured, my ears filling with density, like the muted stampede of a trillion red ants biting and stinging my body, and they pound out a prophetic thought: I am...I was...I will be, forever and ever. Amen.

I embrace my ego, and in frequent ways, I attempt to impose it on the silences pushing up against me. This has always been my secret success for living out loud. I avoid the too much, the too obvious, and I give birth to a subtle prudence. Even here there are liquid forms of principles and mores that agitate the guilt I file away, and even if it comes from a place I have never understood, I succumb to it and dissolve. I spend multiple eternities tunneling through my flawed skin to stretch it into recognizable forms. I am unceasing in my persistence, in the unrelenting obsession it takes to find the costume designer who passes out this flesh.

I find ways to create twinkles of fascination between my will and my need to scratch out a path that sustains.

The older I get the more I diminish in my blinking world, and the more I expand in a world within myself, solipsistic, but this is too much thinking. Lately, revelations often come down to what I ate the night before, a biological impulse.

I count, I collect, and I take inventory of nothing in particular. It's all mental masturbation. It's like counting the alphabet in a less than random order and an anxious suspicion tells me a broken letter has fallen out of the stew and stiffened. Damn it all! There's no time to dilly dally in this confused kitchen, to consider the lost possibilities, nonetheless the demise of a single alphabet; that would be regret, and regret can only rust the literary gears already put into motion.

I consider why the shepherd has empty fields of green grass on a bright sunny day. He picks at his lute on what would otherwise be considered a quiet hill. Sheep are not as soft as I've always been inclined to believe, but thick and stubborn, and they can always be tucked away somewhere for later consideration, like between the knees of a softer savior. My mind is trying to catch the lift of a theme to take me to the next envelopment, like the philosopher's mind that grows wings, cloud to cloud, to my next journey. Even writing it all down on paper disturbs the purity of each confused moment, like when I follow the lines of purple in my veins, up my arm, until my blood escapes the skin to meet the cold oxygen, suspended in the cold air, turning red. The purity of the blood is always compromised the moment it mixes with the air we breathe.

What am I thinking about?

I want to say nothing, but it is everything I nearly know that has not found a home in my blinking life.

How can you be thinking about nothing, you ask?

Did I say nothing? Okay, I meant I try to think about a nothing that I don't have to explain, but somehow, I always have to explain everything, and it comes out like drivel, disconnected, void of reason. It's a persistence that always finds a way to disturb each vulnerable moment. There's no way to ignore the clarity of awareness, even if it does suspend the revelations I've always been hurried to embrace. It comes slower, like drips, constant, and it irritates my skin.

It's like when I stare at an indiscernible point in front of me, beyond me, at a blurred something I can't focus on, and someone close by always finds the conviction to break my concentration. It is the only disruptive moment I've ever had that compelled me toward an understanding that, in the end, someone really does care about what I am doing. Empathy is the invasion of the most private moment.

I prepare to slip into sleep. I belt my will so tightly I can't think, and it becomes as light as an imagined kiss. I am afraid to allow my thoughts to rein free: consider the things I am likely to say. I want to manipulate each moment. I know the delicate implications, even if I can't articulate them. Falling asleep is like trying to grasp the night before it means too much.

I reach for the big idea like the forced revelation of the great Plotinus, who seethes in his own spiritual ambition without knowing it. I try not to limit my potential to the "One" thing.

What I crave is much different than what I want and my mind turns out the desire until I can't understand what I truly need. And then, I finally give in, letting it all go, falling into a deep sleep.

Conticinio, the dead of night, the night's perfect oblivion. *I wait for the veil of a Venezuelan lover to be dragged across my skin, a song that tears up while I wait for the purity of night to settle around me.*

A love chirp from a lone cricket addresses the quiet of the still-dark of the early morning air. Stars reflect like glass. The yellow-stained moon freezes in time. The void undresses all expectations, and my mind ferments in its own soft rime, its own perfect peace. Call it the great universal bus stop, Nirvana, but I'm not a religious man. But surely, given the slip of a little reason, it is a taste of the eternal moment I have heard so much about that is always so suspiciously diverted to eccentric paths where no one chooses to travel, an unkempt road filled with wild daisies.

How could death be so different, especially, if we are constantly sliding in and out of spaces that compel us forward to an irreversible surrender? None of it lasts quite long enough for my benefit, but it's a reminder of where I belong, of where I once again will be.

In conticinio, I am naked, vulnerable, and I truly believe.

The Dream

I was living in an old Streamline trailer with Joan Crawford, an obsessive woman, who tried to control every detail of my tentative thoughts. She was the old Joan Crawford, not the young Joan Crawford, some kind of odd Freudian filter working through my conscious to configure issues I have never addressed in my past, or so I've been told. She stomped through her small terra like the matron of a dusty estate. The inside of the trailer had an often ruminated cleanliness, emasculated by pink paneling and lots of wooden hangers stacked neatly on the counters. The carpet was lavender.

"Did I say lavender?"

Anyway, it smelled new.

I believe I dream in color and receive scents. My mind is slicing out realities, portioned to serve, easy to handle with the delicate fingers I brandish in this uncertain space. Self-deception has a certain romance to it, and I embrace it like someone I pretend to remember. It is always good to see mists of my past that soon disappear. I have no way of really knowing, and not knowing completes the reckless connections I make with all the small things I continue to wrestle with throughout my blinking life.

There was someone else living in the trailer. She was a younger woman, and

I didn't see her face at first because she was quietly filed away in a distant room. She started to scream about something darting through the trailer, something terrible. So when I did finally see her for the first time it was through the eyes of Joan Crawford, sifting through my reality to make sure I didn't see anything pretty enough to store in my future recollections. But some things you just can't hide like the obvious.

"There is an alien in the trailer," the young woman cried. And she threw her arms around me searching for comfort.

"This is not fair," Joan Crawford accused. *She could hear the other woman's thoughts piercing my mind like a sharp blade. It disturbed all her sensibilities. Joan Crawford was everywhere like the thick air around me, omnipresent. There was no room for others.*

"This is an overt attempt to position your sympathies firmly on a privileged list you don't belong on," Joan Crawford accused.

The young woman ignored her, looking through her imagined importance.

"I saw the hideous thing creeping along the wall," the young woman said.

"How big was it?" I asked.

"This big," the young woman said.

She held the palms of her hands vertically apart about the length of a milk bottle.

"How strange," I said, "that you didn't define the length of the alien horizontally, like most men do when telling a big fish story."

"Well, I'm not a man," the young woman stated. "I have the resources to expand."

The young woman was an innocent lamb, ripe for the slaughter. She never learned the advantages of a well-placed lie.

"I don't know why you insist that there is anything here other than you and me," Joan Crawford said. *She squeezed herself between thoughts that diverted my attentions.*

"It has to be here somewhere," I said. "You can't have an idea about something that doesn't exist."

I never gave it a second thought. Descartes would have loved my resolve.

Joan Crawford stomped away, stalking the hint of perfume drifting through the trailer.

I ran to my bedroom and grabbed a gun out of the dresser drawer. Joan Crawford caught me as I started to walk down the hallway.

"Where did you get the gun?" she asked.

"I have kept it at bay, saving it for these accumulated moments, for these distressed periods in history when action is fully required," I said. "So back it

11

off. I have man's work to do. And there is no counting the impatient seconds that include your involvement."

I pushed my way through each door, through each room, smelling the stifled air that assaulted me everywhere I went, and finally, there it was, standing helpless against one of the bedroom walls, looking up at me. Its big black eyes were as empty and as thoughtless as a dried up well. It looked like a small alien, but how was I really to know what an alien looked like? At least it was the alien I imagined. Descartes would have demanded references to make this connection and I was certain that the damned thing didn't have a dime to its name. One thing was for certain; it didn't look like anything I have ever seen on the television set, and this was the ultimate standard for all the truths I embraced. I wanted a heaving Martian, complete with a Roman dress helmet, chasing a talking rabbit to the edge of a slice of cheese.

I herded the little critter into the guest bathroom, a room that was never used, backed it up with the barrel of my gun into the bathtub where I shot it twice. Pop. Pop. It sounded like the death of a distant god, but then I never really entertained the sanctity of the same selfless instincts embraced by torrents of the dispossessed. I could never let myself go on those festive nights, burning with loosened emotions that were difficult to control like a flickering candle, melting, until it diminished into hot pools of revelation. Well, to be honest, I'm afraid I'd drown in my own salvation.

But I have to confess it was a mistake to kill the critter because I put a bullet hole into the fiberglass tub, goo splattered all over the pink tile, and when Joan Crawford walked into the bathroom to investigate the noise, she got mad, accusatory, like what I had done went against all natural instinct. I should have just kicked the damned creature out the back door when I had the chance, dusted off the soles of my shoes, and let it burrow a new life in the brush that grew along the property line. Could have, should have, the best things to do never really unveil themselves at the most appropriate times. My life is full of hindsight.

I guess it was some kind of a pet to Joan Crawford, at least she knew the little critter well, called it by its name, Augustine, the forgotten truth, and she made me clean up the mess with a vacuum cleaner that had a clear canister, and when I turned it on and moved the hose toward the alien it suck up the alien's body and swirled it around in the container, making it into a dulled-green smoothie. I left the vacuum cleaner by the front door.

"I'll take it out in the morning with the trash," I said.

"You've said that a hundred times in the past," Joan Crawford accused. "Promises are a very relaxed endearment in your predicaments."

I looked at the hair on my wrist and paced nervously along the paneled wall. Why is pink such a claustrophobic color?

"Listen, it's time for me to go to school," I said. I can't be late."

"School?" Joan Crawford asked.

"Yes, school," I said. "You surely didn't think I would be living here under the current conditions without numbered reasons?"

She looked hurt.

"You never went to school before," she said.

"I never thought I would need to go to school until now. This is something new under the sun," I said. "I'm tired of drowning in my own ignorance. I can't swim fast enough to keep my head above the pages."

My moments are like a splendid inertia. They race faster than the speed of reason, and my thoughts bend.

"You are coming back?" she asked.

"I can never tell," I said. "I don't have any other spaces to go, but things are certain to change. Given the misfortunes I have piled up I am certain to be slipped a promise or two."

"That's good." She sounded satisfied. "I will order some Chinese take-out. Can you grab a bottle of Pepsi on your way home tonight?"

"Pepsi?"

It was as clear as the mist in my eyes; the Pepsi bottle was my ticket back into her moment, back to the younger Joan Crawford, complete with all the psychotic passion and abandonment, and it surrounded her more likeable successes. It was very tempting.

"Do you want regular or diet?" I asked.

"It doesn't matter."

Ah, now I get it. She broods for my demise.

I walked across the campus. It was looming with kids half my age. I was stopped by a custom Jesus dragging a cross through the middle of the campus square.

"Blessed be the Lamb of God who takes away the sins of the world!" he cried out. His words stuck to the bodies that past him like a limp threat. I was told his comment was a Hebrew proverb meaning, "mutton is served."

I ask him where I could find the Fine Arts building. He scratched the scalp between the thorns in his head.

"Oh, I think it is on top of the hill on the other side of the University," he *said. "It's on my way, so follow me."*

So I did follow him for an uncertain period in time, at least until I was able to navigate my own way, to my own hill, and we parted friends. I promised him I would write if I were ever consumed by my own distress, but I never did. It was easier to just fight the fight, balls to the wall, in my own way, through all the disappointments that tried to confuse my efforts. But it didn't stop me from wondering, now and then, whatever happened to him and his cross. He bared it well.

I stumbled into a part-time job as a cashier in the campus bookstore. It was a huge store with rows and rows of checkout lines stretching out into a disappointing horizon of light, and the store had a small brown and white beagle training people how to do their jobs. I was certain that it was a daunting responsibility for any dog, nonetheless a beagle, but he appeared capable of rising to every occasion.

The cash registers had a lot of complicated buttons, pictures, and the dog was the only one who had access to all the codes. The wheel of power and control consumed his every twitch of a whisker.

Every time my fingers hung nervously over the keyboard the beagle stood on all four feet and wagged his tail for the go-ahead. It was unnerving. I began to feel an increasing uncertainty, and it strangled all my initiative, and so each time I began to punch in a cash sale I looked over at the beagle first for validation to make sure I wasn't doing anything wrong. The dog gave me blank looks, his tongue lapping with satisfaction, tail wagging, which told me I was doing fine, or at the very least, average, ensuring the conventional performance review needed to keep me humbled.

Inevitably, those damned impulses that always overcome my reason, those damned struggles for the extension of the individual inside me careening for expression, intervened, and I keyed in a series of pictures before consulting the beagle, hoping to slip through a lazy sale, and the dog barked. Arff. I jumped, nearly wetting my pants, and then I turned to one of the other trainees next to me and said," Damn it, that beagle is good."

There is an approaching awareness that swims through my body, and it lifts. I'm paralyzed in my bed, wanting more. I can travel a million miles each night just lying here, beneath the covers, in the comfort of my blankets, like

Oblomov watching the world dust up around him. I can see for days in front of me when I dream. So I wait, and disappointed, like the feeling I get at the end of an amusement park ride, I peel the bedcovers away from my body, and I rise.

Mundo lived in a broken-down trailer house across the street from the First Christian Church of the Forgiven Believers. I imagined the bells, in the scarred gothic tower, shaking his family's small tinderbox three times a day like a tin can full of jacks, rattling glasses and plates in their cupboards and loosening every screw and bolt that held their fragile box together.

Mundo's family didn't attend church. That might have been part of the problem. They were distanced from the faithful. They professed to be Episcopalians, but there wasn't an Episcopalian Church within forty miles of our small town. So, in many people's minds, they had excommunicated themselves from the grace of God.

I can't remember anyone from our church ever inviting Mundo's family to Sunday services, even though they lived just across the street. I figured it was probably embarrassing enough for most people that they lived right there, in front of the church, eyeball to eyeball to God. They kept themselves separate from the community like recluses. They only socialized through mandatory school events, parent/teacher conferences, but inside their trailer there were continual outbursts of life that echoed down the street and into the homes of their neighbors:

His father: What the hell is wrong with you son, can't you use the brains that God gave you?

His sister: Mom, Mundo is playing with my underwear! I don't have any privacy!

His father: I can't find a damned thing around here!

His sister: I hate you; I wish you were all dead!

His mother: Please! Just stop it!

Their arguments were so loud that even the most ardent believers in the First Church of the Forgiven Believers had difficulty concentrating on Sunday prayers and hymns, turning the pages of their Bibles nervously and whispering their displeasure just under their breath.

"Oh my, such a horrid family."

But for the most part, Mundo's trailer was shut tight against the morning chill while the congregation poured into their pews on Sunday morning.

I have only been in Mundo's trailer a handful of times. He usually made me wait outside while he went briefly into his home to get whatever he needed. But the few times I went inside, the small trailer was warm and thick with human proximity. It was dark and dull, and light bulbs, hidden behind dusty lampshades fought for a breath of space.

His mother was usually sitting at the kitchen table crowded by clutter, her legs spread open to balance her lazy stomach, her dress drooping between her white knobby knees. There were plates and opened boxes of cereal in front of her. The entire kitchen counter, on either side of the sink, was piled with dirty pots and pans.

"Trace, can I make you something to eat?" his mother asked.

"No Ma'am," I said.

"I wish you would eat, dear," she said. "You look so thin."

"That's okay, Ma'am," I said. "I had lunch before I came over."

"Call me Mom, please," she said. I could tell this was important to her.

"Okay, Mom," I said. She gleamed.

I was always embarrassed for his mother, and so was Mundo. But she was always kind to me, and I know it was important to her that Mundo and I stayed close.

His father sat in the living room, his newspaper snapping in front of his face. An unlit pipe hung in his mouth, and his feet scooted to the edge of the coffee table which was piled high with old newspapers, books, and drinking glasses.

I remembered Mundo's older sister coming down the hallway in an over-sized T-shirt. She was soft looking. She had pink cheeks and her breasts bounced behind her thin T-shirt. The T-shirt sneaked up the side of her hips. It looked like it was trying to crawl up her body. Her thick legs were already mature, like an older woman's legs. They were ripe. We always looked at each other too much when I was there. She was two years older than I. I don't ever remember her having a boyfriend.

"I can't find any clothes," she cried. A pouting scowl inhabited her round face.

"Look in the hamper, honey," her mother said.

"I want clean ones," she demanded.

"They are clean, dear," her mother insisted. "I just haven't had time to put them away."

"Oh God, I wish I had a new family," she muttered. "This one is too embarrassing."

She grabbed the open box of cereal off the kitchen table and put her hand up to her face, hiding her nose, and then she turned around and disappeared back down the hallway. I watched the wrinkles of her T-shirt across her back move, inching up. I couldn't help it. I wanted to steal all the peeks I could.

"Oh my goodness, she is such a handful," Mundo's mother confessed, almost singing.

"Are you ready to go?" Mundo asked.

"Yes."

Mundo's father was always very quiet when I was there. He never said anything except: *It's good to see you, Trace.* His tall lanky body poured into his chair like a threadbare blanket. His round glasses wrapped around the back of his ears. His baseball cap lay on the edge of the armchair. He never went in public without it on his head. The blinding white of his thin-haired head looked lonely. He was like the clutter in the trailer that everyone carefully pretended wasn't there.

At the end of every service, Pastor Flack ensured that the two front doors of the church were always locked. He checked them, his hand gripping the tarnished brass handle like he was pulling the heart out of a dead carcass, rattling the doors in the jamb to make sure they were shut tightly.

Sitting on the church steps, we watched him secure the building against those tempted, people he believed needed to be watched, people like us. And he always gave a quick glance over to Mundo's trailer before he left to let us know he knew Mundo was waiting to dart across the street.

"We must never present an opportunity for temptation," Pastor Flack inserted in every sermon. His eyes scanned each of our faces, looking for weak hints of guilt. "It is only by the grace of God that man can rise above his inherent nature."

Inherent nature--- to us, to me, had something to do with what we got from our parents, like hair color. In his mind, out of his sight, we were capable of all sorts of malevolent acts. The interpretation of the words we heard from the pulpit had many dimensions of understanding in our daily lives. And everyone in our town knew that the way people perceived your family pretty much determined your moral condition. It was inherent.

"An undisciplined mind is a stew of the most corruptible schemes waiting to come to fruition," Pastor Flack liked to say.

His parishioners spent endless energy looking for ways his sermons applied to those they found suspect, those lacking in direction, those they deemed capable of doing anything, given the opportunity, and finally those who needed proper guidance.

Pastor Flack was on watch twenty-four hours a day for the cause of community and Christ, steering our little world into eternal certainty, like a big ship making its way to a lit horizon. In our town, Pastor Flack walked on water. His sermons were the measure of the temperament of town gossip and his words gave an eerie credulity to the convictions of our aging citizens. Talk of small town values always gave me a creepy feeling inside.

"Children, you need to go home pretty soon," Pastor Flack warned.

"Yes, sir," we assured him.

He hesitated momentarily, waiting for us to bolt down the street, giving us a discerning stare that let us know that if something happened, even a single nail pulled from the peeling trim around the windows or the most wobbly shingle missing from the roof of the church, he would know about it, and he would exact payment for the infraction. We knew he would be there, too. His spiritual aura transcended the simple lives that unfolded daily in our community. He was omnipresent.

We watched him pack his cheap wooden pipe with cherry tobacco, pushing the stringy weed deep into the bowl with one of the many keys he had strapped to a metal ring on his belt.

"Somebody is always watching, you know," he warned.

"Yes, sir," I answered.

"God?" Melinda burst.

"That's right, Melinda. Him, too," he said.

We watched his bony hand clench the keys, rattling them in his fingers, reattaching them back to his belt ring. His stern face looked down on us, and when he felt his message had been sufficiently received, he let himself down the church steps with a heavy hesitation, walking away up the sidewalk, the cherry smoke of his pipe floating above the top of his head like a halo. The aroma of his pipe drifted back to where we were sitting, settling in the air around us. We watched him until he vanished into the night, beyond the oak trees and bushes. But his presence always lingered in the shadows like the Holy Ghost. We never said a word until we believed he was completely gone.

Mundo, peeking through the crack of his trailer's doorway, waited for one of us to raise our hand and wave him over, and then he shot out the door to join us on the front steps of the church. He always looked disheveled, like he had been lying in his bed fully dressed, the hair on his head spiked like wet weeds. And then the four of us, me, Mundo, Becky, and Melinda, just sat there, frittering away the remainder of the night.

Mundo liked Melinda, a small thin girl with short brown hair and large breasts filling out her tight pullover blouse. She always wore a long skirt to hide her virtue. She was studious, but she had an eye for mischief. Her eyes were lit with curiosity. He flirted with her endlessly each Sunday night.

One particular night, she sat on the steps of the church, against one of the rails, chewing gum, her pocket bible sinking into her lap. She pushed her brown-rimmed glasses up to the top of her nose when she thought no one was looking. It was after a revival meeting, and Mundo sat next to her. She scooted to his side, and he put his right arm around her shoulders. Melinda and Becky didn't say a word. Both of them were as stiff as corpses, but I could tell the insides of Melinda were bubbling over with feelings and anticipation. The revival had wakened her sexuality.

It was a cool summer night, dark, and a choir of crickets laughed in the tall prairie grass surrounding the cinder block foundation of the church. The shadows of the houses lining the broken street in front of the church rose up like solid monuments, except for Mundo's trailer, which was wedged between them like a frightened stepchild. The sharp snap of a branch echoed in the night. Gusts of wind descended through the trees to excite the leaves. Melinda held her small pocket

Bible in her hands, folding the cardboard binding back and forth, her nervous fingers weakening the pages. She rubbed the damp palms of her hands across the embossed gold print on the front: The Holy Bible, King James Version.

"So what did Flack have to say tonight?" Mundo finally scoffed. He always called the pastor simply "Flack."

"He happens to be a man of God," Melinda said.

"Oh, then what did God have to say tonight?"

"Things you could never understand," she snubbed.

"I understand a lot more than you think," Mundo said.

"About God?"

"Especially about God," Mundo said.

"Like what?" Melinda asked.

"Like he probably doesn't hear people as good as they think he does," Mundo said.

"See what you know, trying to be all sacrilegious, making fun of everything, like you know something everyone else doesn't, always pretending. You're going to hell, Mundo," she said.

"That would be a change," he mumbled.

"Oh, you." Melinda elbowed him.

Becky and I listened to them tease each other.

"You're not too cold are you?" I asked.

"I'm fine."

She pulled her thin sweater tight around the front of her body, the black curls on her head suspended over the top of her shoulders like delicate springs, her waxed white face reflecting the street lights. Her dark eyes looked past me. It was hard to find things to talk about. We moved in different circles during the daytime, at school. I was sure Melinda had to convince her every Sunday to stay.

"Stay. Please. I don't want to be around that boy by myself."

"Why do you want to be around that boy at all?"

"I don't know. Just because."

"Just because?"

"He's kind of cute in a poor way."

"Don't expect much out of me."

"I know. Just be there."

"You're going to get in trouble one of these days, Melinda. You'll end up with babies."

"No. I just want to see what he wants."

"He wants trouble. That's what my parents say. He's nothing but trouble scheming to come to fruition, if you ask me. You're being tempted."

"Tempted?" Melinda laughed. "He seems harmless enough to me."

"Melinda, his father drives the bus!"

"Oh, hush. You put on so."

"The night is cool," I said.

"Yes." Becky looked down at her hands, playing with her fingernails and picking at her cuticles. "I like the feel of the day, right around seven o'clock, just before it starts to cool off and turn dark."

"Sunsets are pretty."

"No, not the sunset, just how the day feels before turning to night," she corrected.

I didn't know what she was trying to say, not that it mattered, I thought sunsets were sunsets, and it all felt the same.

"It's really getting dark," I said.

"The time of the night when bad things start to happen," Melinda jested. She raised her eyebrows and looked into the trees.

"Too dark," Becky continued. "There's no moon. I don't like moonless nights. It's dark like it is when we go out to the Grange, black all around us for miles. I like to be able to see what's around me. Too much darkness confuses me."

"Shh! Did you hear something?" Mundo mocked. "I think it's... Flack!"

"Oh, you!" Melinda blurted. She slapped his shoulder.

Gnats and potato bugs flew into the lone street lamp that hung over Mundo's trailer, and the light showed the corrosion around the metal windowsills and along the bottom flashings. A sudden gust made the panels tremble and buckle. The wind pushed up against the windows of the church, making the glass shake in the frames, echoing a warning. The doors wrestled to pull themselves away from the building.

Both girls screamed. Becky grabbed my arm. I listened for the brass bells in the church tower to ring out and tear through the night like a knife cutting through a window screen so I could dart for home. But they never did. Then the wind calmed. Mundo and Melinda gave each other uncertain flirts, and she slapped his knee while he whispered into her ear.

I wished that tongues of fire would blow across the church steps, sweeping Becky and me into the black of the night, revealing the things unsaid, so we wouldn't have to suffer the awkwardness of this whole thing. I imagined Pastor Flack taking note, peering at us through a cluster of bushes up the street, waiting to jump out at us at the first misdeed. Becky continued holding my arm even after the wind settled down. I could feel her soft fingers sink into my bicep, and I stole an occasional glance into her nervous face; at that moment, I thought she might even like me. We stood against the galvanized handrail of the steps leading to the church doors. There was white paint peeling off the metal. We didn't know what to say to each other, so we just stood there, silent and content. But I liked her touch on my arm. And I liked the silence because it meant the moment would linger.

Mundo reached under the back of Melinda's arm and touched the side of her right breast with his fingers. Melinda gave a short gasp and raised her right hand up to her mouth.

"I can't believe you did that!" she burst.

She jumped up wrenching her body away from Mundo like she felt a spider crawling up her leg. She lunged at him, slapping him across the face with the palm of her free hand. Her pocket Bible was pressed tightly against one of her breasts with the other hand. The crack against his cheek ricocheted down the empty street and disappeared.

"Let's go, Becky," she exhorted, one hand on her hip, the other pointing her Bible at us.

"Sorry," Becky said.

"Now, Becky!" Melinda snapped. "Let's go!"

"Bye," Becky said. Her eyes looked at me with regret.

"Bye," I returned. What I wanted to say was "Stay."

They ran like awkward children hooking each other's arms, giggling, like they had just tangled with the devil and survived. It was the first time I had ever seen Becky laugh, and it bothered me.

"Shame on you, Mundo!" Melinda shouted, turning toward us

skipping backwards, her hand cupped around her mouth. "Shame, shame on you! You're a very bad boy!"

She might as well have pulled the bell tower rope, screamed rape in the night, waking the whole town. I looked for lights to go on up and down the street, and Pastor Flack to jump out from behind any of the bushes along the street.

"Ah, I have you now!"

But nothing happened. I was certain the curtains were moving in houses all over town with hands clenched tightly to those linen hems.

We sat there on the church steps, not a sound but the crickets filling the silent space between us. Mundo pulled out a pack of cigarettes, pluck one out and lit it. He took a long slow drag and let out small disturbed circles of smoke. His head dropped between his legs. It was the first time I thought he might cry. He wiped his right hand on his pants and cracked his knuckles.

"I fucked up," he stated flatly.

"Maybe she likes you," I said. "You know girls: No means yes and all that."

"No, I don't think so. I think 'no' meant 'no'," Mundo said.

"She was skipping away, that had to mean something," I said.

"She was making fun of me. She just wanted to see what it was like to be bad."

"You're hardly bad, Mundo."

"I know, but the idea that I am seems to stick to me."

"Oh, come on, now you're being dramatic," I said.

"I don't think so." He let out a sigh. Then he took another long slow drag on his cigarette. "I'm going home."

Mundo walked across the street to his trailer, his weathered dingo boots dragging across the loose gravel in the street. He pulled hard to get the front door opened. It took a definitive tug to finally snap it free from the frame. He tossed his cigarette to the dirt and disappeared inside. I sat on the church steps staring at the small box he lived in until all the lights went out.

"I don't think so either buddy," I whispered.

I continued to listen to Mundo making a ruckus outside our house.

I tried to lie still for fear that the creak of my box spring might float through the open window, giving me away. I watched the yellowed wallpaper on the ceiling in my room, following the subtle line of flowers where it pulled away from the wall. I hoped for the final chop of the ax, the sign that he was tired of yelling up at my window, going home. I knew he wouldn't knock at the door. He would never knock at the door. He would rather annoy the neighborhood endlessly by yelling up at my window.

"Would you go down and see what that pathetic boy wants?" my mother's sleepy voice scolded through the crack of my door. "Goodness. Doesn't that poor child think to take a break from anything?"

"Okay Mom."

I didn't want to see Mundo, not today. I wanted to sleep. But Mundo was my friend. He had been my friend his whole life. I can't remember not having Mundo in my life. And in a town of 496 people, give or take a few births and deaths, a friend was an awful lot like having a relative: You might not like your relatives, but they were there, constantly, the cousins, second cousins, and the whole incestuous lot. I don't think you picked your friends in small towns; they were thrust upon you like a responsibility. It was what it was, and that was it.

Galvanized lampposts poked out of the ground on dusty corners blinking in the night with unsteady persistence. Tired telephone wires dropped into the large oak trees that line Main Street. There were overgrown brushes in yards with owners too poor to care. Vacant brick and wood-paneled businesses lined the tired street. The names of each business faded in the lime-crusted glass. Stale, boarded-up houses and unused propane tanks showed the outdated lives of people, stained by years of Grange meetings and 4-H meetings. There were farmers crippled by years of overworked bones drying beneath their overalls, hanging out at the feed store, sporting red co-op caps soiled by sweat and field work. The scent of cracked field corn lingered in the heavy summer air. The owner of the local gas station desperately held on to his rusted out gas pumps and dusty packages of Dolly Madison cinnamon rolls, stacked by the cash register, untouched. The town was smothered by acres of wheat and brome, framed by barbed wire fencing. And always, there were the reluctant friendships, laden

with a responsibility that propped up the meaning of the town's daily existence.

"Trace! Get your ass down here, now!" There's smoke!"

I looked out the window. He had the back of the ax handle resting on the top of his right shoulder with his free arm pushed into the torn pocket of his overalls. The short hair on his head stuck up like thistles.

"Smoke?" I shouted. "Where?"

"It's rising out of the west. That way!" He pointed the ax out over the top of the chicken shed. The clear blue sky was white with clouds that were soft like pillows and floated peacefully past the town. The smoke must have been further west. "It's coming from the reservation. Let's go."

"Hold on to the horses, won't you?" I said. "I need to get my pants on."

"Hurry up. I don't want to miss anything," Mundo said.

"Right."

I slipped on my blue jeans, T-shirt and tennis shoes, grabbed the keys to my 1965 Dodge Dart and ran out the back door of the house through the mud porch and dandelion-covered yard.

"It's about fucking time," Mundo said as he lit a cigarette.

"Hush up," I scolded. "You can at least wait 'til we get out of the driveway before you light up. My parents already think you're flaky."

"Everyone's asleep," Mundo said.

"Don't be too sure about that," I said.

"What do you mean?" He cupped the cigarette behind his back looking at the windows of my house. "Why would they be up?"

"The whole fucking neighborhood is probably up. Jesus."

The chickens, tucked safely in the corner of the shed at the back of the garage, braved the morning chill to steal a peek at the maniac shaking the morning air. They inched out of the shed like tired, blinking children on a damp school morning. Their heads jerked forward, looking at us with their one eye, and then pecking at the ground for missed morsels.

"Smoke, huh." I said.

"Yeah. Over there." He pointed.

I looked west, cupped my hand over my brow and saw the faint plume of black smoke rising over the houses and trees on the other side of the alley.

"Yep. It looks like smoke," I said.

"Or one hell of a Powwow fire," Mundo said.

"Smoke," I said.

"You know what they say about smoke," Mundo said. His eyes looked crazy like glass, the stare he always got when ideas began to clash in his head. His eyes were shards of wet ice, bleeding the myriad of colors around him.

"What?"

"Where there's smoke," he chose each word carefully, "there's fire."

I looked at Mundo, and I thought for a second that I saw his madness, his brain spinning out of control, the very thing everyone else saw and I ignored. It was obvious that he was itching to get out across the highway, down the dirt road leading to the reservation, to the smoke. But I wasn't sure if he wanted to help put the fire out or to fan the flames to consume the entire Kansas plain. I was convinced he had his reasons. I half expected him to put cans of gasoline into the trunk on my car, calling them a fire fighting tool, slapping the side of my door, saying, *Let's go, I have my revenge to exact on this damned place.*

But, of course, those were my thoughts, not his; Mundo had no guile.

"Ready?" I asked.

"Shit, yeah. Think some damned Indian burnt down his shack?" he asked, throwing the ax into the back seat of the car.

"We'll have to see. What's with the hand ax?" I asked.

"We might need it," he said.

"Are you going to chop the fire out?"

"Don't be funny, Trace. You can't chop out a fire, but we might have to clear wooded areas to stop the spread of the fire."

"You're going to clear wooded area with a hand ax?" I asked.

"When someone asks who has an ax I'll be there, ready to clear the area. You really shouldn't make light of this shit, Trace," Mundo said.

I knew that most of the land around the Indian Reservation was owned by white farmers. What was left for the Indians was an acre here and there with small tin-roofed houses, boarded windows and tar shingled siding, which sprinkled the plains around the Powwow grounds. And if they didn't live on these small parcels of land, they moved into broken apartments in town. Some of the Indians, lost, just wandered the dusty downtown late at night with no place to go.

The Prairie Band Indians of the Potawatomi tribe had settled west of town on a 30-mile square parcel of land around the middle of the 1800's. They came from Indiana and Illinois, pushing their way through the state of Iowa. They were always a small huddle of people, dropped into this area out of circumstance rather than conviction.

Tourists pulled through our town all the time asking where the teepees were. I used to try to explain to them that there were no teepees that the Indians lived in houses, somewhat, like us, but they never believed it. I was just a kid in their eyes, I supposed, so I just pointed toward the Powwow grounds and let them figure it out.

I tried to imagine the anticipation in their eyes as they pulled away and shot across Highway 75, down the dirt road leading to the Powwow grounds. I imagined them driving back and forth on the road, stirring up dust, trying to figure out how they missed the teepees, seeing only bruised farms and shacks ready to blow over with the slightest Kansas wind. I was sure they pulled to the side of the road, craning their necks every which way to find the Indian campsite, looking into the tangle of hedge and cottonwood trees, and finally stumbling upon the broken down country park, a dusty wooden sign hanging by a reluctant nail, with faded red lettering saying: Powwow Ground.

Even if there were teepees, the Indians didn't want to be bothered by these tourists. So, go figure.

By the time we reached the edge of town, the firehouse siren started to pierce the air of our sleepy town.

"We're going to be the first ones there," Mundo cheered.

"It looks like it."

"We raced across Highway 75 onto the dirt road leading to the Powwow grounds. We could see the black cloud of smoke in front of us piling into the sky like a mad storm.

"Faster, Trace."

"I'm trying."

We watched barbed wire rip past us and the wheat in the fields spin wildly from the wind. Gravel spit out the back end of my car snapping against the metal of the undercarriage; the tires whipped back and forth across the road like a bull snake running scared for a hole. There was the uneasy slide of rubber on rock, the crunch like a rolling pin across a bed of corn flakes. A morning shade, caused by the clouds moving in front of the sun, crawled across the fields like a blanket of sweet darkness. It was as if the hands of God reached down to touch the earth. We spun and peeled across the gravel like crazy drunks on a lazy afternoon. Mundo pounded his right hand on the dash of the car.

"Do it, Trace!" he shouted.

Suddenly, we began to slide in circles of dust, our eyes burning our world turning end over end, the snap of barbed wire, as we slid on the roof of my Dodge Dart through the furrows of sun-dried wheat bouncing off clods of dirt chunks and the slapping of flax under the hood of the car. The hand ax Mundo had placed in the back of the car flew past us into the windshield. And then finally, the car came to a stop. Fluid dripped from the engine onto the back side of the hood and onto the windshield. Small plumes of smoke bled through the dash of the car.

We heard the siren of the fire truck whistle pass us and the swish of each subsequent car that followed it, gravel spitting and hitting the grille of each car. My car lay upside down like a dead turtle. Our bodies were crunched into the roof.

"It doesn't look like we're going to be the first ones to the fire now," Mundo sighed.

"Nope," It was all I could think of to say.

"Sorry, Trace."

"No need to apologize, Mundo. I was driving."

"I am surprised that no one stopped."

"It doesn't surprise me."

"I suppose. But we could have been killed."

"But we weren't."

We heard the sizzle of liquid on the engine, then smelled smoke and for a moment, we were both silent. We both had our hand on the door handle, ready to fly out of the car at the slightest disturbance. Then the sizzle stopped and our grips eased. We just lay there.

"Don't worry, Trace. Smoking cars never..." Mundo said, blinking

dust out of his eyes. The front wheels of the car clicked to a stop. "…
burst into flames."

Cherry and mulberry trees huddled near the entrance of the farm. Bad
fruit stained the ground beneath the trees like a dirty rain. Deep muddy ruts
lined the drive of the property and along the rusty barbed wire fencing leading
to the pond. The fence was strung loosely through gnarled hedge posts that poked
out of the ground like crippled men. A broken-down barn half filled with rotted
hay from a summer cut years ago gave off a heavy stench of mildew. Rusted hay
hooks and scythes hung from nails on the side of the barn. Mundo jumped off
the back of the pickup truck to open the barbed wire gate that was secured by a
leather belt pulled tightly around two hedge posts. He jumped into the bed of
the truck as his father drove through the gate without stopping.

The pond was quiet and brown. It nestled in the center of tall cottonwood
trees. Mundo's father pulled the pickup truck along the tall grass which
encircled the pond.

"I used to go fishing here when I was a kid," his father called through the
open window.

"Right," Mundo called back.

After they had stopped, he took his tackle box and pole, put his unlit pipe in
his mouth, and started to walk away from the truck.

"I think I'll go to the other side of the pond and sit under that shade," his
father said.

His long legs lifted above the high grass and he tripped through the dried
mud holes left by the long-gone cows. When he found a comfortable spot, he sat
down. Mundo watched him untangle his line as it wrapped around his arm,
and when he was through sorting it all out he baited his hook. His father tossed
his line into the water and sat on the ground against a stump.

Mundo dug through the back of the truck and gathered his tackle. After he
got his pole into the water, he lay back and watched the clouds in the sky float
by like a carousel of cotton swabs while his line lay limp in the water.

A sharp gunshot startled him about half an hour later and he looked across
the pond to where he last saw his father. He glimpsed the empty stump; his
father's body lay in the tall grass and a wisp of smoke from his pipe floated up
from the grass. He didn't know what to do, so he sat there and fought back tears.
He lay back in the truck bed and his mind raced through all the things he

might have done, listening to the flick of bullfrogs jumping from the shore into
the water, exhausting himself until the fell asleep, until the weight was gone.
He lay there asleep until the dusk turned to night and night turned to morning.
It was the first time he and his father had ever gone fishing together.

I watched Mundo and his family load the back of their pickup truck with all the personal belongings they thought they could comfortably haul. They were leaving town. I volunteered to help them, but his mother was too embarrassed to have me walk through the debris of their life discarded on the floor throughout the trailer. She said that they weren't sure what they were going to take, so I could help load the back of the truck. I stood outside, leaning against the pickup, while they carted box after torn box out of their trailer. His sister complained about all the things her mother wouldn't allow her to take.

"Mundo, make sure you get all the boxes out of the kitchen," his mother sang.

"You're making me leave all my things," his sister cried. "I need to take my makeup cases and my records. I want my bed."

"We only have so much room, honey," her mother said.

"But Mom!"

"Your father is dead for God's sakes!" Mundo's mother cried. She slumped down on the two-by-six steps outside of the trailer. She looked helpless. "Can't you just show a little respect?"

"Geez, have a cow," his sister mumbled.

Mundo had two pillow cases stuffed with dirty clothes.

"Is that all you're taking, dear?" his mother asked. She wiped tears from her eyes, pulling herself back to her feet, and then she tried to get herself back to the immediate task.

"I got everything I need," he said.

"Then can I bring my records and makeup cases?" his sister asked.

"Yes, dear, you can take your things."

His sister and I looked at each other with each trip she made out to the truck. Once she got her records and makeup case safely tucked into a place she felt they wouldn't be disturbed, she took her time getting back to the trailer for other boxes. She found ways to stall. And when she did show up with a box, it was small, the lightest one she could find, and she tossed it into the back of the bed like unwanted trash. She wore a white string-sleeved blouse and shorts, and I saw the lines and lumps of her bra through the top.

Finally, they piled into the pickup truck, his mother behind the steering wheel. His sister dropped herself into the passenger seat, slumping down so no one could see her. Mundo climbed into the bed of the truck on top of all the boxes.

"Hey, you stay out of trouble," I said.

"Yeah," he returned.

"Call me."

The truck started to slowly pull away.

"By the way," he shouted, "my sister has a crush on you."

"Mom!" A scream came from inside the truck. Mundo laughed.

No one ever asked if I ever heard from Mundo again. Melinda's life never missed a stride. She started to date a basketball player within a month after Mundo was gone. She wore his letterman's jacket everywhere she went, her hands safely hidden in the long leather sleeves. Becky and I exchanged courteous hellos at school and at church, but we never again shared those lingering dark nights on the church steps after evening services.

Our town never changed. Mrs. Motts found a new villain to keep her discerning eye on, and the curtains in the Mitchell home continued to move suspiciously behind the windows. It was as if Mundo had never lived here.

"Let the dead bury the dead," Pastor Flack always said.

His family's trailer was bulldozed and the remains hauled to the dump outside town. A new two-car garage replaced it within weeks.

As a community, we gathered twice a week at the First Christian Church of the Forgiven Believers and listened to the exhortations of Pastor Flack; his sermons continued to temper the convictions of our small community, and any hint of Mundo's life disappeared into the thick sky, like smoke rising from a burn barrel.

The next time I saw Flip, he had a girl on each arm as he walked through the chaotic crowd of the Jackson County Fairground. Sounds of piped music filled the warm night air, and stars disappeared in the bright ray of neon lights.

The festive sound of screams faded, then escalated, and mixed with the encroaching chug and spit of the electric motor on the octopus ride. Its long bent arms pushed and pulled each bucket into circles, then jerked them toward the naked ground like a carnie slapping the bottom of a pack of cigarettes against the side of his hand.

The laughter of families and friends, huddled together in tight circles, detailed their night. Entangled couples walked through once-white barns scraped gray by years of harsh weather. The buildings lined the back of the fairground lot like forgotten grandparents.

The hint of buttered popcorn and cotton candy and hot dogs lingered above the chaos. Duct-taped wiring and plug-ins lay limp, exposed, across the dirt like tired snakes. The trashcans over-flowed with waxed Coca-Cola cups and paper plates and plastic forks and pieces of funnel cake. Half-eaten hamburgers lay on the ground like stomped playing cards.

A chain link fence separated the inside of the park from the parking lot. White-walled cars packed the parking lot, an orgy of shining metal and glass with spacers in the shock coils that jacked their asses into the air like dogs in heat.

The night throbbed with the anticipation of sex.

A broad smile inked its way across Flip's face, his hands firmly wrapped around the thin waist of each girl. The white girl on his right he introduced as Debbie, and the Indian girl with plastic rimmed glasses on his left he introduced as Maya. They shifted their hips and looked through the crowd of people walking past us, through disheveled heads of hair and smiling faces and handfuls of popcorn splashing from hands to open mouths, hitting lips and falling to the ground.

I stared at the girls and their flexed bare high-heeled legs, smooth and unblemished, tightly muscled, modeling in front of me as they crossed and uncrossed them over their ankles. A hint of strawberry perfume floated under my nose. Makeup caked across their faces like watercolors from a cheap tin tray.

Their dresses were short, very short: Debbie's was bright orange and Maya's was black. The hems of their dresses were pasted just below the arc of each of their butts, butts as round and ripe as melons on a hot day. I didn't know how to respond to them except to raise my hand slightly and to say hi. The girls squeezed out listless smiles and a big dry wad wedged in my throat like the bite of a corn dog.

Maya was beautiful. I tried not to stare at her, but every time I looked her way, she looked back at me, her dark eyes reading every silent thought I balanced in my head. My thoughts were confused, and they competed with all the whistles and shouts that filled the fairground. Every burst sounded like it was directed toward me, a knowing mock. I wanted to tuck the wrinkled tails of my sweat-drenched shirt into my jeans. Instead, I brushed my hands across my hair in an attempt to look less fraudulent, more normal and presentable.

It was her glasses. She looked smarter than I. But lately, I thought everyone looked smarter. But the way she stood, erect and comfortable with her body, herself, mature-like, as if the whole thing was nothing new to her, like she had been through this drill before and it made me feel like a novice. She was used to everything, world-wise, letting the boys play their roles, boys being boys, boys groping and boasting; boys like Flip.

Maya reached up to straighten her glasses, not just a poke of the finger, but she grabbed them with conviction, using her thumb and index finger, and she shifted them on her face. And while Flip showed off his ability to nab the girls, she jabbed the points of her high heels into the dry dirt.

The longer we stood in the middle of the fairground, the more the girls pinned their hopes on Flip. And the longer people walked around us like we were lamp posts planted in the middle of the throughway, the more apparent it became that Flip intended to leave the fair with both girls. Standing in the middle of the fairground, people all around us, Flip showed off the spoils of his hunt. The girls were his trophies like stuffed heads of Elk above a fire place.

I wanted to ask him what gives. Whatever happened to share and share alike, the obligation of friendship and all that? But I didn't have the right. I despised him for waving these two girls in front of me, pulling them close, holding them out like big stuffed bears he had won at the midway, letting me, and anyone else who happened to look our way know that they both belonged to him, that he had procured them fair and square, that he was up to it, or thought he was up to it, though I wasn't sure what he intended to do now that he had them.

And the girls, well, they were patient enough considering the circumstances. They just stood there waiting, their arms crossed in front of them, daring the moment. Maybe it didn't matter to them like it mattered to us, like it always mattered to boys. They had been through all this before, but in different ways, availing themselves to the limited enthusiasm of male passion, singularly focused and shallow. All they had to do was listen to us brag, and agree.

The crowds moved through the fairground like cracked billiard balls, aimless, drawn to the irresistible itch of the midway rides and games, seduced by the tattooed carnies that dotted the fairground like greased smudges on a mechanic's shirt. Carnies spied each person as they passed, looked through them and into their heads and searched for weakened moments, for flaws in human thought, and the perfect time. They beset each passerby with entreaty and played upon the vanity of each victim.

"Come on! Hey, you! Yes, you! Win a bear for your girl! It just takes one ball to win!" they shouted. "One ball to win! Three balls for a buck! Anyone can win!"

The captain of our basketball team was there with his freshman girlfriend watching people toss coins, trying to land them on small glass plates. He let his right hand slide down her back, brushing against her butt, and she reached down and pulled his hand back up to her boy-like waist. He stared ahead, rooting for the coin throwers, and then he looked at his girlfriend with a guiltless smile after she had firmly put his hand back up to her waist the second time. He kissed the top of her head. And then, minutes later, he slipped his hand back down to her butt, and this time she let the hand stay.

If you wanted girls, you came to Holton. You chased the road up to the old swimming pool from the top of the hill at Rafters Park on weekends. Huge oak trees loomed over the sloping park, lush with green during the summer months. And young boys, churning with want, pulled along the curb of the park and honked their horns at bikini-clad girls lined along the chain-linked fence looking like the disparate flavors of snow cones. Their bikini bottoms were tied in bows at their hips. Their fingers hooked into the spaces of the fence above their heads as they peered to the top of the hill where the boys stood looking down on them. They giggled, whispering into the ear of a friend and pointing, their other hand covering their mouths.

Or, there were the nights at the skating rink standing at the top of the stairs of what once housed the armory, looking out over the warped wooden floor, hearing the rumble of roller skates rasping and scraping at the bubbled wood, ogling the girls they knew, or at least the ones they had met before, an excuse into their innocent world.

Groups of pubescent teenagers gathered at the far corner of the skating rink in secretive council and exchanged phone numbers and made dates, passing messages to friends of friends, or to someone they saw or to someone they liked. The skating rink was filled with young girls with small breasts that poked out from behind their tight T-shirts like chocolate kisses, at once both anxious and reluctant, but willing to test their new-found sexuality.

You could drive around and around the downtown courthouse, pull into parking spaces along the tired row of red-bricked Victorian buildings, stop in the middle of the bricked street trading romances like little boys traded baseball cards, and ask, "Where are you from? Which school? And do you know...?"

The girls squeezed their chances each weekend as they cruise the streets in their friends' cars at the downtown square. They whistled at boys while hanging out of the car windows, the summer wind twisted through their hair. And then they parked, when gas got low, and sat on the hoods of their cars and watched the flash of shining metal passing by over and over.

There's nothing like sliding through the passenger window of a 1963 Chevy Impala onto the smooth vinyl seat and rubbing the palm of your hand on the metal dash, the AM music spilling out of the radio and out the windows in the twinkle of monosyllabic sounds--Lightening Striking Again and Again; and they all sang, stretching their lungs beyond the clarity of the song.

The next school day these same girls huddled in circles and asked who their friends were with on Saturday night. They flicked out details, stories, and, finally, admitted to the telephone numbers they had gotten---a basketball player in Mayetta, or a senior from Valley Falls who was going to K-State in September.

They lived each weekend to get telephone numbers that were packed carefully away in small shoeboxes on the top shelves of bedroom closets, wedged between ice skates and pom-poms, personal diaries, and stuffed animals. They were faded pencil marks, numbers and names, on wrinkled strips of envelopes or grocery bags that would never be used.

How did Flip meet these girls? I was only away from him for maybe thirty minutes, just long enough to go to one of the portable potties at the edge of the fairground entrance and stroll back through the midway. I pushed carnies away who tried to separate me from the last three dollars in my pocket. I was distracted for moments of time I could not account. I was overwhelmed by the sights, sounds, and scents of the fair. I stood in the middle of the fairground and stared at the neon racing through gas tight tubes of rides that swirled around me. I listened to the organ music of the merry-go-round, and it was all so magical. It cast a spell on everything around me and created a world where the rules were lax, unimportant, where anything was possible.

The next thing I knew, apparently out of thin air, Flip stood before me with two girls he had never even met before, and it didn't take long for me to conclude that neither of them knew the other. It was as if he had just scooped them out of the chaos and brought them along. Only Flip could find a way to scrape a couple of girls out of the crowd faster than I could take a piss.

The girls played a waiting game, hoping the other would bow out, see a friend and break away. They kept to their own counsel like a well-devised plan.

Was I jealous? Of course I was jealous.

Did I want one of these girls?

Most definitely I wanted one of these girls, (specifically Maya) and I wanted to touch one (her). Every boy wanted to touch a girl. It's what consumed his evenings, his ever-waking and dreaming thoughts. The problem I had with Flip was that he wanted to touch all the girls, and in the end, he'd tell everyone about it, give out all the details of what had happened the night before, and it always made me angry that the girls still wanted him, that they couldn't see how he used them, their feelings having no relevance to his needs. Instead, they encouraged him, almost giggly, when he was busted for sharing with others the intimate details of their night together.

Yes, I was jealous. But then, he had a car and I didn't. And having a car was what made him attractive, it was his leverage, and transportation was important to any teenage girl. It got you away. It took you where you wanted to go. It was your freedom.

Two freshman girls sat in the back row of the wooden bleachers at one of the summer little league games. It started as a dare, challenging Flip and Davis with the idea that they didn't have the nerve to meet them. They laughed and cupped their hands over their mouths, their elbows on their knees, and leaned into each other and blew out smirks.

It was a hot July night and fireflies blinked in the spaces among tall cottonwood trees behind a lit baseball field, while a hush of anticipation settled over the infield where the players waited, tense, brushing their cleats through the dirt with their toes, waiting for the batter to slice at the ball. No one seemed to be in a hurry for anything to happen, settling into their seats with blankets and pillows and small Igloo chests filled with sodas and snacks. Mothers grabbed their children by the ears to get their attention, slapping the sides of their heads. There was the occasional interruption by the announcer sitting at a planked table behind home plate, reiterating the umpire's calls on the makeshift PA. "Ball two," his soft voice said. There was a silence, then the crack of electricity coming from the PA, "It's two and two," and like an afterthought, "Two balls and two strikes." Everyone was ready for the game to go well past midnight and into the early morning. It was part of small town Saturday night. And talk, in a small town, any kind of talk, could take you a long way in the space f one night.

"We'll be there," Flip said to the girls, winking at David, giving him a quick elbow. And they were.

The girls, heavy-set and anxious for their first peek into romance had heard all the stories about Flip. For the boys, it was purely physical, selfish, like all sex to teenage guys. It was about curiosity and the first exposure to temporal ownership.

David fumbled with the heavy girl's blouse like someone feeling through a grassy patch trying to find a contact lens or lost change, touching and fingering anything that responded, especially the metal connectors on her bra. He teased and let her know where he wanted to go, what he wanted to do, and after a tiresome amount of sloppy kissing to the point where his lips grew numb, she sat up and unbuttoned her blouse, pulled her shoulder straps down and slid the back of her bra around to the front and unsnapped it, letting her pale breasts hang below her freckled chest. The white of her body filled the night like a neon moon.

He discarded her face for one of her breasts, moving his hand to the top of her jeans, inching his fingers down the tight hold of her belt around her waist and under her stretched panties until his fingertips tickled the soft tangle of her pubic hair and into her slippery fold.

"Do you like me, David?" she asked.

"Yes," he said. "You feel so good. This feels so right."

"I like you, too, David." she said. "I hope you don't hurt me."

"Why would I hurt you?"

Flip told everyone at school that the girl he was with Saturday night was easy and gave head. And although her face was red-wet for the next two weeks at school she puppy-dogged him for months after that night.

David never said a word to the girl he was with after that Saturday night and he never shared his experience with a soul, embarrassed and ashamed that anyone would even know he was with her, and she hated him for it.

I looked at Maya and tried to detect an ache of embarrassment, but never saw it. Debbie, on the other hand, was all glitter and perky. She wanted to pull Maya away from Flip, tugging on his arm, talking to him endlessly, pushing her face into his shoulder, keeping herself in the center of his attention:

"Like my hair?"

"I did it special for the fair."

"Do you come to Holton a lot?"

"Where do you hang out?"

"Do you ever go to the skating rink?"

And when his attention began to wane, wax toward Maya, she included me in her conversation.

"Do you go to the same school as Flip?" she asked.

I nodded.

"Same grade?"

"Sophomore."

"Oh. That's nice."

"Yeah."

"Do you have a car?"

"No, but I'm going to get one."

I looked over at Maya. She was numbed.

"David helps with the gas," Flip said.

"Both of my brothers have cars," Debbie continued.

"How old are you?" I asked.

"Thirteen."

I looked at Flip.

"If they're old enough to bleed, they're old enough to breed," he joked.

"I'm 16," Maya offered.

"My parents let me date," Debbie returned.

"I don't have parents," Maya said.

"Are they dead?" Debbie asked.

"No. They're just gone."

"I have a 1963 Chevy Impala," Flip said. "It's in mint condition."

"Nice car," Maya replied. She smiled. I couldn't have been more disappointed.

"Oh, crap! Ten o'clock!" Debbie pulled away from Flip apologetically. "My brother's waiting for me at the front gate. He's a senior. His girlfriend's a sophomore. He's going to K-State when he graduates."

Maya rolled her eyes, turning them to the sky just above our heads.

Debbie pushed up on her tiptoes and kissed Flip on the cheek.

"Call me?" she asked.

"I got your number," he said, reaching up to his front pocket with his free hand. Maya squeezed his other hand and tugged on his arm.

"I have yours, too," she said holding up her closed fist, the small fleck of a crinkled paper peeking out between her thumb and index finger.

"Call me or I'll call you," Flip said.

"It was fun. Bye Flip, David," Debbie said. She skipped away, turning in circles through the crowd, parting people like a mist of Lysol in a smoky room, and she disappeared before I had a chance to respond.

Maya moved her arm around Flip's neck, taking possession of his attention. The tug of her dress pulled her skirt higher.

"You ready to go?" Flip asked, and I wasn't sure if he was talking to me or Maya. I hoped he was talking to me, and I said yes.

"Sure," Maya said. I felt awkward.

Her small body lured him with anticipation. It lured me with longing. I could only watch.

"Yeah, we better do something," he chuckled.

"I need to be home by one o'clock or I'm in big trouble," I reminded him. Flip looked at me like I was a liability.

"It's the weekend of the Jackson County Fair," Flip said. "Our parents will understand."

He was right.

"Maybe yours will, but I've been through this before. Remember? My parents already think you're a bad influence on me," I said.

"Bullshit. We don't drink, and I drive like an old man," he said.

Maya's pretty face was curtained by black straight hair, and I looked at the space between her legs, the shadow of her dress barely hiding what I pretended not to look for. Actually, I stared. I couldn't help it, my eyes drifted. They tried to see everything, and I thought that Flip didn't deserve any of it. She caught me looking, and I turned red.

It seemed like I always wanted to touch what I couldn't have. The girls knew it, and it made me look weak.

One year before, David took a class at the fairground to learn how to drive a tractor. The classes took place outside, on the same strip of land which ran

along Highway 75, where the carnival rides were erected every year at the fair.
He needed to get his driving chit in order to work in the hay fields that summer.
It was early spring and small patches of grass dotted the open space where the
tractors sat ready for the eager boys to test their aptitude.

The driving chit was his passport into summer employment, his freedom,
and his rite of passage. He was saving his money to get a car. He passed the
written test on the different operating parts of the tractor, and then he was led
to where the new tractors rested for his driving test. He climbed onto the metal
seat of the Super C, the fresh smell of grease and paint drifting into his nose, the
stick shift rising between his legs like an invitation.

The teacher stood on the back hitch, balancing his frame, and the front of
the Super C heaved slightly as he guided David through the clutch, gears, and
brake. David crunched the gears trying to push the stick shift into low, and as
he let his foot off the clutch the tractor jumped forward. Eventually he was able
to make the slow transition between low to second gear, then second to third, and
his confidence grew with the changing of each gear. And finally, he was ready
to work in the hay fields.

After David got his driving chit, he tucked it safely between two inserts
in his wallet. He bought his first hay hook and a pair of leather gloves at
the Farmer's Co-op at the end of Main Street, which sat along the rusted and
abandoned railroad tracks. The new gloves smelled like oil and he pushed them
up to his nose. He couldn't wait to spear his first hay bale, heaving it onto
the trailer. He lay in his bed the night before his first day of work poking his
fingers with the point of the hay hook until he fell asleep.

"Well, let's drive around the courthouse and see what's up," Flip
said, and we walked toward the parking lot.

I was behind Flip and Maya and I watched her body move next to
him. I almost told Flip I was going to stay, that he could pick me up
later. I wanted to make my way back through the crowd at the fair,
looking for the real Maya since I couldn't have this Maya. I knew the
magic of the night would deliver. And I felt like Flip was ripping me
away from any opportunity. The night laughed.

There were girls at the fair, lots of girls, alone, or maybe with a
friend, and they ambled through the crowd of people looking for boys,
skipping between the music and lights, spilling into the spaces that

made them accessible, places that put them on display, places I had yet to discover.

I wished I had a car. I wished I had more than a tractor chit. I needed a driver's license. I wished I could touch Maya. I knew I could touch her differently than Flip. I could love her. And I believed it. She was my first real crush. I wanted to tell her not to hurt me.

I sat in the back seat of the car watching their heads. Maya sat as close to Flip as she could and my chest pounded. Nobody said a word, the sound of *Long Cool Woman* by the Hollies filled the car, and I couldn't help but whisper the words of the song.

We drove around the courthouse, from 5th Street to New York to 6th Street to Pennsylvania, and over again, the pale, lifeless windows of the turn-of-the-century businesses looked out over the square of cars filled with kids. A white Galaxy 500 honked at us and a handful of boys shouted out the window with every circle we made.

"Do you know them?" Flip asked Maya. She shook her head.

The next time they passed us, one of the passengers in the back seat, hanging out the window, motioned for us to pull over, and Flip did. All four boys jumped out of the car. Two of them ran toward us while two of the boys sat on the hood of the Galaxy. All the windows of Flip's Chevy were rolled down.

"What were you doing with my sister, you asshole?" one boy shouted while the other jerked Flip's door open.

Flip looked at Maya. She shook her head, looking into her lap.

"Not her," the boy continued, "Debbie!"

"Nothing," Flip said. "I just met her tonight. I never touched her."

"Then what are you doing with her?" he asked. The boy pointed at Maya. Maya sat silently at Flip's side, not saying a word. This was guy stuff as far as she was concerned.

"I ought to kick your ass," Debbie's brother said. "I picked her up and she started telling me about this guy she met from Mayetta with a 1963 Chevy Impala and here you are with this damned Indian chick."

"Hey, I just met your sister at the fair tonight," Flip said.

"Well, she seems to think there's something more to it."

"She didn't give me a chance to make something more of it," Flip said.

Debbie's brother reached into Flip's car and grabbed him by the top of his shirt and jerked him out, pulling him over, and pushing him up against the fender.

"Get your fucking hands off of me, you son-of-a-bitch," Flip demanded.

Debbie's brother put his finger in Flip's face. I tried to open the back door on the driver's side of the car, but the other boy had walked over to the door and leaned back against it.

"If I ever hear that you touched my sister, your ass is mine," he said.

"You and whose army?" Flip challenged.

Another car, a Rambler, with two girls in it, honked and pulled in alongside Debbie's brother's car. The two boys slid off the hood and immediately burrowed into the girl's windows, laughing. I could hear the banter.

What's going on?

Nothing. Just a couple of assholes.

From Mayetta.

Giggles.

Clint's going to kick their asses.

Get 'em Clint.

Giggles.

Whew!

What'd he do?

His sister?

I feel sorry for the poor bastard.

Who's the girl?

Fucking Indian.

Oh,

Gutsy little prick.

Other cars were driving by, hooting and whistling at Flip. I slid across the seat to the other side, got out of the car and leaned over the top.

"Stay out of it," the boy on the other side of the car warned. "Clint?"

"No one has anything to do with this except this guy," Clint said.

He poked his finger into Flip's chest. Clint's friend looked at me and shrugged. I placed my palms on the top of the car and drummed with my fingers. I was embarrassed.

"Maybe both of these Mayetta assholes need to stay out of Holton," Clint said.

"You can't keep us out of town," Flip bravely defended.

Now, I'm thinking I might have to get ready to fight these guys. I looked over at the other carload of girls as they pushed their way out the windows flirting with the other boys, the four of them having already forgotten about us. Another carload of girls pulled up alongside them, and I'm starting to think that I'm on the wrong side of things. I have always been on the wrong side of things.

I'm wondering if Maya knows any of these kids. And maybe she does, but they don't know her, and if they do, they don't say anything. They're white, all of them. Nobody yells out, "Hey Maya, how are you doing?" Or, "What are you doing with those two jerks?" She doesn't appear to be embarrassed.

She's invisible to everyone but me, and I wished at that moment I could have told her this. She looks straight at the closed doors of one of the businesses in front of her and goes to another world, to a place where there is music and neon, and nobody cares who she is.

Flip, on the other hand, was bent on standing up, balls to the wall, to the whole town. Clint pushed Flip once more.

"Just stay away from my little sister," he warned. He motioned to the other boy. "Let's go!"

They made their way back to the Galaxy 500. The girls in the other cars whistled and laughed and honked their horns. Clint looked over the top of his car and started laughing at Flip.

"Hey. You're okay, man. I mean it. After you dump that Indian chick, you'd better give my little sister a call, asshole," he shouted. The other boys laughed.

Flip gave them the bird, a bold boner flying high above his shoulders. The boys just laughed. He slid back into the car and Maya put her arm around her hero's shoulders and reached up to touch one of his ears.

"I'm not afraid of those guys," he assured us.

What a fucking idiot, I thought.

"I'm ready for a little action, now. Bring the fuckers on," he laughed.

Maya whispered something into his ear, looking at me while she stroked his neck. Flip turned at the next corner, leaving the square going through the dark tree-lined neighborhoods. Without a word, she pointed to a side street, and Flip turned again, then to another side street, and then another turn. Finally, I heard Maya whisper, "here."

Flip slowed the car, inching along the curb.

She looked at one of the houses. It was dark, no lights, and when she was satisfied that no one had seen us she slipped out of the car and walked up to the front door. She walked sluggishly, her heels striking the sidewalk in awkward claps all the way to the front door. Then she disappeared into the black of the porch. The house was a small paint-chipped bungalow, wood-worn, and white-spotted like an aspen tree. The lawn was scraped brown and a big ugly dog was chained to the side of the house, barking and pulling on his chain to get at us.

"Shut up, Mongo!" Maya snapped with a sharp reproach. I was surprised to hear her scold the dog with such authority. Then there was the creak of the door, followed by a soft thump.

"Maybe we need to go home, Flip."

"What? This is my lucky night. I'm getting laid," he said.

"Haven't you had enough excitement for the night?" I asked.

"I can't help it that your girl went home."

"My girl?"

"Yeah, I was going to let you have Debbie."

"That's not the way it sounded at the fairground," I said.

"That was all show. Once we got to the car, she was all yours."

Yeah, Flip was a real piece of work. We listened to the radio while we waited for Maya. I didn't say another word.

We heard the door open and out came Maya, walking toward the car, stuffing something into her purse. She slid back into the seat next to Flip. "Okay, I'm ready."

"Where to?" Flip asked.

Maya pointed, and Flip drove. He kept driving, through the dark neighborhood, by each sleepy house, the streets lit by pale yellow lamps, peppered by bugs. Maya kept pointing until we were out of town.

The lights of the city were a sedate glow over the cottonwood trees behind us.

We do not belong out here, I thought, nothing good will come of this. We hould never have left the fairground. I'm afraid.

"Pull in here," Maya said.

We stopped in a simple field dotted by cattle standing still like big
black wraiths. Dry mud crevices etched along a line of trees. There was
a crumble of dirt beneath the tires. After we got about one hundred
feet off the dirt road, Maya said, "stop."

Flip couldn't wait; he was all over Maya as soon as the engine of his
car choked off, his arms wrestling her close to him, smothering her face.

"I'll go for a walk," I said. I was humiliated.

I walked up the gravel road lined by barbed-wire fencing, kicking
rocks into the ditch, looking through the distant black of the night,
hedge posts gnarled into the wire about every eight feet like twisted
arms.

How long did I have to wait out here?

I tried to smell the air and walked backwards, looking up at the
stars. I felt the breeze coming from the direction of the car. I tried to
catch the hint of Maya's sweat, the first time smell of sex. I tried to
inhale it all just to get a taste of her, and I imagined my head filling
with their activity, strawberry and cotton, skin like Nestle's chocolate
wrestling in the front seat of the car. I imagined Flip smirking with
pleasure as he peeled the buttons off the back of her dress, desperately
grappling with her body, trying to hike it up around her thin waist, his
hands fitting her like a square peg in a round hole.

When I imagined Flip touching her, Maya, his hands pulling at
her skin, snapping the bra off her breasts the way tired men flick the
rubber bands off a Sunday newspaper, I started to feel ill.

The thick air of the late summer night made me dizzy. I thought
I heard a woman's voice scream in the distance, and then float up to
the stars. I couldn't determine which way it was coming from, only
where it was going, but I was certain it was a woman's voice, like the
squawk of a crow, a death rattle breaking through the darkness with its
primordial scorn. I looked around me, twisting on the graveled road,
then standing still, listening, hearing only the drone of crickets.

Do it again. Make the noise. Give me a chance to hear it better.

There was nothing. Dead silence. I looked back at the car for movement.

Did they hear it, too?

I wanted to run toward the voice, find traces of it in the humid air, smell it out, and find its source. I didn't know what I would do once I found it, but I felt I needed to be there, where there was pain, to help, to save whoever was in distress, if there was distress. I ran further along the edge of the road, away from the car, frantic, scanning the fields for a light, signs of movement, a car, a house, or people walking. There was nothing. I stopped, and my heart pounded behind my ribs, palpitating in trepidation. I leaned over, tired, placing my hands on my knees, breathing hard.

Nothing. There was nothing. It got away from me. It all got away from me. I should have listened better the first time. But I never listened the way I should.

I turned and I looked toward the car. I was too far away. I needed to get back. I needed to stop running away. I felt the guilt of distance. Nothing truly disappeared. A part of it always stayed in the air.

The voices and the music from the Jackson County Fair passed over me in the breeze like small shocks of the past. I turned to feel a gust of wind blow past me. It sounded like a girl's innocent whisper: *I like you, David. I hope you don't hurt me.* A pain went through my chest like a blunt pipe. I fell to my knees and started to cry.

Growing up hurts.

When Tyson and Melvyn dared Jake to eat the fly, neither of them thought that he would actually do it. He shook his closed hand, put it up to his ear feeling the buzz of the fly against his palm, held it up, teasing them, and then in one quick motion, he put his hand over his mouth.

"You let it go," Melvyn sniped, his dull eyes peering out of his bean-shaped head.

After a little jostling of the fly in his mouth, Jake rolled his tongue out through his teeth, and there, lying on his tongue was the wet fly, shriveled up in his saliva, the slight flutter of its wing waving at the two young men. Their lower lips dropped, staring at the black bug. He pulled the fly back into his mouth and swallowed, then rolled his tongue back out for Tyson and Melvyn to see.

"Gone," he said.

The two men shook their heads. Jake washed the fly down with a swallow of beer from the red plastic cup in front of him.

"You're one sick bastard, Jake," Tyson stated.

"It wasn't much," he said. "But you have to get past certain assumptions before you can do it."

"That it's gross!" Melvyn burst.

"Something like that," Jake offered.

The other two men laughed.

It was a wedding party in the country, complete with cows and sheep and horses riffling in the background, their feet mixing a muddy stew, looking out over the crowd of people in dumb wonder. Larry walked arm in arm with his bride, Lucy, through the cut brome of their immense front yard, her blonde hair entwined with daisies and wild columbine picked from the ditch along the dirt road in front of their small gothic house. The dry, chipped paint spotted the old home, revealing the baked gray of the aged wood siding. Chapped scales hung from the bay window like nervous icicles. The sound of Van Morrison's *Astral Weeks* pushed its way through the rusty screened-windows. The house grimaced with the weight of time and the punishment of harsh weather. Huge cottonwood trees draped over the gravel-packed road, their long, angular arms reaching out, bouncing in the hot wind.

It was a small forty acre farm with the barn and sheds surrounding the house like a tired wagon train. The bottoms of the once sturdy red buildings pushed their way out from the dirt foundations. The doors and windows hung by rusty hinges and nails that rattled with any hint of wind. The fragile walls leaned in toward each other to keep the edifices from collapsing. The patchy wood shingles on the roofs were littered with mildew, clinging like tired fingers as each tile lay delicately under the one just above it. Barbed-wire fencing, coppered with age, engulfed the property, strangling the crippled hedge posts that poked out of the ground.

The preacher was a young man. He called himself Thaddeus because he didn't feel his birth name of Robert Olmstead was dignified enough for his profession. He wore Oshkosh overalls, a tie-dyed T-shirt and a black derby he bought at a party shop. He carried a small black Bible in the front pocket of his overalls and worked the crowd like an unashamed car salesman, shaking hands and slapping backs, holding onto the back of people's shirts and blouses, squeezing their wrists and biceps until they gave up their names and a small nugget of their personal life. He liked to tell the story about the time he was held up in an old stone cabin, without electricity, plumbing, or the normal sense God gave any man. He was fasting and praying.

I had just finished supplication and was about to partake in a humble lunch of black bread, bologna and tea when a grizzly bear, bigger than the meanest of Philistines, began to slap and scratch on the planked door of the cabin. The cabin shook like a Portuguese maraca. With much wrestling, the bear finally knocked the door off its hinges, splintering the doorjamb. I wasn't sure what I

was going to do and I said, God, if ever I needed a divine intervention, it would be now. Then, like the crack of a lightning bolt in the eastern sky, the Holy Spirit descended on the situation, and I moved the heavy hand-hewed table and chairs between us, and I held up my Thompson Chain of Reference Bible, the King James Version, mind you, like the holy cross of Jesus in front of me. Praise the Lord! That bear stood on his back haunches swaying like a drunken sinner, sniffing the hot air inside the cabin, but he didn't come in. I felt the fireplace blaze behind me. Be gone, you big beast of burden! I shouted it with all the force of the Holy Spirit I could find in me. The bear let out a roar, then dropped to all fours and walked away. I had held him at bay with the literal word of God. Praise Jesus! I'm glad to be alive to tell the tale.

He squeezed his open Bible, his thumb pushing on the pages and his white-knuckled fingers pressing on the outside cover. He moved his other hand across the pages of the small book.

"Jesus is coming soon. Halleluiah! There is power in the word of God," he said. He closed the Bible, slapped the top of the binding and snapped through the razor thin pages with his thumb. "Bless you. It is good that you could make it to Larry's and Lucy's wedding on this beautiful summer day."

He called himself an inter-denominational minister, and quickly added, "I'm presently without a doctrinal inclination, mind you, continuing my search for the right fit of church, God, and parishioners."

He worked with Larry on the cut floor at the packinghouse. Today, he was in his element, the small church in the woods, Larry's home.

Thaddeus stood in front of Lucy and Larry. A shock of dust blew behind them, and Thaddeus blinked. He waited for the wind to die down, his hand on top of his derby.

"It's a windy bugger out here, today," he smiled. Everyone laughed. "I want to welcome you kind people. Thank you for taking valuable time away from your personal lives to share in this wonderful celebration. Larry and I work together every day pulling loins. I told him he needed to wash down good before the wedding." The guests laughed obligingly.

"So, this is an especially happy day for me, to see my friend make this commitment. Lucy, are you sure you want to marry this rascal? You know you can do better."

"Amen, Reverend!" a voice shouted.

A rumble of laughter rolled through the front yard. Everyone was sitting at their makeshift tables and had turned their chairs toward the preacher. The kids were restless, running across the lawn. Lucy nodded.

"Okay, you can't say you weren't warned."

There was more laughter.

"Lucy, do you take Larry to be your lawfully wedded husband, in sickness and health, and all that other stuff?"

"Yes."

"Larry," Thaddeus smiled. "How about you, you're not going to back out at this stage, are you?"

"Yes, I mean no," he responded.

"Gotcha didn't I?"

He waited for the laughter to calm.

"I now pronounce you man and wife. Take good care of each other."

The audience applauded, and cheered with whistles, raising their plastic cups of beer.

There was a skinned lamb on a spit, the sacrifice for the ceremony. The sweet smell of barbecue sauce laced with garlic floated out over the tables fitted together like a patchwork quilt throughout the front yard. Flames licked up under the belly of the lamb, searing the flesh. Thousands of flies, crazy with indirection, swarmed around the spit and tables. The guests shooed the flies with their hands and their makeshift wedding programs.

The cows, a contented audience, lined the driveway fence, chewing alfalfa while the flies spotted their backs like burnt freckles.

Lucy danced in smooth circles in the dirt with her new husband, dust clinging to the ruffles of her calico dress, kicking up small balls of powder from the yard punished by the hot August sun. The flowers in her hair were beginning to wilt. The humidity was thick, sticking to everything, and wet Rorschach designs of perspiration clung to each guest's shirt and blouse, sending a dank smell through the crowd. People had pulled their clothes off minutes after the wedding vows were breathed, laying jeans across the makeshift tables, giving way to T-shirts, light cotton shorts, and halter tops with logos across the breasts like "Big Mama" or "Incurably Horny."

Lucy looked into the face of her new husband with great pride as they moved in circles around the yard.

"If Jake can do it, I can do it," Tyson said flatly. He reached out across the table and clobbered a fly mounting another fly. Their legs clung to each other like tangled black thread. He picked up the flies and threw them into his mouth.

"Well, I'm not sure that counts," Melvyn stated. "They were dead ones. Jake ate his fly while it was still alive."

"Flies are flies," Tyson said, "dead or alive."

"You didn't have to feel them tickle your mouth."

"But I ate two."

Tyson took a long, deserved swallow of his beer and placed his plastic cup in front of him. A wicked grin of satisfaction cut across his face like a crooked river. Then he wiped his lips.

"There," he said.

People grabbed their partners, making their way to the clearing in the front yard to dance alongside Larry and Lucy.

There was Greg Huska who pulled bellies off the sides of hogs on the cut floor, and his wife, Janet, who worked on the night shift, in the curing department, slicing bacon. She complained constantly to Greg about the brine in the curing juice getting into the small cuts on her hands and burning her fingers all day long.

Even with the rubber gloves, I don't know how that stuff gets in there. My hands itch and sting all day. I asked the nurse what I could do, but she just gave me some cream for my hands and told me to keep them from getting wet. Keep them from getting wet? Shit! They're wet all day long. The bacon room drips with brine. I've tried talc, cotton gloves under my rubber gloves, rubber bands around the open ends of the gloves, everything, but nothing seems to work. The brine is everywhere. It knows where to go. The first time I take off the gloves, at break, or to blow my nose, it's all over. My hands are always peppered pink. Just look!

She pushed her hands out in front of her and they shook.

I just want to cry. I hate bacon, but what can I do, my kids love it!

Greg and Janet saw very little of each other throughout the week and even less of their children, but they saved on babysitting bills, they reasoned. Their two girls shuffled from one parent to the other at the changing of the shift, thrown from her car to his pickup truck in the middle of the night, their sleepy eyes wondering what was going on. The weekends were pep rallies to prepare them for the monotonous ritual of the week to come.

Brad Bartok and his girlfriend, Grace, swam through the crowd of dancers building on the dirt dance floor. Brad's heavy body lilted through the sea of cutoff jeans and tank tops, pushing his girlfriend through the scattered tuffs of dead brome, his big hands cupped around her knuckles, navigating her small body through the plank picnic tables and chairs. A small group of boys and girls, at the edge of the table line kicked a rubber ball into each other's stomachs. The ball hit Brad in the right knee and bounced off to the side, to the edge of the property line.

Brad slit the throats of hogs on the kill floor. He liked to tell stories about his job, stories that were coarse, making people with the strongest of constitutions waver.

58

People, having never been in a packing house, he said, can only imagine the things that we see in the course of a day. There is blood everywhere. I remember the time I missed the jugular of one of the hogs.

Well to begin with, the hog is stunned by this machine. We call it a stunner. Ha! And there is enough electricity shooting through the animal's head to make it punch drunk for sixty minutes. The hog is pulled up onto the conveyer where the grappling chains are wrapped around each of its back legs, then the hog is pulled upside down in front of me, and I slit its throat. Like this. Ha! You have to pull the knife down, not across, and you have to hit the throat just above the Adam's apple. It's like ripping through a piece of canvas. Ha! The hog moves down the line to David, who cuts off its front hooves, right at the ankle joint. You have to put your knife right on the ankle to feel where it depresses, and then with a quick slit, angling it through the joint and off it comes. There is blood everywhere. Ha! I'm standing in a concrete pool of it, about two feet deep in the blood that drips from the hogs necks. I got waders on up to my hips. The blood squirts out over my vinyl apron that covers my chest and down the side of the waders, and it's greasier than a fat Louisiana whore on a warm Saturday night. Greasy little whores! Ha! They're sticky as hell. Well, the hog wakes up after David takes off its hooves, and I'm thinking I must have missed the jugular, dull knife or something, because it starts squealing to beat all hell and everyone further up the line can hear it, and they back up off the line to see what the hell all the commotion is about. Someone stops the conveyor, and there's a long screech, and the hog starts swinging back and forth on the chain, wiggling like a worm on a hook. Ha! Blood is dripping where its front feet used to be. One of the hog's legs slips off a grappling chain. Oh shit, then the other legs slips off, and the hog falls with a thud to the concrete below breaking one of its back legs. It tries to stand up on the greasy floor, but it can't, because it is slipping every which way but up on its front stubs. It's like watching a baby on skates. Ha! It's all bloodied, and it starts scraping across the floor, the long shrill of its bony joints sliding against the slimy concrete. Ha! It's a fucking eerie sound. David grabs the bolt gun hanging on the wall, cocks it and walks casually over to the hog, puts the barrel of the bolt gun flush against the hog's head while it gags and convulses, and he pulls the trigger. Ha! Just like that. Pop! Two inches of good old American steel is shot right into the skull of the dumb animal, putting the poor bastard out of its misery. It's instantaneous. The beast slips to the floor like a limp plant on a hot summer day. David washes the bolt gun with a pressure hose, reloads it, and hangs it up on the wall. Someone starts the conveyer back up and away we go. Quite the sight, I must say. The things we do for pork chops. Ha!

David and his wife, Nancy, danced alongside Brad and his girlfriend, Grace, stealing smirks as they twirled in the dirt. David was the only person still wearing his jeans. David always wore his jeans, no matter how hot it got, no matter where he was at, no matter what the season or occasion. And he wore his old scruffy Dingo boots, the straps broken across the top of his left foot. His scattered hair was pulled back under his AC/DC cap.

There were mostly kill and cut floor workers at the wedding, except for Mark who had recently moved from the boning department to the cut floor. In the boning department, they used small flexible knives, Chicago Cutlery, to cut the bones out of the cold hindquarters of the hog. He had worked in the boning department for six years before he poked a vein in his left arm with the point of his knife. The blade pierced his skin and cut into a raw bone; blood squirted across the conveyer belt filled with cold meat. He put his finger on the hole in his arm, standing on the line for a minute until he could collect himself, and then asked his supervisor if he could go to the nurse. The rest of the guys teased him as he walked off the line, so he took his finger off his arm and squirted blood at them.

"Yeah, I used to be a boner," he liked to jest. "But now, I'm just a big prick."

Mark always wore a freshly pressed cowboy shirt, one of those with the artificial pearl button snaps and embroidered pockets, along with a pair of dark blue designer denims. Every time Larry had a party at his farm, he always came dressed to kill. His hair was greased back behind his ears, dripping with enough smelly stuff to kill a mayonnaise jar filled with Nebraska mosquitoes, and he coupled with Larry's younger sister, Charlotte, at every party. From the first big party that Larry threw to the present time, and as sure as a Midwest rainstorm, by the end of the night, people were asking where Mark and Charlotte were hiding. And though they only lived about an hour away from each other, they never saw each other outside of these parties. It was as far as they would ever get with each other, the best they would ever do, at least in Charlotte's eyes, and she puppy-dogged her brother from the time she arrived with questions about Mark and when he was going to be there.

"Did he say when he was going to come?"

"What time?"

"Did he ask about me?"

The twinkle in her face could cool a hot Nebraska day.

There was Quang Tran, who worked next to Larry pulling loins, and his quiet wife, Lu. They were doing their best to fit in, to be American. Lucy made special attempts to make them feel like they belonged, strolling over to the table where they sat alone in the middle of the party to make conversation, commenting about how nice it was that they could make it and how Lu had pretty hair, black and silky and straight like a horse's mane. They looked like a hole in a donut.

"Only in America can you own land without fear of losing it," Quang liked to say. Larry helped him paint the inside of their small house. Quang handed him a can of midnight blue for the bathroom while he and his wife worked on the bedrooms.

"Dark blue for a small bathroom, are you sure?" Larry questioned.

Quang smiled, shaking his head. "You paint."

Larry found out that Quang was sending large portions of his paycheck to his family in Vietnam. His wife worked in a small garment factory on the edge of town. And though they had no children, they seemed to live as close to the bone as anyone else who worked at the packing house.

There was a small scattering of both Lucy's and Larry's relatives from out of town who huddled around separate tables at opposite ends of the yard. Both families stuck out like newly-ironed patches on old blue jeans, but in different ways.

There was Lucy's bald father, dressed in a tuxedo, after she had made it very plain in her invitations that this was going to be an informal affair. He sat stern in his metal folding chair, his tuxedo jacket draped over the back. It kept sliding awkwardly down the front of the chair until he was sitting on it. And every time he pushed the jacket's shoulders back up to the top of the chair, it slipped back down. His bowtie hung with disappointment from his shirt. He looked straight across the table at his refined wife, Cleo, having a silent conversation, holding back his discontent, their eyes looking through each other.

We should have paid for this damned thing from the beginning, not taken no for an answer, and forced these kids to have a wedding with some dignity. I told her we would pay for it. They would have thanked us later. This place looks like an Appalachian circus.

Cleo could see it in his eyes, the restraint and the fire.

The rest of his family, his children and their children, sat quietly in their chairs, hands tucked safely under the table, looking at each other and knocking on the bottom of the pressed board table with their knuckles, kicking their metal chairs with the tops of their feet.

Shh! Cleo waved.

They lined up along on the other side of Lucy's father and Cleo according to size. A table full of wedding presents of every size lay undisturbed at the table next to them. A lot of the presents were in grocery bags with ribbons stapled to the top.

Larry's parents were loud. Their grandchildren crawled over the tops of the tables and chairs like picnic ants. His curly-haired father was laughing and making jokes.

"I'm ready to eat some dead sheep."

He wore orange plaid shorts and flip-flops, a white polo shirt soiled with beer stains, his belly hanging over a pair of white bony knees. His wife, Darlene, wore a pair of big round white sunglasses and khaki shorts. Varicose veins lined the backs of her legs like rivers on a map. She was grabbing children off the tops of the tables by the seats of their pants, smacking their behinds, and dropping them into the dirt.

This was the whole shebang: the wedding, the reception, and the honeymoon---everything. There were no limousines and white rice. No tickets to Hawaii with seven days and nights stay in a beachfront resort. No giggle sessions among mother and daughter and sister. There was no three hundred dollar wedding cake. No champagne.

Monday everyone had to be back at the packing house in their white overalls, knee deep in pig blood and wet meat, pulling the fat off loins, trimming jowls, boning hams, and sawing the back quarters off frozen corsos of hogs kept in a below-freezing cooler. They would endure the drone of conveyer belts clanging and humming, the grinding of the bone augers, floor jacks, the hypnotic melody of the freezer blowers circulating the hint of ammonia which danced through their heads all day. The smell of fresh meat would stick to their skin long after their shifts had ended.

"I suppose a fly is a fly no matter how it's eaten," Melvyn said.

"Damn right," Tyson said.

Jake reached out across the table and caught another fly and scooped it into his mouth.

"I'll be damned," Melvyn laughed. "He did it again."

"I suppose you could eat flies all day long," Tyson said.

"All day? I wouldn't want to ruin my appetite," Jake said. "I mean, there is still the lamb."

"It's sure taking a long time," Melvyn said. He turned to look at the spit, and then he cupped his eyes and looked at the sun.

"You ever eat lamb?" Tyson asked.

"I don't think I have," Jake said.

"Me either," Melvyn agreed.

"They say it's greasy," Tyson said.

"In what way?" Melvyn asked.

"Like all things that are greasy. I don't know," Tyson said. "But it sure smells good."

He turned his chair to look at the flaming meat.

"I like a good hamburger," Melvyn said. "But I suppose meat is meat like flies is flies."

The honeymoon couple left the dance floor. Larry walked over to the spit and started turning the lamb, squirting water on the flames and dabbing more barbecue sauce on the meat. Lucy fidgeted with the food table. There were bowls of potato salad sprinkled with paprika and slices of hard boiled eggs, a relish tray of celery sticks, some filled with peanut butter and some filled with cream cheese that were already starting to soften in the cut stalks. There were radishes cut to look like flowers. Black olives and Spanish olives filled small bowls. Pork 'n beans, with limp strips of meaty bacon lay across the top of each bowl. Opened bags of potato chips, regular and barbecued-flavor, lay on top of small stacks of napkins. There were bags of white bread, twisted shut, with a bowl of hand shaken butter sitting next to each loaf. A pile of paper plates and plastic spoons, forks, and knives lay on the edge of the table. A keg of beer rested in a large galvanized washtub filled with ice.

"Are you going to eat a fly, or what?" Tyson asked Melvyn.

"Well, I'm not sure."

Tyson smacked one just as it landed on the edge of the table.

"There," Tyson said. He pointed at the fly.

"It's all smashed up and bloodied," Melvyn complained. "I'm not going to put that thing in my mouth."

"Well, there's less guts to eat," Tyson said. He wiped the guts off the table and held the fly up by one of its wings. "See. Flat. All the nasty stuff is gone."

"That's just plain gross," Melvyn laughed.

"Get past the assumptions," Tyson said.

He tossed the fly on the ground and swatted another one.

"There. This one is just stunned. It's still twitching," Tyson said.

"I'd like to get my own fly if you don't mind," Melvyn said.

"Well, you can have your pick," Tyson said. He looked around at the swarm of flies circling their table.

"You don't have to eat anything," Jake said to Melvyn. "Don't listen to him. He's just pulling your rope, man."

"I don't want to be the only one who didn't eat a fly," Melvyn said.

"It's not like we're going to go to work tomorrow and say we ate flies and Melvyn didn't," Jake said.

"That's not the point," Melvyn said.

"What's the point?" Tyson asked.

"You're my friends," Melvyn said. "And if one of us eats a fly then all of us should eat a fly."

Charlotte floated through the crowd, her Kodak Instamatic camera cord wrapped around her wrist, pulling it up to her eye and snapping pictures. She told people to smile, to cluster together, and they did, along with the paper plates filled with half-eaten food and tipped-over plastic cups that lay in front of them. And when she compressed everyone into the frame of her camera, she took their pictures.

"Wave and squeeze in tight. This is for the wedding album."

Charlotte pantomimed what they should be doing, framing her face with her hands and smiling. She was a short, squat woman, with pink flabby forearms and a pretty face. She wiggled her way through the crowd like a blue gill through the muddy Big Blue River. Her white makeup made her look soft, innocent. Her eyes sparkled and lit up any group. She looked over the heads of each cluster of people she photographed, trying to find Mark, but he was nowhere in sight.

Larry's father and mother were now dancing, doing some kind of perverse watusi, raising their hands in celebration, rasping out divots of dirt from the ground. Their grandchildren ran through the dance area like crazy demons, chasing each other, bumping into dancers and falling on their butts in the dirt. They tore at each other's clothes in frenzied hysterics. Larry's father kicked one of his grandchildren with his left foot, sending the child face down into the dirt, and then he grabbed his wife, spinning her in circles. She laughed, but then she slapped him in a spurt of moral clarity.

"Treat your grandchildren better than that," she scolded.

"What?"

"You know what, be good."

Melvyn's hand lay flat on the table over a fly. He took a big swig of his beer to sterilize his mouth and thought about the little pest before he finally scooped it up and squeezed it slowly, enough to cripple it, and then he ate it.

"Cold,"Jake said.

Melvyn started to choke.

"See. That wasn't so bad," Tyson said.

"The beer helps," Melvyn said.

"Without the beer, we wouldn't be eating flies in the first place," Jake smirked in a final burst of revelation. "That's the secret."

Lucy's parents stayed long enough to have a small picnic plate of roasted lamb and potato salad, and then kissed their new son-in-law and daughter on the foreheads, giving them a sizeable check that was tucked inside a wedding card, and left. They herded their family into the two minivans parked at the end of the driveway and launched gravel with their rear wheels to make their escape. They left a trail of dust from the dirt road in front of Larry's and Lucy's farmhouse to the dirt intersection a quarter of a mile up the road. The dust descended over the dancing area, hanging in the air. They never said hello to Larry's parents.

Quang and Lu danced a nicely choreographed waltz. They kicked up only small puffs of dirt. They spun in soft circles on the tips of their toes like they were on an oak ballroom floor. Quang's fingertips pressed lightly against his wife's back, and his left arm held his wife's right hand high in the air. She held her head gracefully extended past her shoulders, and they moved with dignity and modesty.

"Classy," Jake said.

"I wonder where they learned that stuff," Melvyn said.

"They got some kind of finishing schools that they have to go to before they can come here. I mean so they can fit in with the rest of us Americans," Tyson said.

"You know, Quang traveled across the country by bus with just the name of our town and the name of the packing house pinned to his sweater," Jake said. "At every stop he'd have to walk up to the bus driver and flash the front of his sweater to make sure he was going the right way. The only word he knew in English was "Work."

"Since Quang showed up at the packinghouse, a lot of other Vietnamese started to come," Melvyn said.

"I don't know where they come from," Tyson said. "They just keep showing up. I had to wait a couple of weeks before I even got an interview. But that was five years ago. I guess things have changed."

"They're coming from California," Jake said. "I think they are hired before they even hit American soil. I don't know how."

"They're like ants to the picnic," Tyson laughed.

"Yeah. Big families of ants, all living in one bedroom apartments," Melvyn said. "My place smells hot with fish every night. And I always see different people going in and out of the apartment downstairs. I think there are about ten people living there."

"Everyone we know at the packing house is quitting," Tyson said. "They're being replaced by Vietnamese people."

"No one wants to work in a factory anymore," Jake said. "It's too hard of work."

"I don't understand. We have a lot of freedom," Melvyn said.

"Freedom? What the hell are you talking about? We have to raise our hand on the line just to take a piss," Jake said.

"So, there are always rules. You just can't let people walk off the line any time they get an itch, even to take a leak," Melvyn said. "I mean, there's a lot of freedom outside our job. No one expects much from us. They ignore us. We can do pretty much what we want to do without the slightest notice."

"Fuck. Cuss. Be rude," Tyson laughed.

"Drugs," Jake added. "Rich people always have to keep up appearances, even if they don't mean it. We live in a cage at work, and they live in a cage outside work."

"Yeah. It's not like any of us are going to be on the city council," Tyson said. "Though I don't know, maybe Melvin's got some designs on power."

"What?" Melvyn asked.

"We've all screwed the same girls two or three times over and no one seems to care," Tyson said.

"Not even their parents," Melvyn said. Tyson and Jake looked at Melvyn.

"What?" Melvyn asked. "I mean, it seems like there is always some woman at the factory trying to hook me up with her daughter. I think it's because we make good money."

"I think it's because they have nowhere else to go, no one to take care of them," Jake said.

"Someone is always sacking out at my apartment," Melvyn said.

"Okay, so we have it better than we'd like to admit," Tyson said.

"At least as good as we can imagine," Jake said.

"I'd like to go to Niagara Falls," Melvyn said.

"What?" Tyson asked. "Where the hell did that come from?"

"Niagara Falls? You got a problem with that?" Melvyn asked.

"No. I just don't see what it has to do with what we're talking about," Tyson said.

"We got it good. And I'd just like to see it. I always wanted to see it," Melvyn said. "I heard that they have a restaurant on the top of a tower that goes around in circles. I'd like to see that."

"Then you should go," Jake said.

"I want to go, but my money always disappears," Melvyn said.

Every Friday, I cash my check and by the end of the night it's gone."

"You need more discipline, Melvyn," Jake said.

"Do you have enough to go to Niagara Falls?" Melvyn asked.

"No," Jake said. "But, I'm not saving for it. I like it right here."

"Oh," Melvyn said. "It's a little hard to have discipline when everyone I know spends all their time at the bar buying rounds."

"Quit pissing and moaning," Tyson said.

"Anyone want another beer?" Jake asked.

The night squeezed around the stars and small pinholes of light filled the black sky. Lightening bugs blinked like soft candles in a light breeze. The crickets hiding along the hedge line and foundation of the old farmhouse chirped. The tables and chairs had all been moved to the side of the yard against the cottonwood trees along the back side of the property line. The house was dark. Tents littered the front yard like a Boy Scout camp, flashlights snapping off and on showing the orange, green and red nylon walls. Snores were coming from one of the large Coleman tents that Larry's family was sleeping in.

Someone farted.

"Gross, Dad," a young boy giggled.

"Brian, go to sleep!"

"It wasn't me, Mom."

"Both of you go to sleep."

Mark's old Chevy pickup truck, the rusty bucket, as he liked to call it, was parked along the dirt road in front of the farm. His flashlight cast light through the branches of the cottonwood trees above him like a magic wand, and shadows from the trees danced over the dirt. There was innocent laughter echoing out of the back of the truck, then a whimper, and the head of Charlotte popped up above the rusty quarter panel, her long hair streaming down into the truck bed.

"Don't hide from me again, mister," her voice scolded. Her words floated like a whisper over the tops of the tents.

Melvyn listened to the lovers play.

Tyson and Jake elbowed each other in their small pup tent, fighting for real estate.

"Your breath smells like fly guts," Tyson said.

"Shut up and go to sleep," Jake said. "We got work tomorrow."

"Turn the other way," Tyson said.

"I'm going to leave if you don't shut up."

Melvyn lay in the pasture on an old army blanket as cows lumbered around him, quiet phantoms, moving their heavy bodies like chessmen, the soft moos filling the sultry night. He looked up at the stars as quiet thin clouds floated across the sky. The small sliver of the moon hid amongst the stars. Even the crickets eventually gave way to the night. The scent of fresh cow pies tickled his nose. He thought about Niagara Falls and how he was going to save enough money to drive out there, go up in the restaurant that went around in circles on the top of a tower. He could do it. He was certain. He just needed to stay away from the bar.

"One of these days this is all going to be gone, our lives and our work," he thought. "And we're going to wonder how everything changed so quickly."

When Wink and I heard the yelp, we were playing cards at the kitchen table. The front door was open to let in any bursts of cool air, but I think we let more flies in the house than we did breeze, and they whizzed around us and pecked at our faces while we tried to pull cards from our hands.

"What was that?" Wink asked.

"It sounded like a dog," I said.

We both threw our cards on the table and jumped at the torn screened door. The old highway heading into Purdy ran right past the house, and sure enough, there was a dog in the middle of the road, yelping. It looked like it had been hit by a car, but there was no car to be seen. It must have just kept on driving after the dog was hit. We walked out to where the dog lay.

"I think it got hit real bad," Wink said.

"Yep."

The dog tried to pull itself free, but its back end was pushed into the road, and it whimpered as it tried to get away. But it was no use. The hot sun mixed with the humidity, and the dog's muscle and hair was like glue stuck to the asphalt.

"Wink, why don't you get the shovel from the side of the house," I said. "Maybe, we can scrape the dog free."

"Then what will we do?"

"Never mind about that," I said. "We can figure that out later. Just go get the shovel."

He was right. I didn't quite know what was going to happen after we scraped the dog free. The whole back of its butt was smashed pretty badly into the road. Its bones were crushed. I hoped it would just somehow be better and run out into the field on the other side of the road, across the railroad tracks, and disappear, but I knew that wasn't going to happen. But, I figured we had to do something and getting a shovel seemed like the first reasonable idea.

The dog started to yelp loudly. It looked up at me, waiting to get some relief from its pain, but all I could do was look back at it. Its eyes were sad, and it didn't understand what was happening.

"Don't look at me that way, dog," I said. "I didn't do anything to hurt you."

"I got it!" Wink yelled, limping back to where I waited in the road. Wink wore a metal brace that wrapped under his foot and extended up each side of his left leg. He dragged his heavy body as he walked, and the metal parts of his brace scraped at the joints. He said that he was born with weak bones and that he would have to wear the brace until he was out of high school. He had had the brace on his leg as long as I could remember and no one in town thought anything of it. It never stopped him from getting into trouble with the rest of us. He just breathed a little heavier, that was all.

He handed me the shovel.

"Are you going to put the shovel under the dog?" Wink asked.

"I'm not all together sure what I'm going to do," I said.

I placed the shovel next to the dog, waited a moment, then, I scooted it near the dog's butt. A sticky pool of blood next to the dog was already turning dark. The dog tried to pull its body forward, but couldn't lift its hind end. As I tried to push the point of the shovel under the dog, it started to yelp again something hideous.

"Why don't you just leave it be!" Wink cried.

"Come on, dog," I shouted. "I'm just trying to help you out. Don't be so touchy."

"I don't think the dog sees it that way," he said.

I pulled the shovel away from the dog's butt and held it up to my chest. The dog looked up at me like I did something wrong to it.

"This ain't going to work," I said. I squeezed the shovel like it was the only truth in the world.

"We need to call the Humane Society," Wink said. "I can't take this dog yelping like it is all day long. They'll know the best thing to do. They're trained for these kinds of things."

"The Humane Society is in Cassville. It could take them over an hour to get here," I said. I knew inside that Wink was right. "And that's only if they cared enough to hurry. I don't see anyone trying to hurry too much to help a poor dog."

Wink put his hands up to his ears. He closed his eyes.

"We got to do something to quiet this dog," he cried. "His yelping is making me crazy."

"Wink, we need to be calm, okay?" I said. "We ain't going to help this dog by being out of sorts. We got to think of something more immediate."

"Okay," he said.

I didn't believe him. The dog's yelping was bothering him real bad. I could tell by the way he looked that he wished we had just stayed in the house playing cards with the door closed.

"Well, one thing is for sure. This dog is hurting real bad, and it ain't going to live too long," I said. "We just got to figure out how to make things easy until it happens."

"We got to move the dog, somehow, before cars come," Wink said. He looked up and down the empty road. "Maybe we should hit the dog with the shovel."

"What?"

"Put it out of its misery," he said. "So we can move it before any more cars come."

"I don't know if I can do it," I said. "Look at the way the dog is looking at us, like it expects us to help."

"Go to the other side where it ain't watching you," he said.

"Why don't you do it," I said.

"You got the shovel," Wink said. "It's in front of your house. You have the immediate need."

"It's a hard thing to do," I said.

"You just swing the shovel hard on top of the dog's head," Wink offered.

The dog looked at us like he understood what Wink was saying. It bowed its head, strumming its paws across the asphalt, and waited. I didn't think I could do it, at least, not while the dog was looking up at us and acting like it was resigned to whatever happened.

"It's hurting real bad," Wink said.

"I know it's hurting real bad."

I turned and looked around us for something different. Mr. Humphrey from the house next door across the lot was running out to where we were standing with the dog. He didn't have a shirt on.

His skinny body was pale and he hardly had any chest hair except for a few stubborn tangles. He carried a .22 semi-automatic rifle that he propped on the top of his right shoulder while he ran.

"Back up boys," he shouted as he got close to us. "It looks like this poor beast is done for."

"We tried to scrape it up," I said. "But it just kept yelping."

"No good. Its whole rear end is smashed into the highway. It ain't good for nothing at this point. Even if you did scrape it up, it ain't going anywhere. So you'd better back up. I'm going to put the thing down. It probably already has rabies."

"Rabies?" I said. "From what?"

"From being hit by the car. Dogs always get rabies when they get hurt real bad," he said.

"Dogs can get rabies by getting hit by a car?" I asked.

"You can't change how nature happens, son," he said. "Nature has its own rules, and dogs are mighty touchy animals when they are hurting."

"Good thing you didn't scrape it off the highway," Wink said. "It might have come after us."

"Okay, back up boys, the bullet might ricochet back at us," Mr. Humphrey said.

Wink and I moved back, behind Mr. Humphrey. He smelled bad, like he had been sleeping in his own sweat, so we backed up further. He put the rifle up to his right shoulder and aimed at the dog; the front of the rifle bobbed nervously, and he pulled the trigger. Pop! The dog let out a loud yelp.

"Did you get it?" Wink asked.

"Damn. I hit it in the shoulder," Mr. Humphrey said. The dog slumped. "I couldn't keep my aim straight. I'll try again."

He put his rifle up to his shoulder again, and he squinted one eye while he tried to aim correctly this time. Pop! Pop! Again the dog let out a blood curdling yelp.

"Damn it all to hell!" Mr. Humphrey shouted. "I keep hitting it in the wrong place."

"You need to hit it right," I said.

"The damned thing moved on me."

"Moved? " I questioned. "It ain't going nowhere with its butt stuck to the road."

"Well, it moved all the same," he said. "What do you know about shooting a gun?"

"I don't know enough about shooting a gun," I defended. "But I know enough not to make an animal hurt so much."

"You can't help the hurting," he said. "The dog's going to hurt no matter what we do."

Mr. Humphrey moved closer to the dog, about three feet from its head, his body pulled back in case the dog snapped at him, and he pulled the trigger. Pop! Pop! Pop! The dog continued to yelp and yelp. And I couldn't stand it anymore, so I ran up to the dog and hit it on the top of the head as hard as I could with the backside of the shovel.

"Come on, dog, die!" I screamed. Wink looked at me like I was out of my head. His big round eyes moved in his face.

There was silence. We all stood and looked at the dog for a moment to see if it would move. It lay in the road, quiet.

"That done it," Mr. Humphrey stated, satisfied.

"Yuck." Wink said.

I handed the shovel to Mr. Humphrey, and he gave me his rifle. He scraped the dog off the highway, like it was a cow pie, and then he handed the shovel back to me. He tucked the carcass of the dog up under his left arm. He took his rifle back and swung it over his shoulder with the other arm like a great hunter. He carried the dog to the woods behind where we both lived. We followed a ways behind him because he smelled so bad. Blood smeared across the back of his shoulders. He let the dog and his rifle down at the edge of the woods, and then he grabbed the dog by the front legs and tossed it into the woods. He grunted hard.

"You ain't going to bury it?" Wink asked.

"Why?" Mr. Humphrey asked.

"Because that's the right thing to do," Wink said.

"Who told you that was the right thing to do?" Mr. Humphrey asked.

"Some things you just know are right, like taking a shower when you smell," Wink accused.

"Hush," I said to Wink.

"It's the nature inside you that tells you when things are right," Wink continued.

"Well, nature is telling me that this dog belongs in the woods, unburied," he said. "And I'll take a shower on my own inclination, if you don't mind, not because you have issues with it. Didn't your parents teach you any manners?"

"It just doesn't seem like the right thing to do," Wink said. "That's all I'm trying to say."

"Son, it's a hard thing to know the right thing from the wrong thing, sometimes. You'll understand that better when you get older. And you're not older yet. Right now, you need to count on adults to do your right thinking," Mr. Humphrey said. "Now, take your shovel and get on back to your house and let it be."

He brushed off the sides of his jeans with his hands, picked up his rifle and put it on top of his shoulder and started back to his house.

"Do you think we ought to fetch the dog out of the woods and bury it?" Wink asked.

"No, I don't think we should do anything," I said. "I don't see any need for messing with Mr. Humphrey's work. Let's go inside."

"Sometimes adults don't always do the right thing," Wink said.

I threw the shovel alongside the house.

"Damn it, Wink," I said. "I don't know anything about how adults think, especially when it's about what is the right thing or the wrong thing to do. It just ain't any of my concern. So, let's go into the house."

Mom left Pop. It was the worst thing to ever happen to either of us, though I must confess, Pop took it harder than me. I came home from school one day and Pop was sitting at the kitchen table with a short glass of Canadian Club, waiting.

"She's gone," he said.

"Who?"

"Your mother, who else?" he said. "She didn't leave a note or nothing."

"Where did she go?"

"I don't know," he said. "She's just gone."

"Well, how do you know she's gone?"

"I just do," he said, and he was right. A week went by and she never came home, and then weeks went by, and still she didn't show up. And after a couple of months, I stopped looking.

Pop spent the days after mom left ghostlike around the house, and sometimes I caught him in his room, his face pushed into the pillows on his bed with angry tears, his fist smashed into the headboard.

In many ways I was glad to see her go. She acted like she weren't here most of the time even when she was here. I could tell she wasn't happy. She spent most of her time staring at the T.V. screen, or cleaning when there wasn't any cleaning needed, or finding reasons to go shopping at night.

"Everything she cooks makes me fart," Pop used to jest. And he was right. She wasn't much good in the kitchen.

She never liked to sit and talk to Pop or me. She was always quiet. She did what she had to do each day. She was like a tenant, an employee. She weren't much of a mother that I could ever remember, not that it was her fault, I never had much to say to her, and I'm guessing she was lacking in the wife side of things, too.

After Pop snapped out of his misery, he came home late just about every night, whether it was weeknights or weekends, drunk, stumbling through our small plastered house, crashing through the kitchen, knocking over chairs and bumping into the table which wasn't far from the front door, the house being a big open room with a bedroom on each end. He tried to pick things up, but usually they just stayed turned over on the floor for weeks until I decided to make it right. He tripped clumsily toward the cupboard to get a short glass to pour himself a strong drink before he made his way to the bedroom. He never shut the bedroom door when he was drunk, unless he was with a woman. He always set his drink on the end table next to the bed before he went to his bathroom. I could hear the sound of the faucet running, the clearing of his throat and spitting, and then he came back to his bed, fell across the scooped out mattress and passed out. He snored heavily through the nights, and I got used to sleeping with a pillow over my head to muffle the sound. The glass on the end table was always empty by the morning.

It didn't bother me to see Pop so messed up. He always stayed out late on weekends, regardless, and even when mom was here he stumbled through the front doorway early in the mornings, staggering to the bedroom where she would help him get his clothes off and tuck him under the covers of the bed. I was used to his strange behavior. It was more important to me that he came home at the end of every night. And he always did.

❋

Wink and I stayed up late the day the dog was run over. We tried to play cards, but Wink's heart just wasn't in it. I had to remind him when it was his turn to make a play, and he would throw cards down like he wasn't thinking. We left the front screen door open, now that it was dark, and a breeze started to find its way through the open room.

"Did you hear that?" Wink perked up.

"I didn't hear anything," I said. "What's your problem? Do you want to play cards?"

"There was a noise at the side of the house."

"It's nothing," I said. "I never heard any noises."

"It can't be nothing," Wink said. "Because nothing is nothing, and I heard something. Noise has got to come from something."

"It's just the wind making the trash cans hit each other," I said.

"They never moved before," Wink said.

"Well, maybe they moved tonight because of the breeze being stronger," I said.

"No, I think it's more than that," Wink said. "I think it's the dog coming back to get satisfaction."

"What?"

"It wasn't buried right," he said. "And now it's coming back for satisfaction."

"The dog is dead, Wink," I said. "It ain't coming back for nothing."

"Everything's got a soul," he said.

"What kind of soul can a dog have?" I asked.

"It has a soul like we got a soul, and it's restless because it was never buried right, and it's coming back until it is."

"Who told you that?" I asked.

"It's part of the Baptist religion," he said.

"I never heard anything about that before," I said.

"That's because you never been to church like me," he said. "There are things about religion that you are ignorant of because you never made the attempt to learn."

"I don't know what not going to church has to do with not hearing something outside," I said.

"You don't believe that we have a soul that can separate itself from the body," he said. "It's the dog making the noise."

"I don't believe in ghosts," I said. "I don't think it has anything to do with being Baptist."

"The soul ain't no ghost," he said. "It's real. It's the spiritual part of a thing that needs to have satisfaction before it can move on."

"Move on to where?" I asked.

"The next place," he said.

"I don't believe that dog is roaming through the trash cans because it can't find satisfaction," I said.

"Every soul needs satisfaction," he said. "The Baptist church is all about the soul finding satisfaction."

"Well, one thing is for certain, I truly believe the Baptist church is filled with unsatisfied people," I said.

"Well, we need to make sure the dog is satisfied," he said.

"The dog is dead."

"Well, it don't appeared to be so; even dogs don't like being thrown in the woods like we did."

"Well, we didn't throw that dog into the woods, Mr. Humphrey did it," I said. "So, if the dog comes back for satisfaction, it ought to make noise with Mr. Humphrey's trash cans."

"Well, maybe it reckons that we had a choice in the matter. We could have buried the dog after Mr. Humphrey left, and we didn't," Wink said. "We need to do something to make it right with the dog."

"What? " I asked. "Mr. Humphrey already did what he did. He's the one responsible."

"We can still bury the dog."

"Wink, it's one o'clock in the morning. Don't you think the dog can wait for us to make it right in the morning?"

"A restless soul knows no time," he said. His wide face was white with worry. He jerked his leg up to bend his knee and the metal on his brace squeaked.

"If we bury the dog now, will you shut the hell up about this whole thing?"

"It depends on whether the dog has satisfaction."

"How are we going to know if the dog has satisfaction?"

"I don't know. I just figure if we bury the dog, it will happen."

I was asleep on the couch when Pop came home late on a Saturday night.

The door pushed open and a stream of laughter poured into the room.

"This is so-o cute," a woman's voice said about our small house. I was lying on the couch in the big room, and I squinted from under the pillow to watch them. I shifted so no one could see I was looking. She was a heavy woman with red hair. She was wearing a short purple dress, tight against her hips, and she pulled it down while she walked. She had a lot of makeup splashed across her face, heavy red lipstick and dark penciled eyebrows. They stumbled, and Pop stopped their fall by grabbing the edge of the table.

"Now, let's wait up, lover," she scolded. "There's a child in the room."

"Oh," Pop stuttered. "He doesn't give a damn. Besides, he's sleeping."

"How do you know he's sleeping?" she said.

"He stays up too late."

She pulled herself free from Pop and walked over to where I lay. She stumbled in her high heels and gave a couple of oops and giggles. I could see holes in her black stockings that had run up the side of her thigh. I liked the way her body jiggled like jelly. I started to breathe heavy like I was about to snore.

"He's so-o cute," she said.

She sat down next to me on the couch and I could feel her pantyhose rub against my blanket. She smelled like flowers and I almost sneezed.

"Okay, so the little bastard is cute," Pop said. "Hurry up, let's get to the bedroom before I bust a nut."

"Shush," she said.

The woman touched the side of my back and ran her fingernails, softly, tapping along my T-shirt.

"Sleep tight, sweetie," she said. She grabbed my arm and squeezed my bicep. She stood up awkwardly on her heels and walked toward Pop's bedroom. I watched her butt wiggle, and I wanted to touch it. She pulled her dress down. "You'd better be ready, lover, because I'm going to give you more lovin' than you ever dreamed you could handle."

"Baby, I was born ready. I can handle anything you can throw at me," Pop said. His voice floated from the bedroom.

"Hmm." the woman smiled.

She pulled the door shut, but I could still hear the muffled sounds of voices and laughter. There was a sharp slap against flesh.

"What did you do that for?" Pop complained.

"Because you needed it," she laughed.

Then there was silence, no talking. I could hear movement, shoes dropping *on the linoleum floor, and then there was a hard thud of their bodies falling on the bed as it scraped across the floor.*

I was always glad to see Pop happy.

I got the flashlight and we went to the back of the house along the edge of the woods. I pointed the flashlight out over the wooded area. The tree stumps all looked like white-gray tombstones, and there was an eerie silence. Weeds poked up around the trunks of each tree.

"Did you see Mr. Humphrey come charging out of the house with his gun like he was the Calvary?" Wink laughed.

"He weren't much use," I laughed.

"My mom says he's the most worthless man in Purdy, by even the lowest standards."

"Did she give reasons?" I asked.

"She never gave reasons, except that he ain't worked in a coon's age," Wink said. "People say his wife supports him."

"I don't know if not working is a good reason for being worthless," I said.

"I think it is for a woman," he said.

"Does he have one of them disabilities?" I asked.

"My mom says he can work if he wants to, but he doesn't want to," Wink said. "She says the whole town laughs at him behind his back. I don't think anyone would hire him now, even if he had the inclination to work. "

"He's a silly man," I said.

"She says the whole town talks about his wife doing everybody in Barry County, Baptist and otherwise."

"Your mom says that?" I asked.

"Not to me," Wink said. "To my Pop, but I can hear it. The walls are thin in the house."

"How does she know stuff like that?" I asked. "Did anyone ever see her with another man?"

"I heard my mom say that she ain't ever home," he said. "What do you expect them to think?"

"Well, I'm just trying to say that if people don't know for certain, then they shouldn't make assumptions about it."

"It ain't no big deal," Wink said. "I don't know why you care so much to defend her."

"I'm just saying people shouldn't talk so much about things when they don't know the facts. Mr. Humphrey is stupid enough without people making him look more stupid."

"Well, one thing is for sure," Wink said. "He can't shoot worth beans. You can swing a shovel better than he can aim his rifle."

We both started to laugh.

"Hush," I said. "People will find us out."

We stopped to get our bearings and looked out into the woods with the flashlight. We saw what looked like faces behind every patch of weeds. Ghosts.

A car raced on the old highway in front of the house, loud music spilling out of its open windows, and it was gone as quick as we saw it. I turned the flashlight off and handed it to Wink when I first heard the car coming up the road. I thought it was Pop.

"Shush," I whispered.

"What?"

"Nothing. I think the dog is somewhere along here," I said. Wink clicked on the flashlight.

"Stop," Wink said. We both stood still. Wink flashed the light out into the trees. "I'm sorry, it's nothing. I thought I heard another noise. It's really scary out here. It seems like there are dead dogs everywhere I look."

"We can still go back to the house and wait 'til the morning," I said.

"No. I want to continue with what we came out here to do," Wink said. "I think the dog is just a little further over there, in that open area."

We found the dog lying on its side in a shallow patch of weeds. Wink put the flashlight on it and bugs had already started to test the flesh.

"Hand me the shovel," I said.

"Okay," he said. He stood over the dog with the flashlight. The dog's eye was filled with gnats.

"It looks really stiff," Wink said.

"Where do you want to bury it?" I asked.

"Back further in the woods so we can't hear it make noise at night."

"There won't be any noise if it's satisfied," I said.

"Just in case it ain't satisfied," he said.

"I didn't come out here this early in the morning not to get this dog satisfied," I said. "I thought you knew for certain."

"I know for certain," Wink said. "I was just trying to make more certain."

"I'm starting to think that the Baptists don't know what they're talking about," I said.

"You wouldn't say that if you were satisfied," Wink said. "You would know for certain, too."

"I'm satisfied enough."

"Pop, she's gone," I said. "You need to forget her. She ain't worth the effort."

"Well, she did say she would love me forever, and then she just up and left. You expect people to keep their promises when they make them."

"The promise was good for that moment," I said. "Maybe she did what she did because it was right for her at the time."

"There is never a good time to go back on a promise," he said. "When you make a commitment, you need to stick to it and do what's right for everyone."

"Well, we ain't everyone."

"We should have been everyone to her."

"Well, we weren't. There ain't much more to say about it," I said. "She's long gone. I think you need to leave it at that."

"What about you?" he said. "Doesn't it hurt you? She didn't even let you know where she was going. She didn't leave you a note. Nothing. Right? "

"I don't much care."

"But, do you want to know why? "

"I said I don't care. As far as I'm concerned, she's dead to us."

"Shame," he continued. "When a woman decides to quit being a mom and a wife, she feels shame. It's her nature. It's part of being a woman."

"Everyone has their own shame," I said.

"But a woman has a different shame," he said. "They're entrusted with keeping everything right, and when they don't keep things right, things get out of control. Men are not good at keeping things right."

He started to wave his arms, and alcohol splashed out of his short glass. He put the glass on top of the refrigerator and shuffled over to the cupboard. He leaned into it, on his tiptoes, and pulled a box off the top shelf. He took the box over to the table, set it down, went back over to the cupboard and leaned into it again. This time he pulled down a holster and pistol.

"Pop. Please."

"You got to know the truth, son."

"There ain't any truth to know, Pop. Just let it be."

"Truth is always important," he said. "Truth is the only thing that matters."

He stumbled around the kitchen table, dazed, like he was looking for something. He slammed the holstered pistol on the kitchen table.

"Where's my goddamn drink?" he asked. "Did you hide it from me, because if you did, I'll kick your ass?"

"It's on the refrigerator, Pop, behind you, where you put it."

"Oh."

"What are you going to do with the gun, Pop?"

"I'm going to clean it," he said slowly. He had a self-satisfied smile on his face.

"Why do you need to clean it?"

"Because I like having a clean gun in the house," he said.

"You're planning to do something," I said.

"What makes you think I'm planning to do something?"

"Because I know you; you wouldn't get your gun out unless you were planning to do something. I don't think you're thinking right."

"My thinking is just fine," he said.

"Well, If you're thinking of doing something, you can't," I said. "You don't even know where she lives."

"Yes, I do," he said. "She lives here."

"Not no more," I said.

"She's confused. She'll come back when she's had enough time to sort things out."

"And you think if you can find her you can help her sort things out with that gun," I said.

"Like I said, I'm just cleaning it. It's been gathering dust in the cupboard for a long time. A pistol ain't any good if it just gathers dust. It won't fire unless you keep it cleaned and oiled. What if someone broke into the house and tried to hurt us?"

He opened the box on the table; it contained a thin .22 caliber cleaning *brush on a twisted wire handle, a .22 caliber barrel rod, a small can of oil, and a small stack of cleaning patches. He set the open box next to the gun.*

"I got to take a piss," he said.

I waited until he was gone, then I picked up his pistol and hid it in the crack of the old couch. I threw the blanket I slept under back over the top in a haphazard way so he wouldn't think anything was wrong and went back and sat at the kitchen table.

Pop stumbled back out into the kitchen and stood wobbling and looking around the room.

"Where's my goddamned drink?" he said.

"It's still on the refrigerator," I said.

"Oh."

He opened the refrigerator, looking for something.

"Do we have any bologna?" he asked.

"We don't have much of anything to eat," I said.

"Oh."

He walked over to where I sat at the kitchen table and stood next to me.

"I guess we should probably go to the grocery store," he said.

"Yep."

Then he grabbed a handful of my hair and pulled my head up.

"Where's my pistol?" he said.

"I hid it," I said. "Ouch! Let me go!"

"I'll let go of your hair when you tell me where the goddamned pistol is at," he said. "So, 'fess it up or I'll crack your fucking skull!"

"No, you're going to do something wrong with it," I said. "And I'm not going to let you."

He pushed my head into the top of the table.

"Where is it, goddamn it?"

"No."

The ground was soft. The shovel slid into the dirt like it was going through dry sand. I reached down after getting a shovel full of soil and pulled the weeds out so we would have fresh dirt to put back on top of the dog's grave. By the time I finished we had a hole that was plenty big to put the dog in and bury it. Wink held the flashlight while I dug.

"Will you keep the flashlight steady so I can see what I'm doing?" I said. "Stop shining it all over the woods."

"I thought I heard something," he said.

"Just keep it on what we're doing. There's nothing out there worth seeing at this time in the morning."

"I'm not worried about the things worth seeing," he said.

There was wetness in the air. A waxing moon floated through an apparition of gray clouds. I put the shovel down next to the grave and walked over to where the dog lay. I dragged it by its front legs until it dropped into the hole. I had a large piece of plastic I found on the side of the house, and I put it over the dog to keep bugs off its face. I picked up the shovel to fill the hole with dirt.

"I never buried anything before," Wink said.

"I never buried anything before, either," I said.

"Do you think we did it right?" he asked.

"I don't think there is a right way to bury a dog," I said.

There was a little dark mound of dirt over the dog's grave when I was finished. I patted the top of the mound with the shovel to make sure it was firm.

"There," I said.

"We got to say some words," Wink said.

"I'll let you say the words, since you have that Baptist upbringing,' I said. "You're the one who was taught all the right things to say in these types of circumstances."

Wink looked up at me confused.

"I was never taught what the right words are," he said. "I have only been to people funerals."

"Well, people funerals can't be much different than dog funerals," I said.

I pushed the shovel into the ground at the side of the small grave. Wink searched the ground for two loose branches. With a string that he had brought from the house, he tied the two sticks together to make a cross and pushed the bottom end of the cross in the ground on the side of the mound.

"Wink, I think it is good that we are giving this dog a Christian burial," I said. "I wasn't much for the idea at the beginning."

"Well, now that we're being honest," he said, "I ain't ever been to a people funeral either."

We both stood at the front of the mound shining the flashlight on the dirt.

"Okay, go ahead and say something," I said.

Wink coughed to clear his throat.

"Dog," he said. "We are truly sorry for how things happened. We did everything we could to make things right. So you go on now, and let us be. Amen."

"Is that it?" I asked.

"Our preacher always says that all that really counts is a contrite heart."

"Let's go for a walk, son."

We got about a hundred yards up the old highway. The sun was just going down over the cottonwood trees. I could smell cows; I could always smell cows at this time of the evening. The smell filled the thick air around the house.

Pop pulled a bottle of Canadian Club from his pants pocket. He tipped the bottle up to his mouth and took a long drink, then handed the bottle over to me.

"Here," he said.

"That's okay, Pop," I said. "I don't need any."

"No. I'm serious, damn it, take a swig," he said.

I took the bottle and put it against my lips and pushed it upside down, I let the bottle hang there, but I didn't swallow anything. The alcohol burned the rim of my mouth, and I was glad I had kept my mouth shut.

"I loved your mother," he said. "I'm sorry she's gone. I did some things wrong; a lot of things were my fault. I know more now that there is distance. Distance is the great go-between for truth. Sometimes we need a lot of distance to let the anger settle. Your mom was a beautiful woman, but I think it's time for me to get along in my life."

"She was never worth the trouble you put yourself through, Pop."

"Maybe, but she's still your mother. And one of these days she's going to show up to see you. You can count on it," he said. "How do I know? She ain't going to be able to live with herself unless she does. It's part of being a woman. And when she does, you love her."

"Okay," I said.

"I mean it, damn it," he demanded. He took the bottle and tipped it up to his mouth, and after he had drawn a long drink, he just held the bottle. "I'm

trying to say something important. She's just confused, and she's going to need you one day. Here, take another drink."

I took the bottle, and this time I tried to swallow a little of the whiskey. It tasted like sweet wood. It burned, and I tried to hide my distaste.

"Burns, huh?" he smiled.

"A little," I said.

"Good." He said. "Whiskey is something you have to get accustomed to in order to appreciate it."

"Why do you drink it if you have to practice so much to enjoy it?"

"Anything worth appreciation needs practice, no matter how much it burns. It's like trying to love a woman. Good things are always going to burn a little. You understand what I'm saying, son?"

"I think so."

"Okay, let me have the bottle back before you hog it all," he said. He gave me a conspirator's smile.

"See that railroad track?" he asked. He pointed the bottle toward the other side of the road. It was starting to get dark. He nearly lost his balance, but he put his arms in front of him to keep himself steady. "Well I used to work on that track. It about killed my ass. It was hard fucking work, lugging new ties out of the back of a truck to replace old ones, taking the spikes out of the old ones, and sliding the new ties under the rails. And even though we wore leather gloves, sometimes on hot days, while we were replacing the ties, we might lean against hot rails with our forearms and it burned us. Do you know what I'm trying to say?"

"That anything worth appreciating is going to burn a little?" I asked.

My Pop waved the bottle in front of him, disappointed.

"No. What I'm trying say is that you should never be afraid of a little work. Okay?"

"Yes, Pop."

"No matter what," he said. "There are a lot of people who just can't work."

"Right," I said, "Like Mr. Humphrey."

"What?"

We stood still in the middle of the old highway and Pop looked up at the sky. The light of our small town fanned over the top of the trees. He tipped the bottle back on his lips and I could hear the bubble of the liquid disappearing. He left a small thimbleful of whiskey at the bottom of the bottle.

"What a beautiful night," he said, wiping his lips. "The stars are so..." He

shrugged.

"Pop?" *I said.*

"Yes son."

"Wink and I buried a dog out behind the house in the woods last night."

"What happened?"

"It got ran over by a car on the highway."

"Oh," *he said.* "You did the right thing. Here take another drink."

I took the bottle and just held it in my hands.

"You know, I've been thinking that maybe we should move to a new place," *he said.*

"In town?"

"No," *he said. He grimaced.* "I have been thinking that maybe we should move out of Missouri."

"Where?"

"Anyplace," *he said.* "Some place new, someplace where we've never been, a good place."

"Whatever you think is best," *I said.*

"It would have to be a place where no one knew us," *he continued. I wanted to ask him why he wanted to go where no one knew us, but I thought differently.*

"California," *he concluded.* "There are places for people in California."

"I love you, Pop," *I said.*

He reached over and ruffled my hair.

"I know, son," *he said.* "I know."

Andy seemed harmless enough when he opened the passenger door of my car, dropping himself into the vinyl seat. A mutable grin was etched across his face like the curve on a super slide. He wore a brand new plaid shirt, still creased from its packaging, and blue jeans, starchy and midnight blue. The bottom hems of his pants were folded up to offset the length, and a red knapsack hung over his right shoulder. A worn stocking cap with frayed ends, coming loose at the sides, was pulled over the top of his head and covered what looked like tangles of jet black hair. It framed his coarse face scarred by a river of lines.

I spotted him sitting in the dry Nevada dirt on the side of the merging lane coming out of the Lovelock interchange in Nevada. He had his knapsack between his knees and he was staring up at the highway as cars flashed past him and disappeared into the flat horizon.

"Where are you going?" I shouted pulling up alongside the edge of the highway. The gravel crunched under the weight of the car's tires. The dust created by the stop lifted into the air and floated back toward the interchange. He jolted, slapping his right hand on the powdered dirt, almost falling further down the hill that supported the exit. Then he sprang to his feet and brushed himself off. The dust swirled up around his knees.

"Pennsylvania," he shouted. He hurried to the top of the road and descended on my car like a gnat to an open wound, grabbing the handle of the door before I could reconsider my offer. "Thanks for the lift."

"You got a long way to go. It's a good thing that I stopped." I gave him a quick look over and merged back onto the highway. "What are you doing by yourself in the middle of the desert?"

"I just got out of the hospital. I'm going to see my dad," he said. He was winded and eager to share the information.

"Well, I can take you as far as Nebraska. That's where my trip ends. You got pretty big balls trying to hitchhike your way across a hot desert. This isn't winter, you know. Do you even have drinking water?"

"A little, in my bag. I never thought about it," he said.

"You're not really dressed for the summer heat are you?" I said.

"The desert is cold at night," he said. He sniffled. "People think it's always hot in the desert, but it isn't. Sometimes it's hot and sometimes it's cool."

I shook my head in amazement.

The things people do.

"When we get to Nebraska, I'll let you use the shower in my apartment. Okay? Clean up a bit before you go on to Pennsylvania. Oh, my name is Tim."

I reached over and grabbed his hand, keeping an eye on the road in front of me.

"Andy," he said. Andy was slow and deliberate, reaching over with what appeared to be a pained arm. He was suspicious, but amiable. He slumped into his seat, and having now finished with all the necessary formalities, dropped his knapsack on the floor in front of him, lay his head back, and let out a low sigh.

I was certain that he felt lucky to have been plucked off the hot, dry clay.

There are myriads of small unfortunate creatures caught unaware, daily in the hot sun, having skittered far from their original havens of safety, and now, lost, looking for a cool hole for respite without success. They stop, resting on flat rocks, tired and confused. Their stomachs heave in fear. And finally, they give up as their bodies start to collapse drying up, quietly, not knowing what is happening to them, while the sand whispers across the desert.

"Thanks again for stopping," he said. "Really, I didn't know what I was going to do. I guess I didn't plan this trip too well. Cars have been passing me all afternoon. I had to sleep under the bridge last night. I didn't want to do that again."

"You were out in the desert all night long by yourself?" I asked.

"I wasn't by myself. I wish I had been by myself. An old man in a dark trench coat hung out in the bushes just feet away from the bridge where I slept. He looked like he was waiting for something. He walked around the desert all night long. I don't know where he came from, but he never said a word, just stood at the edge of the bridge. Sometimes he disappeared, but I could hear the crack of the dry branches he stepped on. It was creepy. I think there are a lot of perverts that just wander the interstates looking for vulnerable people."

"Did you have a way to protect yourself?"

"I had ways," he said, shaking his head. "But the man was gone by the time the sun came up."

"That's good to hear."

"I felt like there were bugs crawling on me all night long. It got real cold."

"I don't blame you for not wanting to be down there again for another night,"

"I've been out on the road for about a week," Andy said. "It hasn't been fun."

"You've been out there for a week?" I asked. "Have you eaten anything?"

"I have a little food in my pack."

"Do you feel strong?"

"I feel fine. Why?"

"I can use a little help driving. My butt's numb."

"What?" Andy asked. He looked puzzled. "Oh, sure, I can do that."

"Did you get enough sleep last night?"

"Yeah, I finally did get to sleep."

"Can you handle a stick?"

"The car I used to drive had a stick shift."

"Well, good," I said. "I've been on the road for over twenty-four hours straight without sleep. Do you want to take over?"

Andy looked surprised, which should have been my first clue, but I thought he had a problem hearing me with the windows down and the air whipping into the car.

"Do you want to drive?" I said, raising my voice.

Andy stuttered, trying to push out an answer. His hands reached up to the sides of his head, touching his temples, rocking back and forth in his bucket seat.

"Um, fine, yeah, I can do that."

"Great."

They always look for cracks between the dry rocks and the cuts in the earth, the lizards and small bugs, places where they can find safety from larger predators. Yuccas litter the landscape with their withered flowers. They are food and they are drink. There is nothing to eat unless they burrow deeper into the coolness beneath the sand and wait, snapping up occasional sand fleas that shoot across the red clay. Survival is always waning in the desert, and the vulnerable teeter into desperate situations.

Why did I put him behind the wheel of my car? I was tired and I wasn't thinking straight. The road and the desert and too many drugs and cigarettes frazzled me. Forget the formalities that accompany two men, total strangers, getting to know each other through the wary volley of casual conversation, establishing the rudiments of trust. I couldn't even trust myself. Where was he going to go? The highway was a straight shot to Nebraska. I would have let a drunken monkey take over the wheel of my car if I thought it could stay on the road.

I pulled my car to the side of the highway, and we both got out to trade places. Andy was sluggish, dragging the heels of his dusty tennis shoes across the asphalt. He launched a couple of small rocks across the shoulder of the highway and down the embankment. He stood still for seconds, scanning the empty spaces of the desert around him. The sun burned the air over the terrain. I watched him, his laziness, and then I looked up the road. Only a small black dot of a car balanced in the distant ripple of heat coming off the asphalt. I touched the hood of my car, and it was hot.

"I don't have a license," he confessed.

"You can drive?"

"Yes."

"That's fine. We're on a long, straight stretch of interstate. Just keep the car at the speed limit and stay between the white lines," I said. I gave him a conspirator's wink and slid into the passenger side of my car.

"The white lines?"

"Yeah, the white lines on the road, out there. If you can stay within the white lines you'll never get in trouble."

"Oh."

He slipped behind the wheel of the car, looked at the dashboard, fingering a few of the knobs like he was trying to familiarize himself with all its functions, making sure he could find the lights and the radio which had been off since I left Los Angeles, and the heater and cool air knobs which he turned on and off quickly. He tried to make look like he had driven cars a thousand times before, that he had actually mastered the technique and wherewithal of car handling.

"There's a lot of buttons," he said. There were hardly any buttons at all. This was a Dodge Colt. He looked at me for confirmation.

"You're doing great," I comforted. "You're practically a professional."

"What?"

"Here, take a couple of these," I said. I had reached into the glove box and fumbled through a pile of plastic bottles. I pulled out a small one which was filled with pink hearts. "I always keep a bottle of these candy in the car for long trips. They always help me stay awake in the early mornings. Caffeine. That's all they are. You can buy them out of just about any male magazine."

"I guess they must be okay if you can get them from a magazine," Andy assured himself.

"Totally legal," I said. "But, they'll make your heart pump like a fucking jack hammer."

"Thanks."

"Don't thank me; thank D & E Pharmaceuticals," I said, looking at the back of the bottle, squinting one eye. "They are the saviors of the red-eyed traveler."

I put two of the pills in the palm of his right hand and he swallowed them with one big, dry gulp.

There are no rocks in the desert big enough for Andy to slip under. He is naked in the night, totally vulnerable. Everything that moves is a potential predator. He has only the icy stars and the coolness of the moon above him to give him solace while he sleeps, while the sand below him moves, watching him, while the man in the dark trench coat skirts his desert bed, stalking, pondering his possibilities.

"Good night," I said.

I put my sunglasses on and flipped the sun visor down to block the yellow-orange rays that angled through my skin. I watched the mescaline shock of black come to life and the little black squiggles move in the liquid of my eyelids.

"Wake me if you have any problems."

"Okay, I think I got it."

I let my attention collapse and my mind melted into a shallow slumber that rocked with the wind as it blew through the open window of my small Dodge Colt. I needed sleep very badly. I had traveled from Los Angeles to Lovelock, stopping only for gas. My thoughts were scattered, filling my head with crazy reasons. I was all over the road, drifting at times beyond the white lines I had created for myself so long ago.

What would it be like to gut a lizard? Slice it up, open it down the middle of its pink stomach, and after all the insides had been scraped out, cook it. It couldn't be much different than eating a chicken nugget.

I turned my car over to a complete stranger, whom only minutes ago I didn't know, whose existence was not even a hint in my thoughts. It was the perfect abandonment of reason. How did I know which way he would steer this small car? I have given him a weapon to wield against me, a power. I gave him a knife with my name engraved into the blade. I relinquish all concern. And I didn't care. Life brushes off the tips of our fingers like a passing thought.

He could take me south, or north, or turn back to California. He could drive my car into a desolate stretch of sand, strip me naked at gunpoint, force me on all fours, walk me through the desert like a lame coyote, and take my wallet where the last three hundred dollars I had were tucked safely between my social security card and HMO card. He could make me beg on my knees for my life, satisfy every bizarre whim that haunted his thoughts, and leave my dead body on the hot sand to dry out like a dead lizard. I didn't even know what he had in his knapsack

"Tim!" Andy's frantic voice interrupted my thoughts.

I looked over at him, noticed his hands, white-knuckled, choking the steering wheel. His body was rigid, eyes popping out of his skull like ping-pong balls, staring out at the highway.

"I don't think I can handle this," he said.

"That's okay, just take it easy and move over to the side of the highway." I guided him, reaching over to touch his shoulder. I dug through the glove box, grabbed the first bottle I could find, popped off the lid, methamphetamines, and I tossed a couple into my mouth. "It's okay. You're doing just fine, Andy."

It was like bringing a wounded jet out of a torn sky for an awkward belly landing. He was a tight-stringed kite on a windy day, waiting for that one fatal gust to tear him to pieces like aged paper. I prayed for his wind to lull.

Who in the hell is this guy! I had pulled over to the side of the road in a moment of physical weakness and fragile coherence, and I let this scamp into my car like I was picking my brother up from the gym. I should have never given him those pink hearts. He looks white, disturbed. He is clearly in a fit. His brain is probably playing handball with the sides of his skull. I'm never going to get any sleep now. The sun is sucking the liquid out of my head, and the desert is just waiting to consume the both of us. There are predators everywhere.

"Take it easy now. You'll be all right, Andy. Good," I encouraged as the car came to a sluggish stop. There was the final jerk of the engine, a death throe. "Put the car in neutral and pull up the emergency brake."

Andy's body raced with electricity. He could barely contain the scared demon trying to find its way through his skin. He raised his right hand to clench his shirt and squeezed it like his clothing was a suffocating shroud. He pulled. He was a nervous little mouse racing to find its hole.

I prodded him to let go of the steering wheel and his left hand dropped to the door handle.

"You're okay."

"Thanks," he said, relieved to have the control of the vehicle taken from him. He got out of the car and leaned against the driver's door, his arms folded across his chest. His body rocked like a crippled man in a rocking chair. A truck drove by and his fragile arms winced to protect his face.

"Are you going to be all right?" I asked.

"I'll be fine," he said.

I didn't believe it. I looked back down the highway for hope and saw nothing but the sweat of the desert heat coming up off the road. Translucent clouds feathered across the blue sky. There was nothing to hold onto. There was no place to stop.

"I'm sorry I couldn't handle driving your car, Tim," he said. "I know you're tired."

He shuffled back to the passenger side of the car. I waited for him to get settled before I got back behind the steering wheel.

"I'm going to take a little cigarette break," I said.

"Okay," Andy said. He sat in his seat like an obedient dog.

I leaned back against the driver's side of the car and took long hot drags off the cigarette. A semi-truck sneaked up on us, and its wind almost pulled me into the highway, into the side of the semi. I touched the side of my car with one of my palms. My heart raced.

It was the last cigarette I had, and I sucked the tobacco down to the filter, then wadded the empty pack into a ball and threw it out into the highway and watched it toss around as cars and trucks passed over it, slapping it into the undercarriage. I steadied myself as the whoosh of each car passed me. It made me want to just let go, allow my body to be pulled into the traffic on the road. There was a stillness between each blast of wind like the world had come to an end and I was the only one here. And then the next semi whipped by, hitting me like a heavy cloud. The sky was as white as the sun, and it squeezed the tired landscape around me.

"Andy, I'm sorry I gave you those pink hearts," I said. "It was a stupid thing for me to do."

"I think they gave me a buzz," he confirmed, grabbing his chest. "I thought I could handle it. But my chest started to hurt."

"Like you drank too much coffee?"

"I don't drink coffee."

"Well, see. There you go."

Andy stared into the thinning sky, and it filled his simple face with meaning. I wanted to ask him what he was looking at, but I suspected it was nothing I could understand.

"Why were you in the hospital, Andy?" I asked. "Were you in a car accident?"

"No. I've never been in a car accident, but my cousin was. It took his head clear off his body. He went through the windshield and his torso hit a tree."

"I'm sorry to hear that."

"It was nothing. He should have been wearing his seatbelt," he said. "It happened when we were just kids. Are you going to buckle your seatbelt?"

"What?" I asked. "Oh, thank you."

"I was in a psychiatric hospital," he said.

"Oh."

"But, I'm okay. I don't think they would have let me out if I wasn't okay. I can try to drive again after these pink hearts wear off."

Fat fucking chance! This damned belt. It always fights me. It won't lock just right. It feels crooked. Snap! I probably pushed this poor bastard right over the edge. He was better off living under the bridge at the Lovelock interchange, slumped away from the cruel indifference of the civilized world. He should have coupled with the greasy old man who wanted to bugger him. They could have wandered the desert together until they disappeared into the sand, comforted each other in their most certain demise and shriveled away on a common rock.

Now he is spit on a string, with no friends to comfort him. His mind is a bowl of soup. Mental hospitals--- who can trust them? They sweep the human wreckage from their hallways out into the street, to be fed upon, making room for new carnage. I'm going to have to keep my eye on him. I don't want him eating the cigarette butts out of the ashtray. Jesus! Don't look at him! It's all coming to me now; I put that crazy loon behind the steering wheel of my car, filled his body full of chemicals and sent him careening down the fucking highway. And then I went to sleep!

I need to keep my eyes open, watch him and watch the road and watch him. Fuck! Don't look at him! I wish I hadn't taken those damned methamphetamines when this whole thing started.

"I'm just glad you're all right, Andy," I said. That's all that really matters."

"I feel fine. I did get a clear bill of health when I left the hospital. At least, that's what they told me. They said, *Son, we've done all we can for you. The rest is up to you. You are free to go.* I think I just had a lot of built-up stress in my life. I feel calm now. The hospital helped me get a lot of priorities straightened out. I just couldn't handle some things. It's hard to handle things when they pile up on you. But now I can handle things. Well, I guess not everything."

"So, you're going to see your dad?"

"Yeah, that'll be good. He's a doctor, too. But, he's a different kind of doctor. I think it will be good to see him."

Andy turned to look at me, his crazy lips twisting out the words. He had a satisfied smile that swept his face. I struggled to keep my eyes focused on the road, catching glimpses of him from the corner of my eye. The muscles in my arms fought to keep the car between the white lines.

"When is he expecting you?" I asked.

"He's not. He still thinks that I'm in the hospital, unless they called him. God, I hope they didn't call him. I want to surprise him."

"You didn't let him know you were coming?"

"Nope," he shrugged. "It'll be all right. I've just shown up at his house a lot of times in the past. He's used to it."

"I'm just thinking he might want to get a room ready for you."

"I don't need people to ready stuff for me. I'm pretty self-sufficient."

I stole a peek and saw him knot his right hand into a fist. He rubbed it into his palm and pushed it into his thigh.

"I mean, he is my dad, right?" he said. "It's not like we haven't had disagreements before. He has to expect stuff like this."

"Well, I suppose so. It's always just nice to let people know when you are coming. People like to know what to expect," I said. "But, I don't know your family situation."

"I suppose we all have family situations." Andy said. "Do you have any family situations?"

"Both of my parents are gone, dead," I lied. I felt guilty telling someone my parents were dead when they were both very much alive.

"I'm sorry to hear that," he said. "It's hard not to have someone."

"I do okay."

His eyes scanned the car, looking for a distraction. He glanced in the back seat and spotted a book lying face down on the top of a folder. He swung around and my heart jumped forward a couple of beats as he reached back and grabbed it off the seat: *Writing Poetry by Barbara Drake.*

"School stuff," I said.

"Are you a poet?"

"Writing is my major in college," I said.

"I write poetry," he snapped.

"Is that so?"

"Oh yeah," he assured. He stiffened his body in the seat, pushed his hand in his pocket and rummaged through his jeans, pulling out pieces of paper, wrinkled and crumpled into little balls, some yellow some white and soiled, some a little brownish like a grocery bag. His fingers fumbled through the small wads opening a few and turning them over, inspecting each one, pressing his face into the faded pencil print. "Want to hear one?"

"Um, sure Andy."

What could I say? No! Keep your twisted thoughts to yourself, you psychotic nutcase. And who the fuck gave you a pencil to squirrel out your innermost confusion? These people must be insane. The insane giving the insane writing tools, weapons, and then sweeping them back into the streets like they were cleaning the kitchen floor.

I listen to the drivel of boring people every day, making attempts to scratch out a little reason from their distressed minds, hoping to find in it coinage, substance. You can't resolve your inner demons with a few metered lines. You have to put sweat equity into it. It's a flesh-to-flesh battle, and in the end, it leaves you too exhausted to think. It's not for the feeble-minded.

That's how I see it. Giving Andy a pencil and an old grocery bag to scribble his thoughts on is like giving a drunk a bottle of Old Crow to help him articulate his despair. So tell me about your pain, Andy. I will listen, and then I will stomp your frittered dreams into thankless oblivion.

"I'd love to hear your stuff," I said. My mind was grinding on words like an auger ripping bone.

"I normally don't share them with just anyone, but since you're a writer, I think it would be good to get some pointers."

"I'm a student," I corrected.

"Well, since you're a writer and we're friends, you might be able to help me with my poems."

"Like I said, I'm just a student."

Friends! Now we are friends! My mind is racing. When in the sweet name of Jesus did we become friends? When? Could it be because I touched your shoulder when you were nearly ready to shit gravy? I never said we were friends. You can't hold me to that. It isn't right. It isn't fair. Oh God, I told this razor-brained idiot he could use the shower in my apartment. This is so messed up. The desert is really scrambling the thoughts in my head. I've got to slow down. I need to stop driving so fast. Holy Jesus, where am I? My map, where is my fucking map? I need a rock to hide under, let the coolness settle my nerves. I don't know if I can go any further.

I'll try, Andy," I said. "But, I'm just a student myself. You know, writing is something very personal. You have to feel good about what you write. My opinion isn't as important as what you think about what you do. What's most important is how you feel."

"Well, I definitely have feelings," Andy said. And with that, he began unfolding more wads of paper. "I'm trying to find a really good one."

"Take your time."

"Oh, here's a good one!"

He coughed a couple of times to get his throat in the right condition.

"Now, you got to remember," he said. "I was really hurting when I wrote this one."

I can imagine.

"You broke my heart," he hesitated.

He looked over at me for encouragement. I nodded, and he coughed one more time.

"You broke my heart like it was nothing, and then you laughed about it, like I was nothing. I don't like to feel like nothing. So I grabbed you by the neck and squeezed and squeezed, until my thumbs pushed through your skin. I could feel the wet of your life, and the meat around your jugular. It was warm, and you tried to swallow, but you could only spit. And when you stopped spitting your life back at me, I took my fingers out of your throat and licked them clean, free from you. I watched your eyes looking back at me in surprise, and I said, '*Who's laughing now.*'"

"The name of that one is *Who's Laughing Now.* What do you think?" *What do I think?*

Shit! I think my brain is leaking reason. I think you are a fucking nutcase. I think you should be put into a padded room with your favorite chew toys and left to suckle them until your lights dim into old age. I think that any fucking institution that would let you out on the street, on your own recognizance, doesn't know their assholes from the manhole in the middle of the road. What do I think? I think too much.

"Fuck, Andy," I said. "I think that was a little intense."

My arms were shaking like an electric paint mixer. It was all I could do to keep the car between the white lines. Everything began to freeze in front of me.

"It was how I felt at the moment. Out of the gut and onto the page, as they say. I think the trouble with me is that my inspiration comes in spurts, odd moments, when I least expect it. And I have to be ready to write when my brain is seething with creativity and certainty. There's not always a pencil handy to write all this stuff down."

"Seething is a good word. I like that."

I need to drop this crazy son-of-a-bitch off right now. I can't take him home. But how do I do it? My arms want to move the car to the side of the road, but something inside pulls me back. I can't stop. I have never been able to think straight in a crisis. I have always been reactive rather than proactive. But then, a crisis never happens when I'm ready for it. My head sizzles with doubt, and it takes me to a place where guilt and regret struggle, wearing me out, leaving me devoid of choices. This is a rock I have crawled out from under before, and it's a brutal task. Life is a craft, not an art form. It takes years of practice to perfect, and I have had to revise draft after draft in my attempts to get it right.

I settle on a single certainty: I need to separate myself from Andy. That is where the Holy Spirit moves. And I try to listen.

"What do you mean?" Andy asked.

"What?"

"You said that seething was a good word."

"Seething? Oh, I was just agreeing with you about the creative process, Andy. The poem was very good," I lied.

"That means a lot to me coming from someone who is a writer."

"Well, I'm just a student, Andy," I said. "I mean, did you hear me? I'm only a fucking student! Okay, I'm sorry."

"But, you write."

"Well, yeah, I write, but anyone can write. I'm learning, too."

"That's what I need to do, I need to learn more. I've got ideas bouncing all over the place in my head. Sometimes I don't know how to get them out. It drives me crazy."

Word choice is always a key to any creative process.

"Don't feel like you have to get all the ideas out of your head. Editing can be your best friend. Don't be afraid to use a little restraint in your writing and in your life."

"Do you think so?"

"I know so. It is always better to trim back what you already have rather than add, I mean, in your writing."

"Do you want to hear another one?"

And before I could stop him, let him know that I had a pretty good feel for his range as a poet he pulled another *good one* from the wads of paper lying in his lap.

"Dead flowers are all I give you, because they make you happy. And I want to make you happy. So I walk hundreds of yards into a field to kill a bunch of wild flowers, just cut them down, and bring them to you, just to make you happy. And you always demand more. I lay them at your heart and all you can do is put them in a jar of water and let them sit there until they wither and die. You self-absorbed bitch, maybe I should cut you down like a field of wild flowers and put you in a jar."

He looked over at me and smiled.

"*Dead Flowers*. That's the name of that one. It's a little shorter, but it has a lot of...I don't know."

"Metaphor?"

"Yeah! See, you know a lot of things I need to know," he said.

"Maybe we need to pull in somewhere to get some fresh air and a bite to eat," I said.

"All I have is one dollar," he said.

"You're traveling across the desert, all the way to Pennsylvania, with only one dollar in your pocket?"

"It's not much is it?"

"Don't worry about it, Andy. I'll pay for your meal."

One dollar. How do you measure the value of pocket change in 1998? I could buy three candy bars for a dollar at the local Wal-Mart. Or two cans of pop. I could get a quarter pound hamburger at the local Jack-in-the-Box, maybe belly up to a cup of coffee and a donut. But in Andy's mind, it was a magic carpet ride to Pennsylvania. It meant he didn't get busted at a bus stop for vagrancy. It meant he could dig through the dusty recesses of his jean pockets, rattle his change, and imagine that he was living large. Or, on the more practical side, he could buy a roll of utility string to use for shoelaces. Or he could roll the bill up to snort a short line of street crank.

What is the value of one single dollar? To me, it is the change I dig out of the crack in my sofa. To Andy, it is his whole life.

We were sixty minutes west of Salt Lake City; I saw a chipped white and black sign rise out of the sand: *Desert Rose Café.* Rows of semis lined the backside of the restaurant like horses in front of a saloon. All I could think about was how I was going to ditch Andy, maybe slide into the bathroom for an inordinate amount of time, and when he was tired of waiting, make my way quickly to the car and spit gravel out of the parking lot.

There are greater issues at stake than the satisfaction of my hunger, one being my freedom: I want to shed myself of all responsibility. Just walk away. Give away the pets or let them run free. Get an unlisted phone number. Watch the dust collect in my apartment. Ignorance is bliss; this is a paradise I hope to regain. Everybody wants to be a virgin again, if only for a day. And so on, and so on...Another is my solitude: nothing gives me greater comfort than being alone. A crowded room can never validate an individual's presence.

As fate would have it, Andy stayed by my side like a casino whore who knows she's slipped into a good place. I wandered over to the sales counter and ogled the clear paperweights with scorpions entombed in the center, and when I picked one up, he picked one up. I scooted over to a line of miniature beer mugs with state logos on the front, and when I picked one up, he picked one up. He was my shadow, attached to the bottom of my soles. He stayed with me stride for stride, souvenir for souvenir. He wasn't losing his new friend. Not here. Not now.

"Are you ready to eat?" I asked.

"Yep."

Eggs, that's all Andy wanted.

"I love eggs," he said.

So, he ordered eggs, sunny side up and runny, the yolks dripping wet, and water, lots of water. He consumed his eggs, slurping them into his mouth like sloppy noodles, letting the whites tickle his tongue before letting them take a sled ride into his stomach. After he was through eating his eggs, he sat quietly over his glass of ice water, slurping the shards and spitting them back into his glass. It drove me nuts.

"Do you want more eggs?" I asked.

He shook his head no.

"She sure is pretty," he said.

"What?" I asked. A spoonful of mashed potatoes hung between my plate and my mouth.

He looked up the restaurant aisle and nodded.

"What do you mean?" I asked.

"I mean I wouldn't mind meeting her."

"Who?"

"The waitress," he said.

"She's probably married," I said.

"How do you know she's married?" he asked.

"Everyone living in the middle of nowhere is married. It's the only way they can stand it," I said. "It's a rule: you can't live in bum-fuck Egypt without having someone to share your misery."

"That's funny," he said. "How do you know this is bum-fuck Egypt?"

"It's as close as you can get without having to buy a first class trans Atlantic ticket."

What the hell else was I going to tell him? Good idea, Andy. Let's make it a double date and ask her to bring along a friend. We can yank them both out of this cockroach-infested grub hole, drive them down the road a bit, both screaming and fighting to kick the back window out of my car, all this, just to give you a chance to have your date. We'll bury their bodies in the flea-infested sand just outside of town, and then we'll bolt out of here like piss-filled dogs looking for a nervous tree.

"She sure is pretty. It wouldn't hurt to ask her," Andy said.

"Whether she's married or not?"

"No. I want to ask her if she would go out with me sometime."

What kind of a knucklehead scheme is that? Go out with her sometime I want to scream into his face. You have a dollar to your whole useless name You're hitchhiking across a sun-scorched desert, no car, living on the charity of a man who knows you just got out of a nuthouse. Oh yeah, tell her your brain is seething with poems that are eulogies to every girl you ever knew and touched with your nervous hands. Tell her you want to touch her eyes, or that you want to take her out into the middle of the desert, cut the tops off yuccas plants, and share with her your terrible talent for love.

The last thing I wanted to do was give Andy any ideas, I mean about whose car we were driving, and whose money we were spending

"We just don't have the time, Andy," I said. "I got to get to Nebraska soon. I have a report to finish before school starts next week I should have been home days ago."

"I suppose you're right," he said.

I couldn't get us out of the Desert Rose Café quickly enough. He ogled the waitress when she put the tab on the table, looking up at her with those goofy gray eyes, trying to figure out how he could love her in the worst way. She smiled. I slid a ten-dollar bill over the top of the tab and she told me she'd be right back with the change.

"Keep the change, please," I said.

"Thank you. You're so sweet."

I grabbed Andy by the sleeve of his shirt and rushed him out of the restaurant.

"'Bye," he shouted back to the waitress. She turned to wave and smiled.

"Come back," she shouted.

Andy stopped and pulled me back through the glass door of the restaurant.

"What in the fuck are you doing, Andy?"

"She told us to come back," he said.

"She didn't mean now."

"Oh," he said. And then he shouted, "We will. We really will."

Not on my goddamned watch.

It was getting dark; the orange sun squeezed into cobalt blue to bring in the night. The black hills on the horizon looked like small breasts popping up into the sage-scented sky. It was getting harder to see the terrain. Andy nestled against the side of the door and fell asleep. I couldn't have been happier, and I determined to make good use of this quiet time to get us as close to Nebraska as possible. My body was ringing like a bell, the drain of the methamphetamines pulling at my nerves, plucking at my courage. I just wanted to get to Lincoln, and I pushed the speedometer as far over eighty as I felt I could without getting stopped by the highway patrol. I thought my little Dodge Colt was going to blow off the road.

That whole night I thought about Andy's poems. I mulled over each one in my head, and the possibility that, just maybe, he could have actually killed someone. I believed he could, that his mind drifted close enough to the end of the dish to oblige him toward action. The edge of the dish: it was the only place Andy has ever been. Who can see him standing in the center of anything?

If he did this thing, I mean if Andy really did this thing, I'm in a car with a killer. And, if he did this thing, then I've got to believe that he has done it a number of times---killed people. He is probably a serial murderer; at least that's the way I see it.

However, one thing I do know for sure, I'm not going to ask him if he's killed anyone. Nothing says stupidity like knowing the worst about your immediate situation. And even if I discussed it with him out of literary curiosity, which was a good way to broach the subject, being his mentor, of sorts, I might get to the nub of this mystery, but in the end, was it something I really needed to know? I didn't want to put him into a desperate position where he felt like he had to do something. The last thing I needed was to make him feel like he had shared too much with me, let his mind bubble with the idea that maybe he had taken chances that were unnecessary. Who knows what floated in that soup he called his brain? It sounded real enough to me. I should accept it for what it is. I mean, people don't write poems about pushing their fingers into other people's throats without a little reference to back it up. Do they?

I looked at Andy sleeping peacefully, curled up like an innocent baby, dead to the world around him. And to look at him, you wouldn't think he was capable of monkey punching the family pooch. I could see Andy getting his ass kicked by any number of people. Most women would be able to squash his head between their thighs. But then, all of these crazy people looked like innocent rubes. Look at Charlie Manson.

Write what you know. That's what my writing professor always told me. And it seemed to me that Andy knew what he was talking about. His poems were filled with a potency that reeked with real experience. He had knowledge that none of us should even think to possess. He knows.

Oh my God, he drank her blood. He slurped it down like runny eggs.

I listened to the relentless drone of the car, its wheels peeling off the warm highway, the hum of the engine pulling us along, lifting the weight of the day. The Wyoming wind drafted through the window, slapping at my face, keeping me awake. I thought I was going to lose my mind. I came very close to pulling to the side of the road and just telling Andy that he had to get out, that he was on his own, that he needed to take his chances on the Wyoming plains. I thought about taking a pee break and compelling him to do the same, then when he had started to make a piddle in the sand, running back to the car and speeding away.

The sliver of a moon illuminated the indistinct line of the distant black mountains.

If I could hang him up by the back of his shorts on the prick of the moon...

And for the first time, I smiled.

I came upon a highway patrol car which had pulled another motorist over to the side of the road. The lights on top of his cruiser blinked like the red, white and blue of a strobe light. A shot of guilt went through me and my arms stiffened. I pulled into the left lane, and as I passed the patrolman, he looked up at us and then quickly back to the business at hand. All I could see was the back of the driver's head bent forward. It could have been me. I eased my foot off the gas pedal just a little.

This was my final chance, and I let it slip past me. Insanity is now certain, I believe. I could have stopped ahead of the patrol car, dragged Andy's ass out of his seat, and told the officer that this was the man he had been looking for all along. This was the man who was probably responsible for every serial murder from Los Angeles to Pennsylvania. I was certain there were articles; handbills with his face splashed on it like a Rorschach print. Push his hands into a bucket of luminal and let the horror reveal itself. There was no doubt in my mind that they would be blue with rage. We should kick him to death right here and now, spare the scales of justice their fickle ways. We shouldn't take the chance that he might get away.

I should have frisked the little scamp and checked his backpack before he even thought about getting into my car. But had I thought about it, pondered all the possibilities, I would never have even considered picking him up. Which brings me to the conclusion in this matter: picking up a hitchhiker, in the middle of a hot desert, or anyplace for that matter, is the most irrational act a person can do.

I tried to settle into my thoughts, but like a dog chasing its tail, my mind went in circles for the rest of the night.

What's in Andy's backpack?

Surely just clothes.

He told me he had ways to defend himself.

Does he have a knife?

What's in Andy's backpack?

Surely just clothes...

All night long, I listened to the wind mix with my thoughts. I looked through the dead bugs smeared on the windshield and past my headlights shooting their beams in front of the car. I thought about his backpack and the weapon and his clothes. It was there, blood stained, like a killer's butter knife, his utility of choice. It was there. I nodded my head in certainty. It was there.

So I sit on the dry rock and wait. The desert night feeds my reason. I smell the weak. I am predator.

Andy hardly said five words to me the whole morning, and then morning turned to afternoon. He just sat in his seat staring out over the green plains.

"Where are we?" he finally asked.

"We're in Nebraska," I said.

"I've never been to Nebraska before, at least not that I can remember."

"Anybody who has ever traveled across the country has probably been through Nebraska. It's the funnel between the east and the west. But there's not much to see."

"Is that corn?"

"Yes it is." My voice was numb.

"It looks pretty."

"But, we don't have any mountains, just small rolling hills."

"What's that?" he pointed.

"Soybeans."

"Oh," he said. He continued to spy out all the little nuances of my home, fingering through what the sparse landscape had to offer, looking for points of interest. "You don't like me, do you?"

"I'm not sure what you're trying to say, Andy," I said. I was too tired to care what he might do. All I could think was *bring it on.* "What do you mean?"

"There are a lot of people who don't like me," he said. "More than I can count."

"How do you figure that to be the case?"

"It's the way people look at me. I could see it at the hospital. Some patients were scared to be around me. The staff couldn't wait to get rid of me. They treated me like a smelly rag," he said. He turned to look straight at me. "That's a metaphor."

I stared back at him.

"I picked you up, didn't I?" I said with a monotone. "I let you read your poems, and then we talked about them. I bought you eggs. You like eggs."

"Yes, I do like eggs."

"And we saw a pretty waitress." I reminded him.

I was ready to offer her up as a sacrifice. The further away we drove from Utah, the more expendable she became.

"I'm going back to that restaurant one of these days," he said. And I believed him.

"She was a nice lady," I said.

"And she wasn't married," he said.

"Maybe."

"She wasn't wearing a ring. I notice things like that," he said. "I think you were trying to keep us apart."

"Why would I want to keep the two of you apart?"

"Maybe it's because I didn't have any money."

"Has lack of money ever stopped you in the past?"

He shot me a spooky look, and then he grinned, shaking his head and pointing his finger at me.

"You're a writer, all right," he laughed. "Yep, you sure are. Or are you a politician? You're not one of them politicians, are you?"

"Nope. I'm just witty enough to get me through the day, not clever enough to shake down a whole career."

"Good. I hate politicians," he said, stoically. "They never tell you what they really think, only what they think you want to hear."

He let out a healthy laugh and slapped the dashboard with one of his hands.

"Hot damn!" he shouted. "You really are good with words. I'm not going to disagree with a person who is good with words."

I was too tired to care at this point. Andy had worn me down.

The sky over the Nebraska plain pressed down on the earth and on each cornfield, after soy field, after alfalfa field, and dilapidated barn, old and scarred, and it was all welcoming me home. I felt guilty for having brought this abortion back with me, to the quiet lives of the farmers and teachers and preachers and café waitresses and packing house workers and small town grocery clerks, and to the pigtailed little girls and freckled-faced boys who lived here. Children scurried in the fields of cut straw. Corn stalks lay broken in the fields without fear of molestation. Andy does not belong in this world. He belongs in a big city where he can disappear into the dysfunction of its daily rage; but here---definitely, no. He was like the echo of a fart off a wooden church pew in a small town. He could do nothing but draw the worst attention to himself.

True to my word, I let Andy use the shower in my apartment. And while I was listening to the water pound against the shower walls like a good Midwest rainstorm, I rolled over in my mind the best way to move him to the next step, back on the road and out of my life. But the longer he stayed in the shower, the more my mind shifted from getting rid of him to disposing of him.

Every writer wants to kill his protagonist or to make him impotent, to neutralize any future threat. It's our obsession. And it wouldn't be hard. My mind searched for the reasons. I could do it. I could go to the kitchen, find the largest knife in the drawer, go to the shower, scare the shit out of him, and when he slipped on the porcelain, I could shove the knife into his body. I could watch the blood wash down the drain. I could wrap him in the shower curtain and dump him in a field. I could do it. He had left his backpack in the car, so I knew I could do it. And the most revealing thing I learned was that I could live with my action. He would deserve it, and no one would ever know. No one would ever care. I could really do it. It's at times like this when I get enthused with the idea of extremes and I begin to understand my true human potential. It's a Hobbesian revelation in its truest form.

The faucet in the shower squeaked off, like the brakes on an ill maintained car, like my mind. I listened to the swish of the shower curtain, the shuffle of Andy's wet feet across the floor. The medicine cabinet opened and closed.

What in the hell is he doing in my medicine cabinet?

Andy sneezed, and before I knew it, he was out of the bathroom, his tangled wet hair slicked back, sniffling. He was ready for me to take him to the nearest truck stop.

The things we think in our idle moments.

I don't think I will ever shake Andy from my mind. Every time I sit down in front of my computer to write, I get a tick of a thought and he slides into my brain, whispering in my ear as I punch away at the keyboard, telling me to write a really *good one*, and I exorcise my demons. I imagine his crooked smile scrutinizing my every word, and he exhorts me to tap into that hidden creativity and certainty. I fill the screen of my computer with dead flowers that drip over every thought that gasps for life. I create.

You son-of-a-bitch, I should have stabbed you in the heart when I had the chance.

Andy was gone. I gave him twenty dollars and helped him into the first semi I could find, occupied by a driver who looked tired and in need of desperate company. I suppose there are times when all of us are in need of desperate company, especially when we are taking a long trip. It's hard not to trust the thoughts that run through your mind as they mix with the hum of the car engine on an empty road.

"Thanks, Tim," Andy said. "And just for the record, I never killed anyone. I know what you were thinking, and I understand. I know I'm not fully well; sometimes I just don't see things as straight as I'd like to, but I know a lot more about right and wrong than you might think I know."

I smiled. I grabbed his forearm and squeezed.

"Good luck, Andy."

I watched the semi snake out of the truck stop, breaking gravel, and onto the merging ramp, launching the tired driver and Andy eastbound on Interstate 80. I had no doubt in my mind that they would become fast friends, because if there was one thing I have learned about truck drivers in all my journeys traveling the interstates, in and out of truck stops---they have an amazing ability to endure, to stay within the white lines of the roads they travel, no matter how intense the circumstances become. They aren't easily distracted. I watched them until they were out of sight while I just sat in my car and played with the keys in the ignition. I couldn't wait to get home, to jump into bed and get some sleep. I was exhausted. I needed to stop at the quick shop for a pack of cigarettes.

Wisps of wind blow through a gray-blurred sky into the next world. At each stop there is rest, an innocent wink to existence. Souls stand on the sidewalk of immortality looking through their past and into their future without as much as a map to guide their way. All things illuminate in their own time. All things constantly move in the stillness of eternity.

My wife walked across the asphalt parking lot which takes up the entire block. The oil stains dotted the pavement like drips of black blood. She was about fifty yards away from me at the Discount Tire Store, and she walked around our minivan with the salesman close behind her. She pointed at the wheels, thumping the tires with her knuckles, stopping to discern the wear on the tread. She stood patiently, her open hand up to the side of her face, asking questions and giving the salesman a studious gaze. That was my wife: the great arbitor of our family business. And she was committed to the task.

Our daughter, Kristi, ran along the line of the bent chain link fence next to the Discount Tire Center. It circled the weathered playground of the Catholic Church which rose up from the ground like a great monolith, stained-glass windows surrounding the sides of the building like a tight belt. Rows of white paint-chipped houses, sporting roofs solid like beaten hats, had dusty windows that streaked each house with a frown. They lined each side of the church. Everything was gray, and I stood in the cloud-blurred sky watching veins of drooping telephone wires criss-cross the tired neighborhood.

Kristi ran in figures of eight, circling through the parking lot, within earshot of her mother. She held a bottle of bubbles, allowing the wind to blow through the plastic wand, lifting wet balloons into the sky. She chased after them, jumping and skipping behind the bubbles as they were caught up into the sky in sudden jolts and popped. She shouted back to her mother, but all I could hear was a stifled enunciation of her words, *"They're blowing up to the sky."* She scooted them higher, heaving her small body up, throwing her arms above her head, encouraging the bubbles on their ascent. She skipped, scraping the asphalt with the bottoms of her red buckled shoes, waving the bubble wand through the sky like she was swatting flies. My wife clapped her hands to get Kristi's attention, but Kristi was pointing at the sky with her small bent finger. She squinted her eye, stretching her small body up. She was looking right at me. She hesitated for a moment, giving a slight grimace, and then she skipped back toward where her mother was standing. She threw her arms around my wife's waist and put her finger in her mouth across the bottom of her teeth.

She was so pretty, my daughter. Her long tangled black hair draped over the back of her shoulders. Her small face was as soft as lotion. Her skinny legs poked out of the bottom of her bouncing dress like popsicle sticks. She let her mother go and her innocent smile pierced the sky above her as she spun in circles watching the fat gray clouds take shape and slowly move. She sent more bubbles into the sky and watched them spin in crazy circles, the spangle of the glassy blue and orange smiling on the wet sides as they snapped into nothing. She stopped just before she reached the garage with her swirling turns and put her nose into the bottle of soap, inhaling a chest full of fragrance.

"It smells so pretty, mommy."

The tire salesman was wiping his hands on a rag that he snatched off a barrel in the garage and walked back to his office. Another man, in a stained uniform, drove our van into one of the service bays. There was the echoed screech of the tires on the concrete, testing the brakes as he stopped. My wife said something to get his attention, and then showed him four fingers. He shook his head in agreement. I never knew my wife to be such a handler of people. And now, there will be many things I will never know about her. I will always be stuck in the knowledge that she had great domestic efficiencies, hardly the qualities that I wanted to store in my memory. She had always been demure, moving around our household in quiet satisfaction. Something, in the end, we both accepted, contentment being her better virtue.

It was my last comfort, to know she was much more than I believed her to be. She turned, perfect, her short hair cropped neatly around her head. It bounced in a way that made me want to touch it one more time. She wore khaki shorts and a pink polo shirt, details I never took the time to notice before, but it meant everything to me now. And she was more beautiful than I had ever remembered.

She looked for our daughter, scanning the concrete along the chain link fence. She walked over to where Kristi stood and hugged her. Kristi pointed to the sky where the bubbles jetted up with each gust of wind. Then she breathed, *"Save some for daddy."* But it sounded like, *"Save daddy."* The words got lost in the hum of the dry breeze that congested the city air between us. Kristi became less distinct to me, a speck like all the other specks on the ground, a dark spot on an undefined landscape.

I tried to swim over to them, but I felt my body pulling back, away from everything, like magnets repelling, as if I were in one of those dreams where I break away from the fingers of people who reach up to grab my toes, missing me by just inches. Everything I tried to do to get closer to them failed. A strong force lay between us, wedging the distance, tugging on my shirt, holding my arms, pulling me to a different place.

It was the last time I saw my wife. It was the last time I saw Kristi.

Sight

The laundry hangs on the makeshift clothesline, strung between a house and a creosote pole, and looks like dusty rags. They snap with the wind as it races up the side of the house and through the alley. The wind cannot see. It is only recognized by what it can do, and it excites everything that it passes through.

He watches crimped newspaper pages and plastic bags roll through an empty street, like guilty children, laughing as if they were fleeing from a crime. The defeated playground across the street, in the same back lot as the Catholic Church, looks like it hasn't been used in decades. Its scraped concrete, bleached by the hot summer sun, sustains snippets of the disappearing yellow lines that once defined a basketball court. There are cracks in the concrete that separate the ground, pulling apart from despair and neglect, abandoned.

Electrical wires vein through the neighborhoods. He sees the broken tips of buildings huddle in the city, scorched by too many hot summers and too many dry winters. It's as if they were waiting, waiting, waiting. They never step up to become anything more than what they are: silent witnesses. Dots of cars, like lost ants, obedient to the landscape around them, find their place to go and disappear.

His eyes can only see the flutter of a world he once knew. It, even now, begins to diminish, to fall away. His vision is becoming less sure, and he strains to see the clarity of the looming elms wedged along the streets, spotted by yellow and green and brown yards.

He looks for his daughter in the world of increasing confusion. He tries to remember her red shoes, how they captured the glint of the sun, how they scraped the ground when she walked, before his eyes are plucked from his head.

My car glanced off the side of a street cleaner. I'm not sure what a street cleaner was doing on the shoulder of the highway in the middle of the afternoon, but it was there. It was just dumb luck. I could see the driver's arms go up, as if taking his hands off the wheel of his vehicle was going to divert the impact, and then my truck flipped, nose up, airborne, and everything moved slowly. I didn't see my life flash before my eyes, but the moment tasted like an eternity, and I thought about nothing but the colors around me beginning to change. The fat gray clouds pasted against the sky, spinning in circles, the razor glint of the sun, the tar-patched highway, and then there was the sudden impact of the roof and bed of the truck sliding on the asphalt, scraping like chalk on a dry slate. It crimped the metal from the truck cab back, and then the window popped. There was the grinding of the engine parts, the flywheel and motor mounts snapping like dried twigs, and finally, the piercing of my body by a mysterious metal bar. I didn't feel any pain, just a quick puncture, and I started to think how lucky I was to have survived this collision. But something was all wrong. My mind was numb, the feeling you get when your ears pop thousands of feet above the ground in an airplane. The box of cordial cherries I had bought for Kristi flew past my face, the chocolates scattering like buckshot from a rifle and out the window. I wanted to reach out and grab the first thing I could. The truck slid to a halt and the fizzle of steam filled my ears like a lullaby. My head rolled to the left side as

I hung upside down, and I saw the torn box of cordial cherries on its side on the highway in front of me. One lone chocolate lay on the pavement by the box; its brown shell cracked open and the clear sugary gel poured out on the asphalt in a small, still pool. In the middle of the pool lay a perfectly good cherry, red and unsoiled, pure. But all I could smell was the sharp, sweet heat of the radiator fluid as is it dripped into the cab around me.

Smell

He sniffs the dust and salt that rise from the sidewalks and streets, from the fences, and from the debris pushing into the walls and bushes. It's the smell of a leftover sky, dulled by the hope of a rain that never comes. There are exhaust fumes, invisible hands of heat, mingling with the hot day and bequeathing silt on every still thing: parked cars, windows, patio furniture, and the scattered toys that litter yards like bits of ash. He never realized how much residue filled the world around him before this moment. It merges with the air, and the earth heaves. Everything has the lifeless scent of a quiet day.

His flawed olfaction makes his head swim, lighter than the clouds above him. The dry breeze lifts him, and his toes point to the earth. Up he goes. His nose becomes as numb as the clay latent in the underlayers of the New Mexico earth. When he tries to breathe, it burns.

"Your wife is supposed to be gone all day," Missy said. "I talked to her this morning. She said something about getting new tires on the van, and then doing some shopping. She has Kristi with her and my husband is out of town. He won't be back until tomorrow. I think we need to put substance to these feelings."

"Substance?" I asked.

"Yes, substance. Listen, do you want to be with me or not? We've been whispering behind their backs for months. It's time to stop the flirting. I want you, and I think you feel the same way. If all this has been a game to you and you're not really interested, then let me know, now. We can end it here."

I thought she was going to cry. I felt pushed, and the immediacy of her demand made me vacillate. I almost said, "Okay, you're right, we should end this right now, before it gets out of control." But I remembered the smell of her hair when she pushed herself into me. I felt weak. What was an hour or two?

I was sitting in my truck, in the parking lot of the Plaza. The engine was off, and I was listening to Missy's pleas. I saw a man and a woman sitting outside the coffee shop at one of the small bistro tables lined along the sidewalk. Their coffees sat to the right of each of them on opposite sides. He wore a dark blue suit that hung fraudulently on his shoulders, and she wore a light summer dress. Her right leg bounced nervously over her left knee, to the side of the table. Her left hand was hidden in the flush of hair that fell over her face. My mind tried to determine the extent of their relationship, guesswork at best. The man leaned forward, one of his hands stretched across the table over the top of the woman's right hand. He looked too young to be her father. He lacked the pride in ownership that invited everyone around to share in his joy (he grimaced), and his hand didn't have that protective movement, the soft pat of assurance that gives a daughter confidence.

He had reached across the table and grabbed the woman's hand with conviction. So, in my thinking, she couldn't be his wife, for their hands would have met in the middle, lovingly or out of habit—out of possession. His firm grasp looked more like an attempt to resolve a bad situation. He reached his other hand over, and she dropped her leg and turned to face him; they cupped each other's hands like they were looking for a promise, a commitment, making a new vow, like they had just discovered how thin a string tied their lives together. Maybe all things had just been played out and they were grabbing the only security they had left in the world. They looked like they were combining the residue of their credibility in order to salvage their worth. Their clasped hands rose slightly above the table, and he shook them, hands firmly grasping the dice, ready to throw, ready to determine their future.

One of them would walk away in the end, I was certain, leaving the other to wrestle with the damage done. I guessed she would be the one. I don't know why; it was just a feeling. Maybe it was because he had reached too far over the table, the measured move of a person afraid.

I knew I could never reach across the table for Missy which, in the end, put me alone in this affair. I would sit back on that same chair, just like the man in the blue suit, but I would watch the tears from her face melt her makeup. My arms would fold across my chest, leaning back, trying to scrape together enough empathy to get me through our coffee, wondering what I had gotten myself into, and then, pressed, I would just let everything come undone.

I don't know what the couple was talking about, but all things imagined have a way of finding a form. I began to have second thoughts. Maybe I should forget this whole thing. I'm just not sure I have the emotional constitution to have an affair. I can't bleed the way some men are willing to bleed. It mitigates my value. Affairs are for the desperate, in desperate circumstances, people looking for a way out of a place they feel trapped. That was the way I always saw it. Me? I just wanted to pad my ego, have sex, something new, a revelation that was difficult to accept. It was a condition that had no resolution, no cure, no way out. It continued without restraint.

"It's not a game," I promised. "I never play games. I just wasn't sure how far you wanted to take this."

"You're starting to sound hesitant. I can tell. You have a lovely wife. I know that. I like her. I consider her my best friend. Funny, isn't it? But honestly, I don't feel guilty about any of this. I don't know why. I'm supposed to. I have always thought that I would be overwhelmed by shame when this day came, but I think I've had too much time to work through everything in my head. I know I can live with it. Does this make me a terrible person?"

"I never looked at it in those terms."

"You scare me sometimes," she said. "The way you think. This is just sex to you. I know. You never had to get yourself into a mental place to let it happen. But what does it matter? This is just a onetime thing, anyway."

Everything is a one-time thing. All subsequent repetition is just a convenience. We live in the perpetual future with the tick of every second. We can never go back. And daily, we are always encouraged in our excesses. So why pretend there is an accumulative value to any of our actions?

Missy and I convinced ourselves that it would be easy to pretend we could get away with it. We would be lovers tonight, and then friends tomorrow, live the rest of our lives, carefully, protecting every detail. It would be like cleaning out a garage filled with pent-up desire, finding a motel, and then dumping our lust like refuse, and then we would go back to our homes like nothing had happened.

I tried to see us like the couple at the coffee shop. I told myself I could bear the weight of this issue, put it behind me, and Missy convinced herself that she knew how to forget. I believed her, because women have a history of forgetting their loss, their pain. Men counted on it. I wanted to believe that neither of us would break.

"Please come get me. We can disappear for an hour or two. Just the two of us, and then it will all be over. This is our brief time. It's a moment I really need."

"You're right," I said. I relinquished all uncertainty. "I'm on my way."

"You can show me that it's important to you," she said. It was like she was looking for a moral advantage in the middle of our sin. "You can at least make this sound like something special. That would be nice, even if it's only for this one time. I do need to feel wanted. "

"I do want you," I said. But it was just sex. I didn't know how to make it sound any more important than that. Our landscape was already filling with the moral wreckage of our decision. It was more important that the smaller sin be swallowed by the greater woe at this point: the fear of getting caught. I didn't want any part of trying to understand why we were doing it. "I have to stop and pick up a box of chocolates for my daughter."

"What?"

"I promised her. You do want me to keep my promise, right? She's looking forward to me bringing them home tonight."

"Okay, but please, just hurry."

"Listen. I want this too." I said. "I want to taste you. I have been thinking about tasting you for long time."

Taste

The day tastes like tainted flour that fills his mouth with desperation. His throat is an acrid knot, and he gasps for a touch of freshness to pour over his tongue. The air he tries to breathe burns and goes through him like fine white sand, sifting through the canals of his body and back out into the wind. It disperses into the thickness of the gray sky, barely discernable. His stomach is empty and churns with the buzz of silence, like anxious electricity racing through old wire. Time is all mixed together. He has a problem knowing where he is. It is difficult to pick out his points of reference, the things against which he measures himself. He spreads out, but continues to cling to his singularity. He looks for refreshment in a hot breeze, but there is no moisture in this sky. It is as dry as powder. His taste wanes, and instead of the satisfaction he seeks, his tongue dips into a pool of dust. He tries to swallow, but he can't. His throat doesn't work. His tongue is knotted. He loses his desire to be satisfied. His only sustenance is the universe around him, and it expands, pulling at his dust, the displacement of his soul. His curiosity widens as his physical qualities diminish.

The day we devised our scheme, I made love to my wife. It was like salt to the wound. She had put on soft music and dimmed all the lights in the house. She was always very good about preparation. There was ice water at the side of our bed and small trays of snacks.

She was always a willing partner and very good at it, which just made things that much harder. It put the spotlight of the sin squarely where it belonged. And it made me see that everything I was doing was the ultimate betrayal of her trust in me. I ran my fingers along the soft line of her naked body, and she moved into me, smiling. A burst of tears flushed my face. She gave me her vulnerability, her trust. She was so perfect.

I pulled my pillow into my face and heaved a couple of uncontrolled sobs. I tried not to let her hear it. She didn't deserve to suffer from the weakness that festered inside me. She asked me why I was so sensitive and she touched my tears with her lips, tasting the salt of my shame.

"Honey?" she asked.

"It's just that I love you so much, it hurts," I said. "I am so lucky to have you."

"You are so sweet."

Why did I love her so much more now than I did the days before I decided to have this affair? The fear of scarcity created her value. I knew this whole thing would end badly, but I didn't know how to stop it. Maybe all men are just too willing. And because of this willingness to cheat on her, I convinced myself that I couldn't possibly love her. My behavior defied its meaning. It was a hard realization. But it was easy to question my feelings once I started to parse my emotions, my intentions.

I was built to fail. Everything I touched ignited.

Touch

He feels the tickle of a dry wind tapping at his body. A cold, like rubbing alcohol, seeps into the pores of his skin, breaking it apart. It is a stinging, searing chill. But rather than cover up, fend off the cold, he takes his clothes off, letting them fall to the earth. They are confining. They are no longer needed. They feel pasty like dried paint on a rag. He looks down to watch them fall apart, turning to soot.

He reaches out to touch the wind and his fingers fall from his hands. His skin is breaking away from the muscle on his bone, dispersing into the air. And then his muscle loosens, mingling with the dust from his clothes. His bone granulates and dissolves in the wind. He is less physical, less himself, something broader, dispersing into the gathering thickness around him, and then he is gone. He has a new skin, though it is not a skin he can recognize, but translucent. He becomes a part of everything around him. And he knows that what he lacks is obvious to the whole.

I watched as Missy's husband pour chunks of charcoal into the grill, and then stacked them into a tight pyramid. He soaked the charcoal with the lighter fluid and let it sit. He looked out over the fence at the park filled with children. It was something my wife and I did a lot, in the evenings, sitting on the patio, just before the sun went down. The laughter and screams floated across the street. Footballs and kickballs crossed the park in crazy lines, and dogs ran and barked, sniffing in the trees.

He and Missy didn't have any children, and she told us that her husband bugged her constantly about having a family, but each time she responded that she didn't think it was an appropriate time for them to start having kids.

He lit the charcoal and watched it burn into coals, graying until the black was consumed.

"Do you want another drink?" I called out.

"Yeah, sure."

I got up from my chair and grabbed his glass and went inside the house. I was mixing a fresh mojita for Missy's husband and me, when Missy came up behind me.

"Do you have enough ice for a third drink?" She asked.

"I can do that," I said.

"I know he can be a bore, but he is a good man. I see how you try to find reasons to keep busy, rather than be left alone with him. He's a mechanical draftsman, not the most romantic employment. He spends his life drawing schematics," Missy apologized. "He's never even finished a full semester of college or trade school. So he's not the most abstract thinker. Everything he knows he got out of a drafting class in high school. A friend of his from high school got him his job with the state engineering department."

"He seems to know a lot," I said.

She shrugged.

"You don't have to bullshit me," she said. "I mean, make no mistake, I love the man. I've spent a good part of my life with him. He's taken good care of me. Most women would appreciate something like that. I just need to have an occasional release. Do you know what I mean?"

I knew what she meant. Real infidelity happened before the sexual act even took place. It started with a compromise of respect.

"My wife is always on me about picking up my clothes," I offered. It was the best I could do under the circumstances. And even though she let out a sigh of disappointment, it was enough to seal our deal. It's funny how women always expect less from men.

"I can tell you look at me," she flirted.

"I do."

"You men like to pretend you have a lust which is pure," she said. "You believe you are forcing the hand of God, pushing him out of his silence, making him create within you a real need to believe in something greater than yourselves. Okay, you can have it your way.

125

I'm not going to analyze it any further than that."

She walked into me, put her hands up to my shoulders, and then pulled me next to her, laying the side of her head on my chest. I put my nose into her red hair and inhaled the sweet scent. It was different than my wife's hair. I wanted more of it. It's too easy to desire something that you have never tasted. Each woman has her own exotic taste, and every man wants to sample it.

"Someone could walk in," I said.

"Maybe," she said, indifferently. "How does it make you feel?"

"Reckless."

She turned around and pushed me into the edge of the sink, the press of her butt against my thighs. It wakened me, and it made it difficult to restrain my need. She grabbed my hand and put it on her stomach, slipping my fingers over the bottom of her red bathing suit, letting me touch the soft between her thighs.

"This is just a tease," she whispered. "Let's make this a onetime thing that counts. Something we will remember."

"I agree," I assured her. I allowed myself to be swept away by her unruliness.

"Good. There's too much on the line for both of us," she said. "When we go back to the deck, it's got to be like nothing happened. No goofy looks that give us away. We're just friends, neighbors. Let's be smart. Is it a deal?"

"I feel like we're planning a murder."

"Maybe we are."

We always know the details of our self-destruction long before it happens. But we march forward and pretend we will be able to divert any adverse outcome. Infidelity is like a runaway train that can't be stopped until it crashes into everything that has value. There is a point where nothing will bring it to a halt, not even reason.

We depend on our pain in its aftermath. It inspires the conscience toward its own redemption. It gives us the fuel necessary to push the act forward. It's a necessary salve. All sin has found its absolution long before the act happened; if it didn't there would be no sin.

She turned me around.

"Let me get a good look at you," she said. She combed my body for evidence, brushing me off like she was wiping the fingerprints off a gun at a crime scene. "We want you to look handsome for your pretty wife and Kristi."

I could feel her breath sweep the back of my neck. She whispered in my ear that everything was going to be fine. The sound of her voice reassured me.

Hearing

His ears ring with the distant buzz of the cicadas. The nervous windows in the old houses across the street try to escape from their panes, but without success. The glass rattles the air. The chained link fencing joins in the dissatisfaction with each gust of wind. The wind starts a whisper of universal anguish, and it swirls around the human experience.

There is the occasional honk of a car horn, and voices. The leaves in the trees crack and dance, then fall to the ground. There are whispers from people, walking, colliding with one another, judging every ticking moment, widening the spaces between each other. It is far away, and it provokes his conscious. All this noise, this excited life, and nobody investigating its true source. And then, it all starts to fade away before he is able to comprehend the connections, the relevance.

He always thought that he would hear a distant trumpet when this moment came, that the sky would rend in the east, and he'd see the glory of heaven pour into his new world. But it wasn't like that at all. He knows now that the only sounds left are the murmur of all things unfinished, and the sounds dwell, tapping at his conscious like the drip from a leaking faucet. The inevitable hush of time diminishes, already squeezing out---lost, and there are fingers pressing against his lips, soliciting silence. It's too late for any starting over in this world and the ending is always met with dissatisfaction. All unfinished business ceases. It's time for his next stop, his next incarnation, and another chance to get it right.

Missy's husband told me about his new project, an arroyo barrier, a project for which he was selected to draw the schematic. We have known Missy and her husband for about a year. They have been over to our house for Sunday barbeques, at least once a month during that time. She and my wife have become very close. They shop together, and I'm sure they know the intimate details of each other's lives. And while they talked about new restaurants and stores, fashion, or just lay out in the sun together, I've listened to her husband rattle on about his latest work projects. Today it was plans for an arroyo, and tomorrow who cares, it was very difficult for me to show the same kind of courtesy my wife was so famous for showing. I could only think that this is a man who understands how expendable he really is, and he craves the attention necessary to dispel his insignificance. It would be too easy for him to lose his worth in the middle of a single crisis. He was talking with his hands, and they obstructed my line of vision to the girls.

The girls: my wife, Kristi, and Missy were lined behind him on their stomachs, lying on sunning lounges. They all wore single-pieced red bathing suits, looking like branched shoots of unpicked cherries. They planned their outfits for our benefits, mine. It was too much of a coincidence. Girls are all about detail. My wife was on the far left, Kristi was in the middle, and Misty was on her right. I could see the bottoms of their feet, buttered legs, and their butts rising above the backs of their heels like moons (except for Kristi---she looked like a strip of bacon between the two women). All three of the girls had sunglasses lying in front of them, and a book, turned upside down on the deck. Kristi, of course, had a Disney Golden book that I bought the last time we were in the department store. The sunglasses in front of her were bigger than her small head and her red bathing suit wrinkled along her frame. But she was committed to being all woman like her mother and Missy. My wife had a respectable derriere, tight in the places that counted and muscled legs. But I had a difficult time keeping my eyes off Missy's butt, juicy and ripe, her red hair floated across her back and off her orange skin. The bubble of her ass moved like an invitation.

It was a bright day, the sun was hot and white, and there wasn't a cloud in the sky. Missy squinted her eye, looking back at me. It looked like she was trying to smile. She shuffled, centering her body on the sunning lounge, and then she spread her legs slightly. I looked at the space between her thighs.

Yes indeed, Missy's husband's whole life was expendable. It was a conclusion that I had long worked through in my head. He had always been two steps behind everything everyone else noticed. And if Missy continued to flirt, we were going to do it, and then his life would be mitigated even more. I can't say I felt sorry for him. I have always believed pity to be a form of weakness.

Religion

The last thing he hears is an old woman praying alone in the Catholic Church. Her soft, indiscernible voice fills the empty room. She is dressed in black, a lace veil covering the top of her head, and she sits in one of the front pews, on a wooden seat chiseled by time. Her rosary wraps around her bony fingers and wrists like a familiar promise. The beads are small lavender crystals. She is praying to the Virgin Mary for a sick child, the granddaughter of her sister, whom she has only met once, last year, when she gave her a pair of enameled red shoes for her birthday. The little girl embraced the shoes like they were the perfect gift.

The old woman looks up at the Virgin, plastered in light blues and white and rose, and the slightly bent fingers over her open heart offer the softness of hope. The church has the scent of myrrh, and Jesus, in the resin stations-of-the-cross, looks down where she kneels. It's a reminder to her that this world is destined to suffer. The Virgin listens to her patiently. The old woman is also praying for the sins of the world, for charity and wisdom, and all the things she believes are good and noble, and while she prays, freed souls drift over of the church to their new life. She believes God abides, daily. He endures all the fears within his creation.

I tried to sleep in late, but Kristi flew through our bedroom door and jumped on the bed. My wife, Clare, had already peeled herself free from the sheets, like she did each morning, with an enthusiasm I could never find, had gone to the bathroom, splashed cold water on her face, and then out to the kitchen to make breakfast. I could smell the hint of coffee in the room.

"Get up daddy," Kristi scolded. "I want to show you my new bathing suit."

She stood on the bed, doing the twist, and then she jumped up and down, a mischievous grin breaking her small face. I pulled the blankets off my nose and tried to see past the blur of my eyes.

"Honey, you look very pretty," I said.

"I know." She strung out the "kno-ow" with a long oh…like she was surprised. "This swimsuit is so-o beautiful. And it looks so-o beautiful on me."

"It definitely does," I agreed.

It was deep red, and it twisted around her small frame like red licorice. Every time she landed, she reached up to push her shoulder strap back up to her neck.

"Come on, daddy," she sang with each bounce. Her voice warbled. "It's time to get up. We have company coming over---Missy and Charles. You have to get the barbeque grill ready."

I pushed myself up along the headboard slightly and watched her bounce. My hair felt sticky and my breath was thick with leftover sleep. Kristi looked alive, a perfectly good cherry, unblemished and innocent. Everything a little girl should be. She was happy, confident, and it poured out of her like a fountain. She threw herself on top of me, and I let out a quick gaff.

"Watch out, princess," I breathed. "Don't hurt me."

She lay on top of my chest, her face staring into my eyes. She kissed me with her razor thin lips, her tiny eyes closed.

"When I get older, daddy, I want to marry a man just like you."

Redemption

He stands at a bus station and his soul waits, looking through his past and toward the future. There are others who, in the blink of this moment, wait with him. They stand open-eyed, wiping the sleepiness out of their new eyes. They wonder if they will ever be here again. They are travelers who break away from the eternal, trading it for a slice of substance, a human world. It's a chance to get something right, to be a greater part of the whole. He steps back, letting the wind blow past him. It's a strong wind that sweeps all of them into a new experience, a new opportunity. He moves past the idea of sin and guilt, and to a place where there is possibility and the chance to become his best self.

I never wanted to climb the damned mountain from the beginning. What was the point? It was my wife's idea. The argument she gave me: because it was there. Because it was there? A lot of things are just there, it didn't mean I wanted to stomp them into submission. The development of a healthy appreciation for the outdoors would be fine, something I was quite capable of doing by flipping through the pages of *National Geographic*.

Ideas that compelled her toward great inspiration usually left me limp, doubtful, looking for neglected chores around the house to hide behind. But, she was relentless, sniffing me out to spring her newest half-baked plan for an adventure. I never felt the need to discover a world already trodden many times over by would-be explorers. There was nothing new under the sun.

I'm a middle-aged man, sporting a belly the size of a good washtub, and I cultivated the aches and pains in my body that accompany it like an earned reward. But my wife, Cyn (Cynthia), all worked up and filled with the spirit of John Muir, determined we were going to have a romantic evening in the mountains sitting in a sulfur-infested hot pool nestled in the armpit of the Jemez Mountains with the scent of evergreen trees assaulting us from all directions. Shit!

And critters! Oh my God! Who knew what beasts stalked these mountains. The thought of spending the whole evening under cover of a foreboding forest in the Jemez Mountains made me want to find a broken tavern on our drive out there to calm my nerves. I could tell Cyn I'd meet her there later that I needed to order myself a half a dozen drinks to pull myself through the night. We have a perfectly good Jacuzzi in our backyard I told her. Cyn's response was, "Don't be so silly."

The problem, of course, was getting up there, straight up, and at my age and fixed disposition and increasing languor, getting up anywhere was a daily struggle against the very gravity that conspired to keep me securely in my place.

But I pretended to fight against that unyielding force with ferocious conviction, as I humped and bumped up the mountain, spitting out the dry air that caught in my throat, while sweat poured out of my pores and my daypack dug into my city-slick shoulders like an unwanted gnat on an open wound. My pack was filled with bottles of wine and cheese and French bread.

We hiked for what seemed like incalculable miles, though Cyn was quick to remind me that it was only about a one mile trek. One mile! How did the earth become so large? It was endless, down the front side of the mountain, over a small trickling river (what we called a farm creek in Nebraska), and then straight up the side of the steep terrain traversing a rock-cragged trail which I concluded would mangle my already brittle ankles into a twisted sculpture. It was a pain that I anticipated to coagulate in my joints, like oatmeal, revisiting my body years later in arthritic nightmares. What's a body if not to dispose of improperly at the end of a not-so-well-managed life?

After we had gone about a hundred feet up the mountain, I thought my heart was going to push its way through my rib cage. I took frequent rest breaks, leaning over my knees, my face growing flush and my head pounding like a manic demon trying to beat its way out of my skull with a ball-peen hammer. When my body seemed rested I pulled myself together and started, again, up the mountain. Cyn thinks that I lack the ability to give, to endure. I beg to differ. My will is an empty sack.

I took in air like a panicked hummingbird beating its wings in a gusty sky. Cyn tried to pretend she was barely winded, flexing her muscles, giving up brief spurts of breath, instructing me on how to get the best out of this trip, health-wise. None of it felt very healthy to me.

"This isn't so bad," she said. I saw the beads of sweat along the hairline of her face. A little more suffering on her part would have been greatly appreciated.

I was certain that beating me in everything that we did together was a very important objective in her routine, a box that needed checking daily. She played it out in her mind: Man versus Woman, another one for the chicks. Yeah! So, I gave her these victories; I succumbed letting her thrash and beat me down in her mind. I allowed her to loom larger than I. It was my gift to her. My life is filled with smaller victories, like finding change on the asphalt in front of the grocery store or a tired thank you from my wife for knowing an obscure fact like tomatoes being fruits rather than vegetables. It compensates me for all the luminous disappointments I encounter in the course of my days. I know what you're thinking—she loomed larger than I regardless of my acquiescence. Okay, someone always looms. Jesus on the cross looms.

"You can't tell me you're not tired," I told her.

"I'm not," she said.

"It's not going to minimize your accomplishment to confess that you're a little winded. Come on."

"Honey, it's okay if you need to rest. I can go on ahead."

Honey, my ass!

Cyn was so good at giving me the classic insult to my already mounting injuries.

"Yeah, okay," I breathed. I reached for short bursts of hard earned air. There was very little of it around me. Or so I believed. "Save me a small mud hole when you get up there. I'll just die right here and let the wild pigs tear at my flesh."

"Don't be silly. There are no wild pigs up here. You'll be fine."

My fingers reached up for inches of compassion, waving her on.

"Yeah, okay. I gotcha. Go. You go on."

Sweat was gushing from my loosened pores. My face looked like a soaker hose, but that wasn't the point. I never pretended this little hike wasn't going to drain my desire to live. I offered the remnants of my life as a sacrifice to my loving wife with each treacherous weekend trip we took. I just knew there was a coffin at the top of this mountain with my name inked across the top in happy black letters. And I had no doubt that Cyn waited for me, too, hammer and nail in hand, to seal my demise. I rest in peace.

I have always capitulated on issues of sovereignty in my relationship with Cyn, and she always capitalized on this abdication with great enthusiasm in order to make me a better person. It is a perfect marriage suited for the values that we both held important to our daily living. I'd like to think we loved each other dearly.

❦

The first little water hole I encountered was large enough to soak my feet, maybe have a little splash party. A trickle of water slimed down the rocks into a green pool riddled with nugget-sized rocks smooth as greased butts. It gave me the initiative to scout further up the rocky trail, an inspiration I desperately needed at this point.

My wife climbed, pressing toward the pinnacle, obsessed as usual with the idea of completing her goal, which included beating me. Now if this was the fountain of youth, I might have pushed my ass a little harder because I'd know that after getting there I'd be able to lilt back to civilization in my newly acquired skin. But all things being what they were, my sagging will, distressed dignity, the complete shutdown of all my bodily functions, the little puddle in front of me was a great enough victory for the moment. I reached down and touched the warm-as-piss water, the reward for my accomplishment.

"Come on!" My wife yelled from somewhere above the rocks which loomed large, cutting their way out of the chiseled mountain and disappearing in the trees. She dared me to push on, tempted me pulling at the last threads of my energy. Never dare a broken man. He will kill himself to prove you right.

"Fuck! What about my break?" I whispered, and then I shouted "Let up, won't you, for Christ's sake. I'm on the precipice of death down here!"

"It's only a little ways up, darling!"

Darling, my ass!

Her voice rolled down the side of the mountain like an avalanche of mockery.

"It's right here!" she shouted.

I sucked in my gut. Actually, I took a big breath of air, pushed my gut back up into my abdominal cavity, shifted the straps on my daypack pulled them into my shoulders, and compelled myself up through the rocks, my tennis shoes sliding down the side of the solid shards poking their way out of the ground. I never thought that toting two bottles of wine, a block of cheese, and a loaf of bread would feel like an eighty pound military pack. But it did, and it took the hunger right out of me. I thought my ankles were going to snap like dried twigs, just like that, and a rescue helicopter would have to be summoned, hover over the incline of the mountain, drop a nylon ladder and sissy seat down through the head of the branches above me, and hoist me out of the wilderness into the six o'clock news where they would display me as the latest misplaced specimen of humanity, inept at backwoods survival, on the celluloid screen for every New Mexican to scrutinize: the guy who couldn't handle a simple one mile hike into the Jemez Mountains. But it didn't happen. Things never quite collapsed around me in the ways I always imagine. Call it the luck of the Irish.

Sure enough, just over the rocks lay a likeable pool of water snuggled in the side of the mountain like a bird's nest looking out over the spans of the mountain area. It really was quite beautiful. Damn, that woman is always right. Cyn has given me way too many opportunities to look foolish in my resolves.

It was green. Everything was green as far as I could see through the limbs of the trees. Cyn was already in the pool setting up our romantic evening, pulling candles out of her daypack, using a flat rock on the edge of the pool for a table, placing the small candles in small red, blue, green and yellow glass cups along the rocks. I set my daypack next to me and took off my tennis shoes and socks and inched my way into the pool. The smell of warm sulfur and French bread rose to tickle the hair in my armpits, and then into my nose as I sank. My weight slumped over the tricky rocks, sharp and slimy with algae. The uneasy maneuver of my toes made my knees flex.

"Jesus."

"Are you all right?"

"Yes. I'm just trying to get used to these rocks."

Five rednecks frolicked in the connecting pool, passing a joint to each other, their arms raised safely out of the water to keep the roach from getting wet. They floated oddly like galloping horses on a carousel, ghostlike, in slow motion, toward each other to make the hand off, thumbs against thumbs.

"Yeah!"

"Whoop-ee!" they shouted.

"I feel good," one of them rumbled.

Under the water they went to wet their faces, wiping their noses and mouths, letting them drip back into the pool.

They laughed. It looked like they had just gotten off work, hard work, their faces packed with the grime of America's highways and back roads. It stained into every line of their skin. They had hands permanently marked and scratched. Not even the sulfured pool would be able to cure their dissipated bodies, though I was certain that they hadn't given it the slightest consideration.

"Howdy!" I said.

"Yep," they all returned in unison. They stared suspiciously at me. It was not an altogether pure howdy, I admit. It lacked considerable bucolic reference, but I tried to be friendly.

"Are you having a séance or something over there?" One of the men snickered, pulling his body out of the water, pointing at my wife, who was lining candles along the rocks.

"We're going to raise the dead over here once the night sets in," I responded with a creepy whisper and raised brow, the fingers on my hands twinkled in front of me like falling rain.

"You're one of them smart asses, huh?"

"I see it more as a whirling accumulation toward my most certain demise."

"In other words, you're looking for a good ass whooping."

"You're correct," I said startled. "But allow me to apologize. You fellows certainly have scholarly inclinations I never anticipated in this wilderness."

"Fuck you."

I started to rise up out of the pool, move closer to my new friends, putting my arms on the rocks that separated us. I looked over to where their heads floated, popping out of the water like rusty buoys. The white strips of their naked asses were illuminated through the pool, the hint of their nubby penises rippling like silvery minnows in the Rio Grande River.

"Do you think anyone ever takes a good pee in these pools?" I asked. I received cold stares. I couldn't determine if it was because I sneaked a peek at their pee-pees, or if it was the revelation that we could be stewing in some stranger's urine. There were complicated worlds at ssue, mixed signals at best, a confusion of realities that needed to be gnored. We divert our attentions daily from the task at hand.

Their faces were like a threat. Obviously, this was taboo subject matter, something no one wanted to consider: peeing in public water. The rednecks looked at each other like I wasn't there, grabbing their cans of beer off the rocks behind them, huddling into a cluster.

"Does a bear shit in the woods?" one of the men finally stammered. They all spit beer out into the water. Two of the men slammed their cans together and foam spilled out of the top, dripping over their hands and into the water. I slipped back into my personal waterhole with my wife, my feet catching the slime on a large rock; I tried to pull at the slime with my toes, and it filled the cracks between my knuckles. I looked up through the thick trunks of the trees, wishing for a pack of wild animals to swoop down on us and put the lot of us out of our misery. It would have surely saved me a trip back down the mountain. I always try to find a comfort in potential tragedy.

"Glass of wine, honey?" my wife offered. This was my reward for making it up to the top, a glass of almost certain dehydration, my preparation for death.

"Sure."

Rednecks in the buff, as long as I live, it's something I'd never see in Nebraska, naked cowboys passing a joint and talking shit. The drivel of their conversation passed between them like Sloppy Joes. I couldn't understand a word they uttered as they giggled like little school girls, all knobby kneed and dangerous, fragment sentence after fragment sentence peppering the air around them like a Haiku poem.

I don't know what they were scheming. Maybe they were rubbing their hairy legs against each other when I interrupted them, pulling on each other's wieners, you know--- good ol' boy stuff. I could see that; beer'd-up rednecks having a little wiener-pulling fun.

And what kind of wine do you bring to an excursion like this, anyway? This was the big discussion Cyn and I had preparing for this hike, discussions that were always inevitable, stressful, and filled with incongruity. I argued white wine, a late harvest German Auslese. I could picture a hot tub full of fat German chefs, the course hairs of their stomachs circling wells of pink belly fat, hocking down bottles of a good Auslese and eating stinky Woolsery cheese with black bread while tuba-blasting farts and baritone laughs echoed through the woods. It could happen, but then, I'm a romantic about things like that.

Cyn hung tough to a good sensible white Zinfandel, in my estimation, always the symbol of a mediocre buzz and shallow suburban living. But this was just a scratch of the snobbery that hid skillfully in the fat of my insecurities. I can reflect—it is one of my few virtues.

"You never know what kind of company you'll get in the deep woods," Cyn argued, always prepared, always the perfect Boy Scout "It's about being hospitable. Everyone likes a good Zinfandel."

I jumped on the kitchen counter, kicking cheese and bread onto the floor sliding on the quickly wetted tile, trying to steady myself. Pots hanging above me dripped like metal rain.

"Honey, the tile!"

"Fuck the tile!" I shouted, taking my stand. "White Zinfandel, what have we become? European! How about taking a solid Liefraumilch?"

Cyn stood back, her hand up to her mouth. She looked at me like I was a madman, dismantling her kitchen.

"Liefraumilch is too tart for cheese and bread," she corrected. "Please come down, honey."

"Too tart? Are you calling the milk from Mary's breasts too tart?"

I kicked a glass across the room into the refrigerator, and it bounced with a thud, dropping to the floor and rolling back into the service aisle. The noisy ceiling fan next to what was left of the pots hanging around me hummed. The children huddled at the threshold of the kitchen door watching their father rattle at the world.

"Does this mean we're not going to have lunch?" my son intoned.

"Come down before the neighbors see you through the window, honey."

I looked out the window to notice the neighbor's dog, head tilted, blinking through the chain link fence. He was breathing hard, and his tongue bounced ildly interested in my hysterics.

I was unmoved, liberated.

"An unexpected pregnancy at a time of razor sharp moral certainty could *our the milk of any young mother's milk. Imagine her consternation, trying to niff out the moments of her past, the exact instant she scraped the semen of some oung man's reckless lifestyle off her thigh. These were curious times, Cyn. In he name of God, they were throwing ducks, weighted with rocks, into lakes in earch of an unsteadied truth. How was she to know that this divine joke was erpetrated with the ignoble design of world salvation? This whole son-of-God hing didn't rear its unlikely head until decades later. As far as she knew, she ould have gotten pregnant on an outhouse stool."*

"Mom, daddy is talking silly again," *my daughter complained. She rolled er eyes, folding her arms and leaning against one of the counters.*

"I know, honey," *Cyn said.* "Just ignore him."

"Are you going to go over my homework with me, dad?" *my son asked.* "Or *an I go outside to play?"*

"I doubt they had outhouses, at least in the way we understand them in *hose times," Cyn said.*

"What's an outhouse?" *my son asked.*

"Hush, your father is speaking."

"You are right," *I said.* "I never considered that. It's much more appropriate *o think of the mother of God as slumping over a fallen tree."*

Cyn was silent. The children started to cry.

"Honey, can we just finish packing our snacks for tonight?" *She asked.* *You're scaring the children."*

"Can't you see it?" *I cried. They all just looked at me with blank faces. t's as obvious as the naked body of Christ being prepared for burial. We live n perfect tombs."*

"Maybe we can take both wines," I suggested, snapping back to the
ask at hand.

"That would be fine."

It's hard to keep my mind from wandering. It is difficult to
letermine which world lacks the substance I need to get me through
ach day. I crave fluff.

And so we did, we took the German Auslese and the white Zinfandel, but after our encounter with the rednecks, I regretted that we didn't pack a healthy supply of Pabst Blue Ribbon beer. We could have used it as a peace offering, or cracked the cans over their heads if they tried to invade our little world.

My wife dipped the back of her head into the pool, going under spitting the sulfured water out when she came up for air, wiping her face with her hands. My first instinct was to pull her out of the green sludge, save her from the certain diseases which infused the water.

"Don't swallow this stuff, honey! There is redneck goo oozing through these tepid waters!"

"Redneck goo?" she asked.

"Through and through like raw sewage."

The rednecks pulled their naked bodies up out of the water and over the rock like confused angry trolls, small philistines, bearing down on me, limp dicks in hand. I grabbed two cans of Pabst Blue Ribbon, raising them high in the air to defend the honor of my wife. It was my moment of clarity.

Sure, it would have been easier to allow Cyn to swallow a little backwood cum. Who would have found out? But that would be too easy. Let's bring an end to this woodsy frolic, balls to the wall, a clear distortion of all my principles. These men had cracker fragile patience, which I was ripe and ready to test. They were willing to spill blood. And as they approached me, I squeezed the two cans of beer, one in each of my hands, until they exploded, showing my resolve and conviction, and then, having made my point, I let the cans drop into the pool.

"Come on, you sons-of–bitches and get what's coming to you."

They converged on me like hungry bears, trouncing my flesh into a Eucharist thin wafer, a New Mexico tortilla.

"Some bread, honey?" My wife said, wiping the water away from the front of her face.

"What? I'm sorry. Just a little. I'm not that hungry. How's does the water feel?"

"Just wonderful."

Much dignity has been restored through closed lips and rumination. Truth should be tendered with considered hesitation.

When the real gay guys showed up, I was relieved. I felt there was realignment of the scales of justice.

"This is a heterosexual pool," one of the rednecks belched from the other side of the rocks as one of the boys peeled off his shorts like an uncomfortable skin.

"Why don't you peckerheads put a lid on it," I said. Okay, so occasionally I do have self-destructive tendencies. "They are at least climbing into a pool with mixed company."

My heart beat like a cheap paper drum.

Tap, tap, tap, the murmurs in my chest ticked like a warning sign and all the reasons and all the excuses and all the meanings poured out of me in one big revelation. All things must converge.

"Peckerheads?" one of the rednecks said. "Fellas, it looks like we have a bleeding butt liberal in the other pool."

They all laughed.

The two boys looked at each other, and then looked up at the rednecks like they were looking through a dark tunnel.

"Thanks," one of them said.

"Assholes," I said. "They are just a bunch of small pecker-pulling assholes!"

"Hey, fuck you buddy!" a voice came from the other pool.

"Honey, hush!" my wife cautioned.

"Nothing like telling someone he has a small pecker to work up a little rage. And you can't claim shrinkage, it's a warm pool!"

The rednecks burst out of the water.

"Stop it!" my wife shouted.

"You'd better get a handle on your little man, lady."

"All of you just stop it!" There was a silence.

"Maybe you should offer them some white Zinfandel," I said.

The two gay boys eased their way into the pool. Their bodies were as white as snow. They had the largest clumps of penis flesh between their legs that I have ever seen on young men, not that I roamed the locker rooms of America to satisfy my curiosities, but I couldn't help but stare, my eyes dropped, stealing peeks at their pricks. Stare and peek. Sexual curiosity is so redundant. I wanted to slap my eyes back to reason.

What is my problem?

"Nice," one of the boys said moving his arms through the water looking like Esther Williams.

"Warm," I said. "Watch the slime on the rocks; I just about twisted my ankle."

"It feels very good."

He was right. The slime felt good on the feet. The way it squeezed through the toes. The gay guys moved closer to each other and traded a quick kiss. One of the young men reached out and touched the other man's shoulder.

"Sorry about the outburst."

They both shrugged.

"Would you boys like some white Zinfandel?" Cyn offered.

"Zinfandel?"

"Or Auslese," I said.

"We love white Zinfandel," one of them said.

She poured each of them a glass. I knew what she was thinking: *another victory for the girls!*

They introduced themselves as John and Luke. My wife looked at me and waited for my smart remark about their names being companion books in the Bible, John, the young and beautiful boy, and Luke, the stern and studious. They were quiet, stoic.

For Cyn's benefit, I didn't say a word about John and Luke's names.

"It's nice to meet you boys," I said.

John was from Belen, New Mexico. They were both students at Colorado College in Manitou Springs. John was a literature major nd Luke was in business applications, what we used to lovingly all computer science. He lived in Colorado. I can't say I wasn't disappointed that Luke wasn't a history major. But history repeats tself in different forms.

Given second chances, most of us would choose different roads. even in the story of the second coming, Jesus bursts out of the clouds vith an army of angels to exact a calculated revenge. No one will be icking sand in his face this time around. He's got his buddies with iim this time. He's pissed and has the scars to justify his ire.

John told us he badgered Luke to come to the Jemez Mountains intil he had to say yes.

"I told him the pools were beautiful," John said.

"New Mexico is the only place I know that turned their ghettos nto tourist attractions," Luke said. "Give them a nice sound. Claim hem to be rustic slices of American history. Call them Pueblos."

"You're not being fair to the significance the pueblos played in the arly development of southwest culture and architecture."

"They're made of grass and mud," Luke said. "Not really the stuff of engineering genius."

"They have existed longer than most modern homes," John said.

"I'm sorry. I'm just being a lazy thinker," Luke said, not wanting o push the conversation further. He moved closer to John and kissed iis forehead.

"Anyway, I finally got him here, though he wasn't too certain about he climb."

"The climb, that was the kicker to me," Luke said. "It is the climb think I was really trying to avoid."

"It's a killer," I said.

"But I guess anything worth experiencing is worth the extra effort o get there," Luke said.

Cyn was nodding her head in agreement, a lesson I'm sure she noped I'd take to heart. I lowered myself into the water and sank up o my chin, bobbed under the water, taking in a little redneck goo and pitting it back past my head, over the side of the rocks.

I knew what she was thinking: I was immature, a child, credentials intended to keep intact until I was safely in the kingdom of God.

"Sometimes you just have to do things you never thought you

would do in order to get the most out of life," Cyn said. Then she turned to John. "You did a good thing getting Luke to come here."

I peed in the pool. It was the most satisfying release I've had in years.

The rednecks were quiet, slumping into the water, plotting a clever exit from the pool. I thought they might throw stones at us on their way out. I tried to stay close to a good ball of slime.

"Faggot lovers," I heard one of them whisper just under his breath. I looked at the boys. Their faces grimaced as they stared into the pool.

I waited for the rednecks to toss empty beer cans into our pool but they never got the chance because a Latin family showed up with their two lovely children like reinforcements, skipping through the rocks, a boy and a girl, who proceeded to do cannonball jumps into the water from a rock hovering just above the heads of the rednecks. They were typical children, restless, and after every cannonball jump, they crawled out of the pool back up to the top of the rock and jumped back into the water, splashing the faces of the rednecks.

The children stood on the rock, fearless and celebratory, dripping wet and shivering. Their lips shriveled purple.

"Geronimo!" They held their noses, gulping big breaths of air before they jumped.

I waited for one of the rednecks to grab one of the children by the hair and neck skin, pulling him close to his naked body: *I'll see you little fart sack tonight. I'll wake you from your sleep, breathe into your face, and I'll...*

The rednecks pushed the window of the little boy's bedroom up slowly, and one by one, they crawled over the sill like fat lizards.

"Shhh!"

They stood, arms in front of them to steady their bodies, and tiptoed, naked in single file, up to the edge of the bed. Their white butts caught the reflection of the street lamp outside and looked like five big bouncing moons lumbering in the dark.

"*Shit!*" *the redneck in the back whispered.*

"*What?*"

"*There's shit,*" *he whispered. "There's dog shit on the tile floor. I stepped right in it. I think it's a big dog.*"

"*Shh!*"

"*Whoa!*" *The redneck in the back slipped and fell on his back. The lights in the room went on at a snap, and the little boy sat up in his bed and looked, confused, at the rednecks. His big black Labrador popped up from under the blanket, sniffing the air, and he growled, baring his readied teeth.*

"*Oh fuck,*" *another redneck called out, and he turned, catching a swatch of doo-doo on the floor, falling and landing on top of the redneck trying to get up.*

"*You're not supposed to be here,*" *the little boy blinked.*

"*Shh!*" *one of the standing rednecks said, tapping his lips with his finger. "We were just leaving.*"

"*Go get them, Blackie,*" *the boy commanded.*

The three standing rednecks turned and tried to make a dash for the window. They grabbed and kicked toys that lay scattered on the floor and hanging from the ceiling. There was a crash that echoed in the room. By this time there was doo-doo smeared everywhere and it got caught in their toes, and down they went on top of their other two friends, tangled in each other's arms and legs. The dog jumped on the first redneck encountered, pushing his snout between his legs, snapping at his penis. He grabbed the redneck's scrotum with his teeth and pulled.

"*Damn it, dog,*" *the man shouted. He tried to bend over to protect himself. "Call your dog off, boy. We were just kidding around!*"

"*Blackie, heel!*"

The rednecks scrambled to their feet, slipping through the smeared doo-doo on the floor, and one by one they jumped head first out the window.

"*Mee-joo,*" *a voice called on the other side of his bedroom door. "Are you okay?*"

"*Yes mom. I just had a dream.*"

Their parents were right there, marshaling them like wary coyotes with newborn pups, clapping as each child put on their own personal show just before they jumped into the water. The rednecks grabbed their beers, putting their thumbs over the opening in their cans to keep the sulfured water out, and they hugged the side of the pool with their free arms. Their heads bobbed in the water like fishing cork.

"Tuck your knees up to your chest, Mee-joo," the father encouraged.

On the top of the rocks, the young boy looked like a dripping rag, his brown skinny body blending in with the dark trunks of the trees behind him. He stood, arms folded. His bony knees pointed inward, he was looking for a good spot to jump, staring into the opaque pool, his teeth tapping a cadence, a countdown.

As for myself, the idea of little Latino children doing cannonball jumps in front of five naked rednecks, who were worried that the two gay guys in the pool next to them were going to pork them as soon as they showed their naked asses in the woods had a certain poetry to it. But then, I'm a romantic about these types of things.

Then Kristine showed up. I couldn't take my eyes off her from the moment she appeared out of the darkness of the rocks at the side of our pool.

"Cute," she said. She slipped out of her shorts and blouse, sporting a purple bikini, and slid, inching her way into our pool, all mother earth, looking at the children, her arms spanned out in front of her fanning the water with the palms of her hands.

Kristine was young, tan and firm. Her naval winked over the top of her thin bikini bottom as she twisted her way into the water, mocking me, and I thought about what I'd do if she started to take off her clothes.

Up to now, all the naked people in the pool had been a mere curiosity, fodder for philosophical rumination. But Kristine getting naked would demand a response. Maybe it was about time we all got naked. The night seemed to demand it. I'm not sure Cyn would want to beat me to the punch on this one, but I was willing to give it my best Webelos effort. I was good at discarding things. It was my second greatest virtue. I imagined a midnight pool of naked flesh and the trickle of sexual juices and energy flowing through the rocks, cracking the earth open, revealing all its wetness. Anything could happen if one believed.

And though there was nothing new under the sun, the night had its own rules, and it leaked out an occasional drop of humanity, like fresh ink, expanding us, stretching us out, and we got to become. For just a moment there was the gleam of a solitary star in the blackened sky. We were known.

Kristine sunk down to her neck and moved her shoulders up and down. She was doing something under the water, undressing, I was certain. I wanted the parts of her bathing suit to rise out of the water and flip over the back of the rocks into the abyss. I stared. I waited. I sensed it. I wondered if Cyn did, too. What would she do if Kristine got naked? It made me smile. How would she find a way to exercise her conservative sensibilities in the midst of such clarity? But she was busy talking to Luke. I heard them say something about different software packages. Thank God for Microsoft. Some people just needed the slight hint of a different wind around them to be distracted. Cyn knew how to compartmentalize her priorities. She was such a good soldier.

Kristine's swimsuit never surfaced. The night whispered a disappointment. The sun gave a sigh of relief.

"The water feels good on my legs," she said to no one in particular.

"I'd take my swimsuit off if there were more girls in the pool," she teased. I looked around at my wife. Please, Cyn, I thought. Kristine was talking to me. I didn't need to know this. But she wanted me to know that she would do it, take off her clothes.

I pulled my shorts off like dirty laundry and threw them into the black forest, catching the tangle of a stiff branch. Damn it all! Kristine did the same. Everyone was sitting at the edge of the pool, and they clapped. Good for the both of you!

"Give the bastards their due," one of the rednecks shouted. He whistled.

I took Kristine in my arms and let the night pour into me.

"I have no idea who you are," she said.

"I'm sure we have met centuries ago, in other pools, on other nights, letting our nervous moments pass in silence. This was bound to happen. History demanded it. The centuries have built up to this. I've been thinking of all the chances I have let pass by. But not fucking now."

We crawled on top of the rocky edge, stared into the abyss and jumped. Up we went, into the night, into the midst of the star-filled sky. A celebration of nakedness, all things released. The smell of copulations, completed, surrounding us.

The universe swirled, including us in its stew.

"What you can touch enlightens. There is a time, and there is a place for all things under the sun, but the night has limitless potential," voices around us sang.

I didn't want to leave this place. I wanted to stay here with Kristine. I wanted the night to last forever, to expand.

"You are so beautiful," I said.

"How can you say that?" she responded. "I'm nothing. I can be summoned and dreamed up on any given night, through any whim of desire. You need to find important things that you can dwell on daily with confidence."

We circled the New Mexico sky, embraced by the freshness of the crisp night just over the Jemez tree line. My veins were filled with cosmic Freon, cool, and we streaked across the sky like burning stars, until we finally disappeared.

"Don't be afraid to imagine," I heard a distant cry. And then everything was quiet.

My wife was lighting the candles in each glass. The pool expanded as big as all New Mexico. If Kristine waded over to me, at this point, and started tugging away at my frumpy shorts, I would pull them off and toss them over the side of the mountain in one big senseless act of carnal foolishness, ignoring the impeding consequences, the loss of a seventeen-year marriage and every honest endearment I ever made to my wife, but most of all, the sacrifice of all reason, the very thing I always told myself I valued above all else. The anticipation of sex strips away the noblest of intentions.

Men know what they are capable of and what they are not capable of in their lives. They push their desire beyond all reason. They can be believed in this area.

My conscience rattled in my head like marbles in a tin can. The loudest thoughts are the ones I always suspect. I always doubt my personal bubbles of enlightenment. I always embrace guilt like a comfortable blanket.

I waited for my wife to see my face flushed with lust. I'm sure that I bled with a desire that could be seen in all its naked simplicity. It's the humidity of my sin, and it accumulates.

You looked at that girl.

She sat solidly next to her door, looking through the smeared window of our car as we drove back home on Highway 4, the thickness of the night engulfing our car. The sound of the motor and tires hummed like a melodic condemnation in my chest.

What? She's a theology student.

Don't 'what' me. You know what you did. For God sakes, she's over half your age. Your mouth dripped down past your stomach. You were gawking. Jesus.

I wasn't doing anything.

You were doing it all. Christ!

We were just talking.

Men never just talk.

I moved over to my wife and put my right hand along the side of her bottom and pushed the encroaching desire away, squeezing it out of my mind. She wasn't even paying attention. God, it was hard not to look stupid. In moments like this I felt responsible for every aberration within a hundred years of my touch. The idea of sin had its lock on me. I fought it daily. I had no problem assuming my share of liability for the transgressions that weighed on the world. Jesus didn't have to go through all that trouble just for me. I'd like to believe that there were others who were willing to bear a portion of the load, too. And bear it with conviction. But I was taught that Jesus was a willing sacrifice, something he was obsessed about doing, and my mother always taught me: *never cheat a person out of a blessing.*

The Latin kids continued jumping into the pool, occasional cracks of their voices breaking the night, splash after splash. The rednecks were flushed out of the water, their limp dicks dangling between their legs like New Mexico ristras. Their wet hair was pasted to their faces, and quietly, without a word, they lined one behind the other, crawling behind the rocks, where their dry clothes lay.

"They're naked!" The boy laughed, pointing at one of the rednecks.

"I see their pee-pees!" the little girl screamed, covering her mouth with her hands. Her pink bathing suit hung over her shoulders, the weight of the water pulling her neck line past the small nub of one her breasts. Her thin brown hair snaked down her back. She jumped up and down on her toes like the rocks were on fire with ants.

"Oh, momma!"

"Here goes a big one," the boy shouted, holding his nose, his cheeks bloated like a bullfrog, and he jumped into the pool, splashing the rednecks as they tried to scuttle past him.

The little girl stood next to her mother with her face mashed into her skirt. Her mother put her hands up alongside of her daughter's face. Her father had his hand up to the top of his forehead; a frown covered his face.

"Are they gone?"

"Shh!"

"But I could see their pee-pees!"

"I know, honey," her mother said, patting her back.

The rednecks hurried past the family and hid behind the rocks.

After the little girl calmed down, the mother herded her children silently down the side of the mountain. The father stood in the night looking at the rednecks.

"You should wear some clothes," he said. "It isn't right."

"We're sorry," one of the rednecks said.

"I'm just saying, you should wear some clothes. Some things you should just know." He shrugged his convictions and followed his family down the mountain.

When the father disappeared below the gray stones, John and Luke pulled themselves back out of the water.

The rednecks were drying themselves off and lighting a joint.

"Damn kids," a voice came from behind us.

There was the snap of new beer cans being opened and quiet laughter.

"I know now why they call your penis the big monster," one of the men joked. "You scare the hell out of little girls."

"Why don't you take off your trunks," John asked me.

My wife put her hand up to her mouth, moved over to the edge of the rocks and spit a mouthful of bread over the side of the pool.

"These?" I asked.

"Yeah."

"It's not that I have a problem with my nudity. When the kids are away, I like to let the stallion out of the corral," I said. "It's just that I got about a two inch dick when he's relaxed, and he's shy around company."

Kristine laughed.

My wife slapped my back.

"He plays with it more than he should," she said. "So it's used to company."

John and Luke smiled.

"I know I shouldn't worry about it," I continued. "It's only flesh. It's not like I'm sporting a couple of prunes. But after looking at you guys, man, I wish I were young again. Trust me; no one wants to look at a fifty-year-old man's penis."

"I don't think you are as worried as you appear," Kristine said.

"I'm just saying if this was an art gallery of genitalia, I would be the least interesting canvas in the room, so why go on display. But your penises are wonderful; I would put them on display, too. If I had a penis like either of you, I would walk proudly down any street in America, my tool in hand. Hey, everyone, look at my penis! Clothes are made for the less endowed."

Kristine pushed her body up just enough to show the arch of her breasts. They poked out of the water like two small beach balls. Those impulses raced through me again, and I tried to find sanctuary.

My wife offered her some white Zinfandel.

"No thank you," she said. She winked at me and floated over to the rocks by the other pool. She climbed out of the water, making her way to where the rednecks were smoking pot and cussing about Mexican people taking over the country.

In my mind, tonight was Montezuma's true revenge. But then, I'm a romantic about things like that.

John's dick lay squished between his thighs like an oyster in its opening shell. The lights and shadows in our pool danced off his body. It was difficult not to look at the two boys. They were quiet and waited for anyone to make a comment. I wanted to just stop the whole charade, apologize, and tell them I just couldn't help it, but my eyes had to steal repetitive peeks at their penises. It was all impulse. Maybe, if I could just hold his penis in my hand, feel its texture, study it - get the whole thing past me...

"Yes, this is a fine jewel."

I live in the Pentecost, in the midst of tongues ignited by a match, burning my inner flesh. My thoughts inflame. I believe it is part of the weight, the humidity accumulated from the past. History is laced with a residue that never burns out. It's an eternal flame.

Well, John never succeeded in getting the shorts off my body, but we had a pleasant evening playing with the idea of it all the same, drinking wine and eating French bread and cheese, and watching the candles light up the pool through the colored glasses. The trees danced in the flickering light and created altered shadows of reality: Plato's cave.

The rednecks surrendered their spit and fire to the warm spring night, whispering more coherently, each testing their prowess with Kristine, trying to finger their way into her bathing suit. All she wanted to do was get stoned. She laughed off their advances. And in the end, it was a very relaxing evening, and everyone settled into their perfect place. What more could anyone ever expect?

My wife floated over to me and put her arms around my neck and we sloshed in quiet circles at the center of the black in the pool, walking over each other's toes as they mingled with the slime on the rocks.

Stars poked through the dark blue night, the crest of a full moon trimmed the edge of the trees, and the mountains on the other side of the road were a large indistinct wall of darkness. John and Luke were as silent as mimes, whispering into each other's ears and smiling, touching each other like lucky thieves.

I could only hear the faint whispers of the rednecks talking to each other about work and the new engine they planned to put in an old pickup truck. In the cover of the night and trees, Kristine had slipped back down the mountain. No one saw her leave. I'd never see her again. There was a selfish pain. I tried to imagine her alone, clinging to her vulnerability, as she slithered past all the rocks in her bikini.

I kissed Cyn, fingering the sides of her slightly bulging waist, slipping my fingers under the sides of her bathing suit. Nothing else mattered in the world.

"I love you," I said.

"I know," she answered.

The walk down the side of the mountain was easier than the climb up, though we did have to watch our footing in the night to make sure we didn't stumble or cut our feet on the path, avoiding the rocks that poked out of the ground. The sound of our bodies brushing through limbs woke the night. My wife, always prepared, always the Boy Scout, had brought two small flashlights that hung around our necks by a string to help us determine the dirt trail in front of us. The forest blocked the light of the moon.

We stopped at an old wooden bridge at the bottom of the mountain and listened to the shallow water dance through the rocks in the night, a teasing samba. It was a new language to add to my vocabulary, and it sounded like the tinkle of liquid glass. It helped to thin the weight of the evening, the weight of history. It told me everything would be okay if I just listened.

I watched the water in the night flow between the two banks, managed nature. Without these boundaries on each side of the river, the water would quickly thin and disappear into the ground. It was like my own life; my thoughts needed these same boundaries, places to dwell so they wouldn't bleed away before they could take root in something substantial, find a page where they could breath, secure meaning and a transitory truth.

"This is nice," I said.

"Yes, it is."

We heard shouts. The rednecks came pouring down the trail like a runaway train, screaming, waving their towels and clothes. Ripped six packs of beer slammed against their thighs.

"Whew!"

"Shit!"

"Here we come!"

"It's the midnight train from fucking Georgia."

"We'd better move," I said. We hid in the foliage, on the side of the trail, the weight of our shoulders pushed into the tangle of tree limbs. We stood there silent until the ranting rednecks flashed passed us pounding out the powder of the trail. Minutes passed waiting for the sound of their tennis shoes and boots to fade.

"You'd better watch your step," one of them called out. "The next time, you're going to fall on your fucking face."

"Nice boys," Cyn said.

"The rednecks?" I asked.

"No, silly, John and Luke."

"Oh, yeah," I said. "They have the pool to themselves, now. I think that is a beautiful thing."

"What happened to the girl?"

"I don't know. I never saw her leave."

"I hope she's okay."

I listened to the screams of the rednecks fade the further they ran away from us, back up the short side of the mountain to the parking lot. They threw something over the side into the brush.

A bunch of mean kids, I thought. Big mean kids.

Or, as my wife likes to say, in a nicer way, meanness is unfocused energy. She would say that they just needed to put themselves to more productive uses. She was right.

I remembered the one redneck asking the rhetorical question: does a bear shit in the woods?

What in the hell did that mean? It was a question that floated in and out of my life in odd moments. It was filler talk. I mean, didn't everyone know that bears shit in the woods? It must mean more. Maybe, I reasoned, when we asked questions like this, deep inside, we wanted more than we intended. I've come to believe that none of us really knew as much as we liked people to believe, so we tried to pad our minds with filler, fluff to help insulate ourselves from insecurities. Knowledge was a wall that protected us from being discovered as the frauds we feared ourselves to be. None of it really mattered.

The only place I have ever seen a bear shit was in a zoo, right on a flat white rock for everyone to see.

I saw news reports on the television about bears coming out of the mountains to torment stay-at-home moms and retired women who lived at the northeast perimeter of the city, along the mountain. They looked for food, but I don't remember hearing anyone complaining about bears taking a dump in their yards.

I felt like I learned a little something that night in the Jemez Mountains, but I didn't know how to define it, except to say that the only sin is ignorance.

I used to be angry with God, until I realized that all the information I had about him came from secondary sources. It forced me to go back, try to redefine everything I have been taught. We see through a glass darkly. How profound. And even though it is difficult to define God, we get glimmers of truth. It is safe to say that God, however defined, gives the world its breath.

I did develop a certain acceptance for things that night. New things do happen under the sun. And I hoped that the next time someone asked me if a bear shit in the woods, I be able to know exactly where I stood. But then I'm a romantic about things like that.

The Wedding Dress

He locked the door of his antique shop hard against the rain and wind, his bony hand gripping the loose brass knob like the shaft of a baseball bat. The door wrestled in the jamb, and when he was satisfied that it was secured for the evening, he pulled his jacket against his brittle body and stepped out onto the sidewalk. He kept his clarinet case tight under his left arm, pulling it close to his chest to keep it from getting too wet. He leaned into the rain as it fell in regimented angles like the onslaught of bullets, pushing him back, close to the wall of his store front. He steadied his body, released himself from the grip of the wind and walked down the wide cracked sidewalk of Main Street with a slow tempered pace. It was five o'clock in the evening, and the lights of each business started to dim. Closed signs flipped in the windows, ending the business day.

People raced, chaotically, to get to their cars parked in stiff angles along the brick-laid street, putting shopping bags over their heads and opening umbrellas that poofed out into the wind. The rectangle windows and doors of businesses along Main Street were like a silent blur of the old brown photos found in dusty books that were hidden in the back rooms of the town's library. Their chipped wooden frames and soiled glass panes looked tired and ready to concede to newer times. Their signs were warped, a weary welcome to the tourists, with lettering that faded as fast as their solvency.

All the old man could hear was the slap of water in the street, making exploding puddles and dripping off the faded canvas awnings that skirted each business like a tired sun visor. The doors of each business slammed shut, the sound of metal keys working their way into each keyhole while the whoosh of car tires hushed down the road. The air was thick with water. The dimmed lights from the street lamps reflected off the crazy wetness of the brick. The businessmen gave each other complementary nods as they made their way to their cars, or to the side streets leading to their homes.

"Dale."

"Webb."

It was almost a question. It was all that needed to be said at the end of a day, the tip of a hand in ritual recognition, a courtesy. It was an aging town, tired, locked in the smallness of its world. And it had learned the wisdom of keeping to its own counsel.

It started to rain harder, so the old man stopped under the awning over the window of the library. He peered through the lime-crusted glass at the Japanese wedding dress, a kimono, called a shiro-maku, pinned askew against the back wall. It was white, pure. His wife had worked to put this display together decades ago. There was silk brocade over the kimono called an uchikake, with colorful cranes and flowers stitched into the arm. On a shelf next to the kimono was the wedding hood, called a tsuno kakushi, complete with combs and straight pins. They sat on a small vanity in front of the dress. The wedding kimono lay against the backdrop of cherry blossom pink and there was heavy black calligraphy on the wall, to the left side of the dress which spelled, "A Beautiful Japanese Wedding." A theater rope was placed in front of the display, supported by two brass poles, a warning to tourists not to get too close to the dress. There was a long table with opened picture books of Japanese gardens and Mt. Fuji, nuggets of Edo culture and the different festivals and traditions celebrated throughout the year. Everything about the display was respectful. And it was a curious thing to see in a small Midwest town.

A young woman sat at an old wooden desk, chipped by time, looking through him and out the window as if she were considering the weather outside. Her black hair was pulled back in a tight bun and he could see the hint of Battenberg lace in the collar of her flower print dress that circled her neckline. She pulled herself away from the desk and walked over to the wedding dress display, straightening the arms of the kimono on the dowel which ran through the sleeves of the dress. It allowed the dress to be seen in all its fullness, flat against the wall, and then she stood back to examine her work. She seemed pleased with what she had done. The old man's eyes remained on the woman as she walked to the other side of the library, picking up books and sliding them back into their respective places. She moved slowly, glancing around the library, looking for things out of place, moving in circles, and then she disappeared into the muted light along the back wall.

He didn't remember the rain stopping. There was only the occasional drip of reluctant water from the roof above him and the trees along the sidewalk. He turned to see that the downtown area had become empty. All the lights in all the businesses were either off or dimmed. The flicker of the street lamps waited for the darkness to sweep through the town. He turned back to the library window to notice that it was dark inside. He placed his hand on the glass and squinted, peering through the window, looking for movement, looking for the woman, without success.

The old man and his wife had found the wedding kimono in an antique shop in Chinatown when they were on their honeymoon in San Francisco decades ago. The dress was going to cost them nearly every loose dollar they had with them.

"What about our honeymoon?" he said.

"This is what I want to spend our money on," she said.

She didn't understand, he thought. This honeymoon was for them, not their community; what were they going to do now, walk around San Francisco, looking through windows the rest of the week?

"But what about us?" he asked.

"You are such a curmudgeon," she teased. "This is really what I want. It is so perfect for the library. Please."

He bought it, but it didn't seem like a good honeymoon memory to him.

"Sometimes I just don't understand how women think," he confessed.

"Then don't try," she said. "You need to learn that you don't have to understand everything."

Most of the books on the shelves in their library had become dusty and obsolete. Paperbacks were bloated by overuse. The library dusted up with disinterest. Nobody came to check out books like they had when his wife was a small girl. She didn't know for sure, but it seemed like people just didn't read like they used to. Maybe they were just too busy. Or, maybe, they just weren't interested.

She remembered seeing pictures of the Shinto temples in Kyoto. Everything was green, exotic, manicured with a precision she had never seen before. She wanted to see Mt. Fuji covered in snow and walk across the Ryogoku Bridge in the middle of a rainstorm. She wanted to see a genuine Japanese garden, participate in a traditional tea ceremony, things she had seen in the picture books buried at the back of the library.

The wedding dress would make people want to come back to the library again. She wanted people to develop an appreciation for the beauty of faraway places, give them a reason to dream. It would give the community a certain degree of renewed pride, an exposure to a culture that they would otherwise never have considered.

"Our town is getting too stale," she scolded her husband. "Everything is so expected, boring."

He nodded, never quite knowing what she was trying to say. To him, boring was good.

And in many ways, it worked. Once the display was in place, newer books were donated, and slowly, curiosity started to bring people back to the library, including day trips by the local grade school, if only to see the wedding dress. The bookshelves experienced a new freshness and local people started to volunteer to man the open hours. The city council allotted a greater portion of their budget to its administrative needs in order to keep it a vital part of the community. It appeared to him that everything his wife touched got a dusting of her glow.

When they got the dress home that first night, she couldn't help it; she had to try it on. She scooted her body into the thin dress with a dance, while he watched, and at that moment, he thought she was the most beautiful woman he had ever seen in his life. The kimono pulled her breasts flat against her body, making her look boyish, and she pulled her hair back and pinned it into a bun.

"Does it work?" she giggled.

"You do know that the dress has to go to the library in the morning?"

"Of course I know, don't be silly. Why can't I enjoy it tonight, while it's here?" she asked. "You worry about too much. It isn't going to hurt anything to try it on. Isn't it simply majestic?"

"On you," he whispered. "It is very majestic."

She put on the tsuno kakushi and tilted her head in the full-length mirror in her room. She pushed at her hair to tuck it in under the hood. She applied makeup and powdered her face.

"It's not a costume," he said.

"I'm just playing. Don't be such a bore."

He walked out of the bedroom, into the front room, pulled out his clarinet, oiled the valves, and then put each of the sections together. He blew a string of notes to *Moonlight Serenade*, making sure everything was working correctly.

"Honey, we need to get another one of these," she called from the back room. "I mean, if we can find one. It doesn't have to be an old one."

He continued to work with his clarinet, polishing the black and chrome.

"Are you listening to me?" she shouted. "I want us to get another one of these kimonos. We need to go back to San Francisco, someday. Or, you can take me to Japan. Is that okay?"

She gritted her teeth in hope.

"Yes," he called. He couldn't understand how women could get so wrapped up in things that were so impractical.

She turned to look at how the dress fit her behind. She liked to touch the silk embroidery on the uchikake. The fine thread excited her fingers.

"Honey, did you know that Japan has the most beautiful full moons in the world?"

Walking past the grade school, the old man saw two teenage lovers laughing and wrestling in the aftermath of the rain by a row of willow trees that lined the side of the property. Two of the willow's branches embraced their innocence with its bending arms, and fresh drops of water fall to the ground. The tree's limbs danced around in the wind, which blew the leafy branches in chaotic circles, nudging the lovers into each other. The girl hopped on the boy's back and tried to weigh him down into the mud.

"Stop it," he complained, but she just laughed.

Their bodies twisted like soft taffy, their hair a tangle of wet strings brushing the drops of water across their faces. He slid through the mud trying to keep his balance, his knees bent to find equilibrium while the uneasy slide of his tennis shoes searched the slippery ground for steadiness. She laughed and pushed down harder on his shoulders, hanging on to his neck, trying to make him fall, and finally he gave in, sending them tumbling to the wet ground.

"My mom's going to kill me," he burst. She grabbed a hand full of mud and brushed the sludge across the front of his shirt in swatches.

"There," she laughed. "Now, don't be such a fuddy duddy."

"You did that on purpose," he complained.

"I'm not sorry," she scolded. "You're always too serious. You need to be more fun."

"You want recklessness?" he dared. She just looked at him, smiling. She raised her brow, waiting. "Then, run away with me."

He tried to grab a somber moment. He looked into her white face, cold from the wind.

"I can't," she giggled. "I have to be home by nine o'clock."

"Don't go home. Let's go away."

"Why should I love you?" she teased.

"Because," he said. "I will take care of you."

"What makes you think I need someone to take care of me?" she asked.

"Because, everybody likes to be taken care of," he said. "You can take care of me, too."

She stared into his face like she was counting the seconds, measuring the moments of her doubt.

"You're serious."

"You should put your hair up out of your face," he continued. "You have no reason to hide it from anyone."

"Maybe from you," she jested.

He pushed his muddy fingers through her long black hair and molded it, and then he painted a smear of mud across her cheek.

"Like that."

"Oh, you!"

She slapped him on the chest, and then she pushed herself up, using the top of his head to steady herself in the mud. She pushed him back, and took off along the line of willow trees, slipping across the ground.

"I bet you can't catch me," she shouted back at him. He got to his feet and chased after her until the old man's eyes gave way, and the couple disappeared into the mist that gathered at the back of the school playground.

An old woman put her umbrella to the side, in the wet grass, and knelt before a grave. It was starting to get dark around her. She gathered up the wet flowers that lay in front of the headstone.

"Esther, I hope you appreciate this. It's very wet out here today, and it is cold to the bone, sister."

Her elbows were bent and she pushed small handfuls of limp stems carefully into a plastic bag and then hid them in a larger red handbag lying next to her. She replaced them with new flowers which she laid respectfully in front of the headstone. She looked up and saw the old man making his way past the cemetery. He never stopped to visit the grave.

From the day that Esther died, he never said more than a few sentences to her sister, or anyone else in town, except a civil greeting in the course of a passing conversation. He wasn't rude, just reclusive.

The last time he spoke to Esther's sister was at the funeral. He thanked her for everything that she had done for Esther, everything that she had done for him, taking her hand and pressing it gently. It was heartfelt, and she knew it. He could never have done all the things that were needed for the funeral himself, and he was glad her sister was there to do things right.

She grunted out a little laugh, watching him attempt to sneak past her. He couldn't move fast enough, his small legs were too weak and he could only shuffle his feet inches at a time. He never looked at her kneeling before the gravestone. He looked at the sidewalk in front of him, hugging his clarinet case with his left arm, and shuffling, step by tempered step.

"The old curmudgeon," she whispered. She raked the grass around the gravestone, clearing it of the loose twigs and leaves that had fallen due to the wind. There were more gravestones in the cemetery than there were people in their small community, and the town kept it spotless. A large blue tarp, still up from a funeral earlier that morning, flapped in the wind, close to a freshly covered grave at the back of the cemetery. The ropes at the top of the four poles fought to keep it from blowing away.

She tried to pull herself up, but she was too slow, uncertain because of the wind and the slippery ground. She grabbed her umbrella and pushed it into the wet earth and reached out to grab a handful of uncut grass with her free hand to support her weight. Finally, after a few grunts, standing on unsteady legs, she straightened her bent back, put her open right hand against her chest, and grabbed the red bag and the inside of her black coat. The fireflies braved their way into the encroaching wet night. They hovered low among the sea of chiseled graves. Their hesitant lights blinked and then faded as the darkness dropped over the community. She waited by a nearby bench to watch the fireflies light up the cemetery. They blinked like Christmas lights, bringing tranquility to the park.

"You have light for the evening, sister," she whispered, satisfied with her scrutiny.

She opened her umbrella and pulled it tight against her scarf-wrapped head in case the rain came back. She looked up at the quiet houses across the street, their meek lights peeking through the thickness of the curtains, and then she limped, briskly, toward her own home.

The day Esther died was a beautiful spring morning. She was in the library early, around seven o'clock. She was pouring over its finances and records, the expenses that needed to be paid for the subsequent month, the library books out, the late notices sent, and the maintenance needed to keep their building sound. She felt tired, pulled herself from her stool and walked around the library, straightening the books on the shelves. She picked up loose paperbacks, placed them where they belonged and gave the place a fresh dusting.

She felt a slight migraine pinch in her head and she sat back down. She put her fingers up to her temples and rubbed. *It never hurt like this before,* she thought. And she grimaced. Then she laid her head on the desk and closed her eyes to get a little rest. She lost consciousness, and she never woke up again.

She was discovered by the second grade teacher and her class as they walked briskly into the library, anxious to see the wedding dress and look at the pictures about life in Japan.

"Esther, are you all right?" The teacher called. She walked over to where Esther laid her head. "Oh my."

The old man stopped on the sidewalk in front of his small Queen Anne house, looking at the rapidly clearing sky. The moon illuminated the street. His house sat on a large lot that circled the corner. He stopped to look out over the wet paving bricks. They reflected white shards of the moon. He walked over to the curb, reaching down to touch one of the illuminated bricks, to feel a part of the white, but his body only bent slightly. In each shard, he saw a portal of light that could take him to that other place where there existed the most the night had to offer.

"Honey, did you know that Japan has the most beautiful full moons in the world?"

She didn't think he had heard, but he did. And he remembered. He was haunted by her voice. It was difficult for him to push through each day without her. The world seemed more a dream the older he got, the greater the distance between his memory of her and his day-to-day life.

He looked across the street and saw the young neighbor woman through the sheer curtains that danced behind her opened window. She was in a pale satin nightgown which barely covered her body, and she brushed out the tangles in her black hair. She looked intently into the vanity mirror in front of her. Her head tilted toward the window as she pulled the knots smooth with quick jerks of the hair brush. He liked to watch her shift on the stool, rife with softness, turning and shaking her head, testing the innocence of her youth. And if she saw him, she never appeared to mind, keeping her window open each night, when the weather permitted, sitting on the same stool, brushing her hair, looking into the same mirror.

The distant honking of geese gave the night a sweet song. Their dotted silhouettes moved through the moonlight like a comfortable skiff. The gray clouds, like soiled ghosts, moved slowly with them across the sky, giving the moon room to fill the land below. The night had a chill that found its way through his jacket and stuck to his skin. He pulled his jacket tight and coughed. There were occasional drips of water off the surrounding trees, and except for the dusty yellow lights that blinked through the spattering of houses around the small town, there was stillness everywhere.

He stood in his dark living room. He had thinned the amount of furniture in his house long ago, trying to keep his life practical, easy to maintain, what he felt he needed in the course of a single day, or night. The illumination of the street lamps came through the bay window curtains. In the rocking chair by the window sat a young woman with her hair tied at the back of her head in a bun. She looked up past him and smiled, and he noticed that she held a Japanese kimono up to her chin.

"Esther?" he whispered.

She moved her hand across the colorful cranes and flowers of the uchikake. She drew her soft translucent fingers across the fine thread in the folds of the kimono, pulling it up to her face, and then placing it, quietly, back into her lap. She looked up and smiled, and then she disappeared through the window into the dusty yellow of the antique street lamp. The light flickered as it embraced her apparition.

"We never went back to San Francisco like I promised, Esther," he said. "I'm so sorry."

The town nestled into a sleep that consumed all its nervous energy. It was just a speck in an ever-expanding Midwest landscape. The clusters of houses were surrounded by soy fields, spotted by cattle that grazed just inside the barbed wire fences that inked the edge of the city limits. Their lows floated through the young green stalks and through the open windows like a soft lullaby. There was the whistle of the wind as it blew through the backyard sheds and wood piles and between the planked sidings, pulling away from the houses that aged along with their owners. The limbs on the trees whispered careful thoughts in the softening breeze.

The old man sat on the wooden swing which hung from the ceiling of his front porch. He removed the old clarinet from its case and fixed each section gently together. He licked the stained reed and squeaked out a couple of awkward notes. He stopped and listened to the sweet voices in the field behind his house. It was a perfect peace, the time of the evening he enjoyed the most.

He put the clarinet back up to his lips and blew a couple of muffled notes of *Moonlight Serenade*. His face contorted with a disappointed surprise as he dropped the instrument, and his fingers reached out in front of him. He slipped off the swing to the ground, holding his chest and rolling into the rose bed in front of him. There was the soft jingle of the chains on the porch swing that sang a sympathetic eulogy that floated in the wind and disappeared. The hint of a hum was left in the night air, and it mixed with the humidity of the night, pressing softness on the lives that slept, reminding the sleepy town that with the passing of every moon their world got just a little smaller.

"I want to go for a drive," Monica said. She looked into my eyes like she was trying to see into a dark place. I fought her intrusion, though she certainly deserved this simple courtesy. I had delayed any idea of marriage for months. I argued that I needed to finish the deck in the backyard. It was my single focus. It was my daily obsession. It was my excuse.

Monica was beautiful and smart. But her greatest virtue was her greatest fault; she was very loyal. She deserved better than what I had to offer, what she got daily from me in terms of endearment. Don't get me wrong, we got along very well, which became the glue that kept us together. She tolerated my distance and I welcomed her intimacy, and I tried not to do anything that would disrupt our perfect union. She wore old faded jeans, which fit her like her personality---comfortably. Her blonde hair bounced just above the collar of her blouse, and she liked to wear thin sweaters. She had a calming disposition, something I tried to appreciate. I don't know why I couldn't make myself more available emotionally. I wanted to put my best foot forward, so to speak, but I instinctively held back. She stayed in the relationship looking for something that was not yet given, something implied. She tried to scratch it out, and increasingly, it was something I wasn't sure I could give. She settled into a long suffering that many women endured with her.

"Any place in particular?" I asked.

"It doesn't matter," she said. "I just want to get out of the house and explore. We never go anywhere. We always stay home like two lazy people. I clean the house twice over and you work in the yard. I'm about to go crazy. I just want to drive, go through the desert."

"I'd rather lay the remaining decking boards on the east side of the patio frame. I'm almost finished."

"Adam, listen to me. I'm very worried that this deck is making you unhealthy. You have to pull away from it. I think you need to take a day off," she said. "Try to be a little more spontaneous."

"Spontaneity isn't always a good thing," I said. "It's an excuse to take a path that leads to great misfortune. I see it happening to young people all the time. They just don't focus their energy on the appropriate options in their lives. Look at all the kids walking the streets, lost, because they never considered the end result of their gratuitous whims."

"Nothing ventured is nothing gained," she quoted. She gave a frustrated sigh. "It doesn't mean you have to hide away. I don't think you've had a misspent youth. So get up, let's go do something. Come on."

"Okay, I'll do it for you."

"Thank you.

Adam got all the tools he needed for the day from the small shed at the corner of the backyard. He laid them out neatly over the top of the picnic table and sat quietly, staring into the morning sky and drinking his hot coffee. Three hot air balloons shushed over the top of his house, attempting to alight in the park across the street. The people in the gondolas waved, and he lifted his coffee cup to his mouth and stared past them into the morning clouds.

He stacked his tools neatly on the edge of the finished deck: his reciprocating saw, cross saw, hammer drill, 3/8 drill, drill bits, hammer, socket set, and the bolts and nuts he needed to secure the crossbeams to the deck frame. He had set the pressure treated four-by-fours in two-feet concrete holes a week earlier. He hammered a nail into one of the four-by-fours at about a foot above grade and placed the end of a fourteen-foot two-by-six across the top of the nail; he leveled the board to an adjacent four-by-four and then hammered another nail beneath this end. The two-by-sixes were slightly warped from the rain the prior night, and they bent out like a large hangnail.

"Pressure-treated my ass," Adam mumbled.

He bolted the end of the first board into the four-by-four and had to push the other end in with his knees to get it above the other nail, leaning into the crossbeam while he drilled a three-eighths hole for the bolt.

"Get through, you bitch!"

The old drill bit barely pierced the back end of the second board and smoke came out of the pinhole opening, and he quickly put the bolt into the hole and gave it a hard slam with the hammer. It cracked slivers of wood from the end of the four-by-four.

"Son-of-a-bitch!"

We pulled into the parking lot of a country club just outside the small village of Cochiti about an hour north of Albuquerque in the high desert. It was a beautiful, pristine golf course with waves of green fairways in the middle of nowhere.

"This place has an inspiring view from the lodge," Monica said. "I used to love just coming out here by myself before you and I met."

"It's hot. Maybe we can get something to drink and just relax for awhile." I offered.

She agreed.

"Just so you know, I would have preferred to have relaxed at home."

"Stop it," she frowned. "Make yourself have fun for a change. Stop finding ways to be so contrary."

"I'll try," I said.

We got a couple of iced teas and sat on the brick patio watching tired golfers hack away on their approach shots to the eighteenth green.

I leaned back on two legs of the chair and rocked.

"We had a man crack his head open last night leaning back on his chair like you're doing," a voice said behind me.

"What?"

An old man with a yellow wring-bucket of soap and water and a mop shuffled behind us. He was thin, tired looking. He kicked the bottom of the bucket to move it over and water splashed over the top edge. The wheels got caught at awkward angles, and the bucket dragged. He wore light blue Dickey overalls and limped up to the table next to us, pushing his mop into the bucket, pulling it out and slopping it across the glazed terracotta floor.

"I'm cleaning up his blood right now," he said.

"It happened last night?" Monica asked.

"Yes, they called me at home, but I told them that there wasn't anything that happened to the floor that couldn't wait until the morning to clean up," he said. "It's just blood. I guess there was an ambulance out here and everything. When I came in this morning, I noticed that there was a hell of a mess. Trash was everywhere. It must have been one hell of a party. I filled two Hefty bags, and I'm on my second bucket of water. I'm surprised that his brains didn't spill out over the tile."

"Did he die?" I asked.

"I don't know. But I'm sure he had a few stitches," the old man smiled. He rested on his heels, the handle of the mop secured under his arm, poking up in front of his right shoulder. He took a large cloth out of his back pocket and wiped the front of his face. Then he reached into his front pant pocket and fumbled through his change. He picked something out of his hand and put his money back into his pocket.

"See that?" He said.

"What?"

"It's right there. See." He showed me the palm of his hand and pointed. He moved his shaking palm into the light to catch the natural sun. "See the little chip, right there?"

"I see something, barely."

"Bone," he said. "I think it's from his skull."

"How do you know it isn't a grain of sand?"

"It could be," he said. "It could be a lot of things, but I think it is from the man's head. I picked it off the tile this morning. It was in some of the dried blood."

"And you think it's bone from his skull?"

"That's what I believe, and what I believe is all that counts."

He put the small grain in the front chest pocket of his overalls and touched it with his liver-spotted hand. He moved the mop, sloshing it across a round area on the tile in front of him until he felt he had gotten all the blood he could, and then, he picked the head of the mop up and pushed it into the wringer.

"I'm just telling you, that's all," the old man said.

"What?"

"You shouldn't lean back on the chair like that. You might fall. But you do what you want to do."

The old man smiled, dipped his head politely, and moved slowly away.

"Thanks for the information, Pop," I said. I leaned the chair back on two legs again while we finished our tea. The old man wheeled the bucket to the front of the clubhouse and disappeared.

"Don't you think you should put the legs of the chair on the floor?" Monica asked.

"What?"

"Put the legs on the tile," she scolded. "The man was trying to help. Show him a little respect. You can at least try to look like you're not trying to hurt yourself."

I continued to rock on the back two legs.

"You can be such an embarrassment," she said. She put her left hand up to the side of her face and pushed one of her fingers into her temple.

One of the golfers had just made a wild swing at his ball hidden in the rough along the fairway. He whiffed the shot, and the ball landed in the same rough about five feet in front of him. He was agitated.

"I told you," his friend shouted. "Just play it out into the fairway. The grass is too deep. Play it for a par. Don't try to get to the green in two."

"Damn it!" The golfer shouted.

"Hey, don't listen to me. I've only been in that grass a hundred times in the past," his partner shouted. "It can't be done. You have to lay it up."

The golfer walked up to where his ball lay and took another wild swing; this time he missed the ball altogether. He stood in the rough looking up into the clear blue sky for an answer. The arc of a translucent moon looked down on him. He tried to see past it. He let his club slip through his hand onto the grass.

His partner ignored him, shaking his head. He grabbed his bag, tossed the strap over his shoulder and walked up to the green.

"See you at the top," he finally shouted.

"What is this place doing out here in the middle of nowhere?" I asked. "Who would drive all the way out here to play golf?"

"A lot of people would because of the lake," Monica said. "It's a weekend area."

"There's a lake down the road?"

"They have vacation homes out here. I suppose some people come here for the weekends just to get away, take a rest. Something you might want to consider," she said.

"Well, golfers are funny people," I said. "They love to live in the misery of a moment. I don't think I have that kind of endurance."

"They're just people like everyone else. They just found ways to relax, or at best, to release the tension in their lives," she said. "Everyone has to find ways to mitigate their stress. Are you ready to go?"

"I think so," I said. I lowered the front legs of the chair safely on to the terracotta tile and walked over to where the old man was standing with a putty knife scratching crud out of the brick wall. He must have come back quietly after putting his wring-bucket away.

"I'll put the chairs back where they were," Monica said.

"I guess some people are just plain careless," I called out. The old man turned, startled, then he cringed.

"I suppose you're right," he said, like he had forgotten our previous conversation. "I just try to keep my life simple."

The deck was perfect, though he still had a few decking boards to lay on the east side---one thousand and three hundred square feet of resort living in the middle of track housing. Adam was restless. He looked for details on the roof not addressed, wrote down notes. Once all the decking was in, he could start the waterproofing. The roof over the west side of the deck looked like an A-frame cabin spiraling up to the point of the house.

Adam built a frame against the wall of the house with folding doors and brackets bolted into the brick where he intended to put a flat screen television Redneck Drive-In, he said to himself. The neighbors are going to love this on a late night. The thought of it made him smile. He ran speaker wires through holes in the wall and channeled them to a sound system he installed on the other side of the brick in the family room. Surround sound.

When he got red-tagged about a week after the deck frame was finished, he stormed through the house for days.

"I know who did this," he ranted. "Well, the bastard isn't getting away with it. He's not going to get any satisfaction. Prick! I'm not tearing down that roof frame, and that is final. This bullshit is going to stop. He has nothing."

"Hush, it's going to be okay," his girlfriend said. "Calm down, you need to just work with the inspector. It's going to be all right."

The inspector came out and measured the height of the roof frame, and he shook his head. He let his tape measure swirl and snap back into the casing.

"Cutting it pretty close," the inspector hesitated.

"The grade slopes," Adam said, flatly. "I think you should measure from the base of the house, not where the front of the deck stops. I'm not responsible for providing my neighbor a view. This is track housing."

"Maybe."

Adam watched the inspector re-measure from the grade in the front of the deck to the back of the deck to the top of the pitch.

"Okay. So it is close," the inspector said. "You could have come a little lower. Did you make those trusses yourself?"

"Yes, if you're going to do something, I believe you should go all the way," Adam said. "Too many people do things half-ass. They can never get themselves to go the whole distance. Anything worth doing should be done with extreme commitment. That's how I feel."

The inspector sighed, shaking his head.

"Restraint can be a good thing, too," he said. "Hey, listen, buddy. Take my advice. Make my job easier and your life easier and get along with your neighbor, okay?"

"Always," Adam finally grinned.

"And by the way, you did a great job on this deck," The inspector said. "I'm jealous."

"Thanks."

After the inspector left, leaving a new permit, Adam took it to the print shop and had it laminated, and then he took a ten-penny nail and slammed it through the center of the permit into the support beam of his roof facing the neighbor's house.

"The fucker."

We crossed interstate 25 and connected to a scenic highway called the Turquoise Trail heading southwards toward Madrid, New Mexico, a small town on the east side of the Sandia Mountains that thrived as a coal mining community back in the mid 1800's. Today it sported a huddle of art shops and quaint little hippy stores.

We drove by broken dry wood mining houses with rusted corrugated tin roofs. Gray splintered sheds dotted the ground around each house. Adobe ruins were etched across the high desert like broken rolls of cinnamon. There were huge slices of red rock pushed into the ground surrounded by cholla plants.

Four Hispanic men in cowboy hats gathered around an open fire that blazed into the clear New Mexico sky. They threw junk into the fire: old chairs, mattresses and dried branches, and then they stood back and watched the fire blaze. One of the men grabbed another man by the back of his shirt like he was going to throw him into the fire and they all laughed.

There was a cinder block building that someone was using as a welding shop. Abstract sculptures sat outside, rusting in front of the building. There were abandoned cars and trucks stacked at the far edge of property lines, or what looked like property lines.

Pinon trees peppered the hills like bunches of broccoli. And in the middle of all this budding decay there was a brand new gas station, teeming with customers.

"Not much here," I said.

"The desert is beautiful, even with all the old rusted cars and old buildings. You need to look past the ugly things," she said.

"It looks to me like people kind of messed it all up," I said. "The lots look like garbage dumps."

"The desert, further out, is clean."

"You don't dig through a trash dumpster for a clean biscuit," I said "You go to the store to get a fresh biscuit. That's why stores exist."

"I think if you look past all the trash, you will see a lot of beauty out here," she said.

"Let's stop for a bottle of water. I'm thirsty again."

"You did a nice job on the deck," a voice came from over the back of his shoulder. It was his neighbor.

Adam turned on his circular saw, and angled it into the corrugated roof panel, and sparks spit out of his electric saw like tears of orange fire. When the saw reached the backside of the panel, he snapped off the metal sliver connecting the two halved pieces. The saw coasted to a stop. He pushed his goggles up to the top of his head.

"Thanks," Adam said, and then he turned back to the metal panels, measuring to cut his next roofing section.

"Hey," his neighbor said. "I'm trying to say I'm sorry about calling the city inspector. It was my wife's idea. She was worried about losing her view of the park. I don't really give a damn what you do to your yard."

Adam stopped his work and sighed, like the inconvenience was taking up his valuable time. He took a deep breath.

"Listen. You did what you felt was important to you. It's done. It's over."

"I'd like us to be friends," his neighbor said.

"Good fences make the best neighbors," Adam said. He picked up the tin and turned it over. "The one I put between our properties before you moved in was built to last. So we're good."

"I just wanted you to know I was sorry."

"Accepted."

"What did you use to make those four-by-sixes supporting your roof shine like that?" his neighbor asked.

"Marine spar."

"Oh. Good idea."

His neighbor stood at the railing of his deck coming off the back of his second story bedroom. He looked for something to say. The children playing in the park across the street sent shrills of laughter into the air, mocking him. Cars whooshed by on the street behind their house. The street separated their house from the park. He waited, craning his neck to see the playing children, and then he turned and walked back into his house.

Adam pulled the trigger of the circular saw and flipped his goggles back over his eyes. He angled the saw into the next panel. The noise of the saw alienated him from the noises around him and drowned out the laughter of the children across the street.

A man, standing in front of us, fingered through the pockets of his shredded jeans for the money to pay for a pizza.

"Eight forty-six," the cashier said. She was Navajo, thick through mid-section with long black hair cascading like a fan down the front and back of her body. She looked through the tinted glass of the store window toward the parking lot and into the hills.

The man put wads of dollar bills on the top of the pizza box.

"That's eight dollars. I need another forty-six cents," the cashier said impatiently, chewing on her gum.

"I'm looking, okay?"

He touched the pockets on his shirt and pants again. He ran his greasy hands through his hair. His eyes looked confused.

"I'm short. Can I owe you?"

"We can't do that, sir. You got to have the cash." She tapped her fingers on the top of the pizza box.

"I got most of it."

I reached into my wallet and pulled out a dollar bill and started to roll it into a small tube. I held it in my closed fist.

"Sorry." She rolled her eyes.

"Son-of–a-bitch…!" the man started.

He was getting ready to explode. He pulled at his pockets. Then he kicked the front of the counter with his boots.

"Damn it!" the man shouted. "What's wrong with you people? If I was one of your Indian friends everything would be just fine."

"Hey, buddy," I called out.

"What!" he shouted, breathing hard, ready for a fight.

I tossed him the rolled-up dollar bill. He dropped it, leaned down to pick it up, coughed and scratched his beard.

"Cool, thanks, man," he said. "I owe you."

"No problem."

He hesitated at the counter looking at the candy on the shelf below it. He grabbed two cherry tootsie pops and threw them on top of the box.

"There," he said, looking at the edge of the counter.

"Eight dollars and ninety- nine cents," The cashier said. He looked up and she stared into his face. He threw the rolled up dollar bill on top of the pizza box and the cashier sighed as she unrolled the sweaty bill.

"Come on, man," a voice in the line said. "We haven't got all day."

She took her time to smooth the bill out along the edge of the counter, oblivious to the people waiting in line, and then she rang the sale up on the cash register and gave the man his penny change. The man took his penny and stomped out of the store with his pizza.

When the cashier got to us I gave her a rolled up $5.00 bill. She glared at me, put the bill, rolled up, in the cash register, and slapped the change on the counter.

"Thank you," she said.

"I know he wasn't the nicest man in the world," I said. "But was all that hassle worth forty-six cents?"

"Store policy," she said. "If I'd let him go I'd get my ass ripped for being short in my register. If I'm short three times in a week, it's a write-up. I'm short enough on my register each week as it is without getting fired for charity. I can't count so good sometimes. I try."

I dropped my coins in the little empty bowl next to the register designated for spare change. The cashier turned away and started to fill the cigarette bins.

"Hey, sweetheart," I said.

The cashier turned back around. She had the look of tired impatience.

"It's all good."

Adam woke up early the next Saturday to the sound of noise in his backyard. It was the neighbor throwing furniture over the side of his balcony railing. Each piece he threw hit the patio with a crack.

"How many chairs are you looking to move out to the backyard?" his neighbor called out to his wife.

"Honey, what are you doing?" her voice cried.

"Helping."

"You're breaking all of our chairs," she said.

"I'm just getting ready for company, dear," he said.

He walked out on the deck with a cherry wood captain's chair held above his head. His wife stood at the sliding door afraid to approach him.

"Where do you want it," he said calmly.

"Please," she begged. "Just put it down. We just bought that dining set."

"Okay," he said. He dropped the chair over the side of the railing and it broke into a hundred pieces. "Do we need any more chairs for tonight?"

"No," she cried. "That's enough."

We passed an old red railroad car garnished with a tin patio roof. The roof stood in front of the double door of the car, propped up by four nervous poles. There were old rusted-out furniture frames that surrounded the car and a sign in front along the road which stated *Madrid Cajita Lodging, nightly or weekly rates.*

"People stay in that place?" I asked. "It's got to have the nastiest beds in the state."

"I'm sure there's a romantic novelty to it," Monica said. "Haven't you ever wanted to stow away on a lazy train like a hobo?"

"Sure, when it's moving. Not when it's abandoned in the middle of the junked-out desert. Rats are probably living under the cabin. There is more novelty to sleeping under the stars in my backyard."

"The low mountain hills behind it are so beautiful."

"And the dumpy house behind the railroad car, ready to blow away, well, it is probably inhabited by the Manson family."

"I think it would be cute to stay here on a nice fall evening."

"Good, we'll come back next Halloween."

"Don't be silly," she scolded. "Oh, look. Pull over there. That looks interesting. It looks like some kind of outdoor museum with sculptures. See the sign? Tiny Town."

"Okay."

"And try to be good this time. Please."

"*Why do you have to be such a mean man,*" *the neighbor's wife said. She stood at the railing of her deck with nothing but a housecoat wrapped around her body. Her dark brown hair tangled down the front of her terrycloth robe.*

"*I don't think of myself as a mean man. That's your observation,*" *Adam said. "I can't help any expectations people might have about me. I never asked to be seen in a certain way. I don't owe anyone an explanation for how I behave. I don't do anything to hurt others.*"

"*I told my husband to turn you in,*" *she confessed. She wanted to see a reaction.*

"*I know,*" *he said*

"*He told you?*" *she asked.*

Adam was silent.

"*He just couldn't live with the idea that you might think it was his idea.*"

He's such a coward, sometimes."

"I'm sure he is willing to do a lot more than turn me into the city to make you happy."

She twisted sideways playfully at the railing. She played with the opening on her bathrobe.

"Do you think so?" she asked.

"I'm certain," Adam said.

"And you?" she challenged. "Would you do anything for your girl? She's very pretty."

She stood still, staring down at him, and he stared back. The seconds passed, and then the seconds felt like minutes. He let the head of the hammer slip to his fingertips, the cold metal balancing against his thigh. They froze in their thoughts, just looking at each other, bathing in their guiltless silence.

Tiny Town lay at the north edge of Madrid on a scorched parcel of land filled with debris rehabilitated into new forms of dignity. We stopped in front of a wire fence that leaned its way across the front of the property.

"More junk," I said.

"Hush!"

A woman came out of a punished trailer house at the back of the lot.

"Shut up, Blackie," she yelled at the dog. It was tethered to a stool which was shaped like a large hand with curled-up fingers for a back support. It sat at the side of the trailer. The dog stopped barking and blinked stupidly at the woman.

We got out of the car and walked up to the entrance. The arch over the threshold had fallen into a pile in front of the walkway leading into the yard. I had to push it back up in order to get through the gate.

There was a rickety donation box at the entrance of the yard. Spider webs circled around the top near the opening. I took a five-dollar bill out of my wallet and rolled it into a tube and pushed it through the web into the slot of the wooden box.

There was a river of glass that cut its way across the yard. It glittered in multi-colored monocles. I saw troubled spirits, plastic dolls with cracked eyes, lying between us and the woman coming out of the trailer. They were naked, on their backs, on piles of shards, and

I watched their souls melt into pools of red. I shook my head.

"Now, I'm fucking seeing shit," I said.

"What?" Monica asked.

"Nothing."

"Maybe we should go," Monica said.

"Look past it. See the beauty, honey," I mocked.

"That's not even funny. Please let's go."

"Let's at least see what happens. We already made a donation to the effort."

The woman stopped, walked over to the dog and grabbed it by the scruff of its loose neck fur and shook it.

"Be quiet, Blackie," she scolded. "It's just visitors."

The dog lay in the dust, its lazy eyes blinked, and then it lay its head on top of its front legs.

"There's a lot of glass," the woman shouted, walking up to us "About this time in the evening it starts to look like gold. I'm Tiny. I have a thing about glass."

"There is definitely a lot of it," I said.

"We can't stay too long," Monica said. She pulled her sweater closer to her chest. "It's starting to get cold."

"I made this river years ago; it cuts through the middle of the yard to show simultaneously the danger and the beauty of glass," Tiny said "Every time I get bottles, I crush them up and dump the pieces into the river. So you can say that it is a growing concern."

She was a toothless woman with terrible tattoos that blended into her tooled skin like smudges of ash, and she branded a smile larger than the scar of glass etching its way across her yard. She wore an old soiled tank top and her breasts wilted like bruised pears down the front of her chest.

"The glass is cool," I agreed.

"The whole yard is my therapy," she said. "I find it very cathartic to just create. I can spend hours out here just putting stuff together. I just let myself go."

"I'm sorry," Monica said. "But are you a little crazy?"

"A little," Tiny laughed. She looked into my girlfriend's face There was a huge space between them, night and day, worlds that would never connect; they would never understand each other enough to share an afternoon tea. "I have to ask myself why the hell I keep coming out here every day. Everything just keeps expanding. I just black out when I work and when I wake up it is dark."

"There seems to be a lot of therapy going on out here, Tiny," I said.

Tiny shared a heart-felt smile.

"Idle hands are the devil's workshop," she said. "Though I'm not sure some people would agree. Some people think the devil is very hard at work in this yard."

I laughed.

"We almost missed this place," Monica said. "It's like your yard just rose up out of the desert as we came over the crest. I never remembered it being here before."

"We are always open if I'm here," Tiny said.

"Your gate fell at the entrance," Monica pointed out.

"Oh, I'll have my old man fix that," she hesitated. "Thanks for pushing it back up."

"Do you get a lot of visitors?" I asked.

"Only the curious stop." She stretched her right hand out. It was an invitation to take in the breadth of her creativity. "I hope you enjoy my work."

Slivered dry lumber, broken into kindling, splintered the yard and formed tired doll houses shrouded by moments of crazy impulses: plastic dolls with cracked skulls bleeding dust and the dried bones of cows. Guillotined Barbie dolls lay like croutons across a rusty grid. There was a mannequin's torso sporting a bloodied pair of football pants. G.I. Joes were wired into a chain-link fence.

Monica put her hand up to her mouth.

"Oh my God!"

I started to look around the yard with a new clarity.

"Cool."

There were rusted knives and scissors piercing scattered bones of animals. A stuffed mildewed rabbit was missing its eyes. Broken ladders lay like bones around the yard. There were rusted-out bicycle frames and wrought iron headboards that twisted like dead bodies against the rocks which stuck out of the ground like razors. A skeleton of a swing set creaked in the dry wind. There were tombstones made from twisted metal that littered the yard like abandoned coffee huts.

A statue of St. Joseph, against the front of the trailer, sat on an old veneered table which was peeling apart, and he looked down on Tiny Town with a heavy sigh.

"I guess we should start looking around," I said.

Monica squeezed my hand. It was limp, and I thought, with just a little pressure, I could crush it like an empty beer can.

"I want to show you my new piece," Tiny said. She pointed to the side of the property. Her voice cracked like her throat was filled with resin. She coughed. "Like I said, I'm always working on something new. I'm nervous with energy, always ready to start a different project. This way."

I followed her over to the other side of the yard. There was a barbed-wire fence that encircled a macabre patio with a black wrought iron table and the frame of an aluminum umbrella, missing its canvas. Spent light bulbs were wired around the perimeter of the umbrella. It was all spray-painted a dull black.

"I call it *Better Homes and Gardens*," she said.

She invited me to come into the display area, to sit in one of the chairs. Monica stood on the other side of the fence, shaking her head and looking at me with a whisper of doubt.

"Honey?" I asked.

"That's okay. I'm fine right here," she said.

"There's nothing in here that will break," Tiny laughed.

"All the same, I think I'll stay out here, thank you."

I slumped back in one of the uncertain chairs and pushed back on two legs. It cracked. I grabbed the unstable arms to steady myself and it started to sink into the ground.

"You'll be okay," Tiny said. "It won't fall."

"I'm not too sure. It's starting to sink."

"It rained last night. It's a little wet. Trust me, you'll be just fine."

"I didn't mean to suggest that it wasn't safe," I said.

Tiny's eyes looked like glassy tears and a crazy smile inched across her face.

"My work can be anything you wish it to be," she said. "Just let yourself become."

"Honey, don't you think it's time to go home?" Monica asked.

"In a minute," I said.

The sun started to disappear, and the sky turned as orange as embers in a fire.

"Do the bulbs light up?"

"Only in your imagination," Tiny said.

"Do you sell your art?" I asked.

"Sell?" she laughed. "This isn't the type of art you can buy. This is the type of art you experience. But I'm always happy to do consignments. I can work on someone's yard if that is what they want. My art is intended to reflect each person's needs."

At the back of the lot sat a burnt-out trailer, void of window glass and curtains. Wind blew through the metal corpse like a whistle in a canyon. It looked like it had caught on fire at one time; black flared out around the windows and the inside was ashen, the walls scarred by indifference. The metal siding had streaks of rust like an old can left in a field.

"Cool. Do you live in that trailer?" I asked.

"Yes. My old man and I stay there in the summer."

"You live with your dad?" Monica asked.

"No, I live with my old man."

"It looks like it could use some window glass," I said.

"It's very cool on summer nights. We migrate to warmer parts of the country in the winter."

"You live on the road?" Monica asked.

"Anywhere we can shack out. We're free as birds, man. We live the way we believe nature intended people to live," she said. "We've been doing it for twenty years."

"Together?" Monica asked.

"Sometimes we live together when it's convenient. Sometimes we live separately when we feel like our individual callings are elsewhere. We listen to the whisper of our spirits."

Tiny's fingers wrap over the top of the windowpane, holding on, digging into the aluminum frame. She is naked and leans over an old exercise bike in front of the window. The bike is missing most of its operating parts, including its pedals and chain. Her head is pushed over the cold steel of the handle bars and she holds on, white-knuckled, while there is the push, and then there is another push. There are subsequent violent pushes, coupled by harsh grunts until her body gives up, and semen drips down the inside of her thigh like a grateful tear. Her cheek lies against the cold metal of the handlebars until it warms her skin. She smiles. There is a quiet outside, except for the crickets which provide a serenade in the calm. The black sky is illuminated by a myriad of micro-lights.

The stench of sweat and ash fill the trailer. She can smell the smoke from the fire that burned out her home the summer before. She had fallen asleep on the threadbare couch while smoking a joint. The roach dropped to the littered floor and a piece of paper caught fire.

She hears footsteps backing away. Then there is the clearing of his throat. Spit.

"I can get a pizza if you want," a voice says.

"That will be fine," she answers. She continues to lay there, her wrists resting on the windowpane.

There is a brief silence. Then she hears the footsteps stumble over the makeshift two-by-eight birch step just outside the trailer.

"Shit."

Tiny hears him stumble through one of her displays. A metal headboard clangs like the bell at an anxious railroad crossing. The soft thumping of boots, the cracking of gravel in the front parking area, the roar of the truck without a muffler, and soon, he is gone. She feels like falling asleep, but she can't close her eyes. Her thighs start to dry. She stares out over the occasional glimmer of glass that reflects in the moonlight.

"The glass is always so beautiful at night," she whispers.

"It has taken me years to collect all this junk," Tiny said. "I go through trash cans around town. Sometimes people just dump their trash at the foot of my yard and I go through it like the eager artist I am."

"People bring you their trash and dump it in your yard?" Monica asked.

"Yes. I use it all. I burn what I don't need for fuel. I have a wood burning stove in the kitchen."

"It looks like you had a fire go haywire inside of your trailer." I said.

"Well, accidents can happen," Tiny laughed.

"And you still live here?" Monica asked.

"It's paid for," Tiny said. "A little smoky residue never killed anyone. It's all natural."

There is a place that I tell myself I will never go, a line that I will never cross. But then, I tell myself, "Never say never." And like a newly found conviction, I walk toward the line. I'm obsessed by a desire that pulls me closer to it. I want to cross over into places that I once considered taboo, reckless. I want to be a part of it all--- Tiny Town. I crave something natural and pure, unblemished by the pettiness of my everyday living, my job, my responsibilities. I want to run away from the structures that protect me. I feel the temptation to destroy it all.

Monica moves away from me. She goes back to the parking lot. She puts her hands up to her mouth and stops for a moment by the car and leans against the door. She is aghast, uncertain. She looks fragile.

"Let's go home," I hear her call out. "Please."

I pretend not to hear her voice. I have the keys to the car in my pocket, and she stands anxiously by the open door. Tiny walks quietly back to her trailer, and I continue to stand in the middle of the yard.

Monica reaches into the front seat of the car to retrieve her purse and slams the door shut. She looks like she might stay for a moment, and I'm hoping that she will look back to where I'm standing, but she doesn't. I watch her start to walk away, and I stare through her to the distant hills that blacken. I notice for the very first time that they arch across the horizon, past the highway in smooth mounds. Monica is right: it is really quite beautiful out here in the desert once you look past the carnage. But it doesn't matter to her anymore. She makes her way to the edge of the highway. She looks up and down the empty lanes going north and south, and she waits. I can hear the vibration of the asphalt as a semi-truck pulls up in front of her and stops. There is the scream and shush of the hydraulic brakes. A door opens on the passenger side and she speaks to the man inside. There is a momentary pause as if she is about to change her mind. Maybe she is waiting for me to call out to her, to tell her that I'm coming. But I don't. I think she is confused. I want her to stay, to come back to Tiny Town and share Better Homes and Gardens, but I know she won't. She shakes her head, grabs the side of the doorjamb and pulls herself into the cab. The door shuts, and I imagine seeing the vague image of her face looking out the dusty window back at me as it pulls away, her fingertips making small circles on the window where she touches it.

I pull a wooden match from my pocket and turn it over and over in my fingers. I'm in the middle of my own tinderbox, the unlit match starts to sweat, and I stand in the comfortable life I have spent years creating for myself. I want things to ignite, but I can't quite get there. My mind moves closer.

I look around at the broken sculptures, watching the pricked souls of all those before me working their way through Tiny's cluttered world. The gate has fallen again in front of the entrance. My car is on cinderblocks, aged; the wheels have been removed. All the windows are missing, and there is rust circling the top of the car. I have prepared my life to meet this moment. I look through the others, past all the feelings I have stored up over the years of what I'm convinced is a misspent life. There is room for all of us in this place, those of us who are tired of moving forward, and Tiny's arms are as wide as the entire stretch of night, and she embraces all of us. It is a release that has been coming for a long time. I strike the match and stare at the flame, and then I smile. I'm there. The flame is pure and white-hot. It looks for fuel. I drop the fire, and everything---my house, my deck, the friendships I had carefully nurtured over the years, my job and savings, all the securities I had protected with precious detail, the way I saw myself--- character, purity, and principles, all of it, every image imagined and real, are engulfed by the flames, and I disappear into the river of shards that cut across the yard of Tiny Town.

I waited.

The Continental Trailways bus stopped once a week at the Vanecek gas station, in Mayetta, Kansas, a lonely store on Fourth Street which lay on the ingress of Highway 75. The small store was in decline, paint peeling around the windows and door moldings. The round tops of the metal gas pumps were rusted from the onslaught of wet springs, frozen winters and the Kansas winds that swept across the plains and punished everything in their stream. Nothing taxes the soul like harsh weather.

At one time Vaneceks bustled with activity, being the only gas station for at least ten miles in every direction from town. It was where families came for propane, fuel for their homes, and each fall Mr. Vanecek made his rounds throughout the community and the surrounding area, in his old truck, filling the gray capsule-shaped tanks that set along each property line. Vaneceks was the first stop out of town for those who worked in Topeka and Holton, or farmers, early risers, hidden in their musty winter coats and stained caps, spending their mornings bantering about the weather and complaining about the local politicians, sipping burnt coffee until they were pushed out of the station door by the need to be back in their fields.

But now, it was only used as a momentary stop along the bus lines route, where packages and special delivery letters, and sometimes, restless people could find their way out of town. An occasional farmer still stopped in the aged store once in awhile to buy a canned coke and snack, but other than that there was nothing else to distinguished the station on a quiet day but dusty windshield wipers and quarts of oil that lay on the half empty shelves, things no one bothered to buy now that there was the new travel center on the highway. The pumps hadn't been working for years, and the meters were locked in time at nineteen cents per gallon.

My hand sweated trying not to lose my bus ticket. I gripped it hard and the smooth surface of the ticket went rough and limp, a flimsy rag, and it wouldn't have taken much at that point for it to fall apart completely. I was afraid to have the bus driver see it, its indiscernible letters smeared across the front. There was unease inside me, the worry that he might scrutinize my ticket, it made me nervous. I didn't want him to question my legitimacy, turning me away, leaving me to stand forever in front of this small place.

The trees were stripped of their leaves by the autumn chill, twisting arms holding up the weight of the gray sky. The old highway alongside the gas station was cracked and filled with bubbling lines of black asphalt caulking. The gravel in the parking lot had long ago been pushed into the dirt making it hard, a perfect throughway for the bus. A single street lamp cast a puzzle of shadows, like ghosts, from the branches of the overgrown tree at the edge of the road. It illuminated the tired gas station and the ground and the yellowed grass along the ditch. And when the street light fluttered at dusk, the shadows danced. The windows in the length of the living quarters at the back end of the gas station were bare except for bed sheets dripping haphazardly over bent curtain rods.

I watched the approach of the bus, a behemoth of guffawing metal, the smell of warm, imperceptible fuel filling the air. It made me light headed. The engine hummed and rattled as the bus pulled in alongside of the old pumps, the scream of the brakes bringing the bus to a reluctant halt. I was overwhelmed by its magnitude as it sidled next to me.

A man came out of the shop; it was Mr. Humphrey. He wore pressed khaki pants and a neatly buttoned shirt. His thin body filled his clothes. He looked clean and taut. A pencil was pushed behind his left ear. He didn't recognize me. He was a different man from the Mr. Humphrey I remembered, the man who ran out, half naked, his rifle up over his shoulder to where a dog was lying in the street yelping, having just been hit by a car. I wanted to call out to him, tell him that we buried the poor animal in the midst of the trees, in back, behind our houses, but to be fair, he wasn't the same man. Well, not quite. I was hard to separate the two men, to explain how I knew them both, how they were both the same men, but not the same men, how the ccupied different spaces in my head. I know it's hard to understand.

He was a deacon in our church, sat in the front row with his dutiful wife, nd worshiped God, listening to the sermons of Pastor Flack with the same keen aterest that everyone else in the congregation listened. He sat on the school board, id everything he could to save our small school from consolidation with Hoyt, neighboring town slightly larger than Mayetta and twelve miles to the south. Ie believed the loss of the school would spell doom for our small community, and e was right. As soon as the deed was done, the town noticeably diminished one usiness at a time, leaving scarred buildings punished by a lack of enthusiasm.

He had left a lucrative job with a big company in Kansas City years ago to ive in Mayetta because he thought it would be a great place to raise kids. He ever told anyone what he did in his past life. He always just shrugged and said, tupid stuff." And after both of his children graduated from Mayetta High chool and moved to Topeka to go to college, they looked for greater opportunities n bigger cities. Mr. Humphrey had bought the only gas station in town at the eight of the economy, before people started moving out of the community, before he downtown dried up economically, leaving only a battered bar.

But he hung in there, opening his gas station every morning, until the station educed to a convenience store, and the convenience store became a diminished emnant of what it once was. The community respected him, even though many bought he was foolish for having fought to save something that he hadn't been orn into, something that he came to late in his life.

"It's all been worth it," he repeated when he talked to his thinning customers. nd they looked at him doubtfully.

If he had only asked any of the farmers who hung around the coffee pot t the gas station in those days, before he bought the place, they would have old him, "Save your money for something more meaningful, something worth eeping."

Mr. Humphrey looked up through the bare trees. He sighed and ;ave a quick glance up both ends of the old highway. He put his hands p to his mouth and breathed heat into his palms, and then he pulled is jacket close to his chest.

The accordion doors opened and the driver stepped out into the cool evening. He looked like Pastor Flack from the First Church of the Forgiven Believers except, instead of filling out a black suit and a white minister's collar, the one I always remembered seeing him in, he wore Continental Trailways uniform. He pulled a pipe and a tobacco pouch out of his gray jacket. I moved to the other side of the gas pumps to get a closer look, to make sure I was seeing right. I couldn't believe it was him. I knew these two men, but they were different. Pastor Flack stood as solid as I had ever remembered, just outside the folding door of the bus, near one of the pumps. He looked around the landscape, spying the railroad track across the road. There was a large apple tree with splayed branches next to the rails, bearing bruised fruit.

"I'll get the boxes, Jack," Mr. Humphrey shouted. Pastor Flack nodded. He pushed the cherry flavored tobacco into his pipe, struck match, and sucked the fire through the pipe. A burn of orange lit in front of his face. He shook out the match and threw it on the ground. The cherry smoke competed with the smell of diesel, but I could smell it through the fuel, and it gave me comfort.

The bus idled while we stood waiting. I wasn't sure whether either of the men had noticed me standing there with my bags. I looked at my ticket to make sure I could still see the words printed across the front in the dark. It was one big smear.

Minutes passed, and Mr. Humphrey finally came out of the store, his hands filled with a bundle of mail and two boxes. He put the packages next to the side of the bus.

"See you next week, Jack?" Mr. Humphrey asked.

Pastor Flack raised his hand, nodding his head.

"As sure as a Kansas rainstorm," he said, grinning into the mail.

Both men laughed.

"Ticket," Pastor Flack said, waving me over. I gave him my limp stub and he tore it in half without looking at it, giving me one section and putting the other section into his pocket. He took my bag and set it next to the bus, pulled the chrome handle, opening the undercarriage, and shuffled my bag on top of a stack of other bags like he was pushing a book into a tightly packed shelf. He set the mail Mr. Humphrey gave him along the metal wall of the compartment.

"Let's go," he said.

"I have a duffle bag."

"It's okay. Put it on the rack above your seat."

I boarded the bus and walked slowly down the aisle, mindful of the seats which were occupied. There was a lethargy that hung in the dark of the coach. I was numb, confused. But they were all there, and I blinked. My past and my future, everyone I knew, straight from my imagination, sprinkled across the bus, like bright galaxies under their personal lights. I hesitated for a moment, and I thought about getting off the bus. I didn't think I was ready for this kind of trip, and I started to doubt the reasons why I wanted to go to New Mexico from the beginning; even more, I questioned why these people were here. They should have been locked securely away in my mind.

"Are you on the right bus?" Pastor Flack asked. He looked through me, waiting. He had never let me down before. He had always steered my life along the proper path, and even though this was not the Pastor Flack I grew up listening to each Sunday morning, the man I depended on, I wanted to trust him.

"I think so," I said.

"Good. Why don't you find yourself a comfortable seat, son."

I touched my back pocket to make sure I had my wallet. It was filled with $500.00 in traveler's checks, everything I had saved from working in the hay fields the past two years, everything I counted on to get me to New Mexico. I had everything I owned in one suitcase and one duffle bag. It was all I needed to start this new life.

An old woman in one of the front seats pulled her umbrella to her chest. On her lap sat a box of pink roses. I looked at the card on the top of the box which inked the name "Esther."

"They're for my sister," the old woman noticed. "She lived in Elk City, Oklahoma. I'm going to visit her grave with her husband. He is such a curmudgeon, not much of a talker, but he's a good man."

She had blue hair that shot in bursts out the sides of her knitted bonnet. Her face was liver-spotted with deep lines that cut through her skin, and when she moved her arm up to adjust the light, it swept the air with fragile hesitation.

She had every right to her frustrations because she was not given the proper

role in her life, stripped of any sexual prowess, reduced to a giver of flowers and consolation. There was so much more, she knew, than spending her precious moments suspended over the monuments to her past.

He walked her up to her house three days a week, bringing her home from the meals-on-wheels at the church. He helped her out of the van and she quickly grabbed his arm, not letting him go. She pulled herself close like they had just finished a delightful date.

"If I were just thirty years younger," she flirted. A naughty smile cracked her thin lips. "I would relentlessly pursue you, young man."

"Esther Johnson, are you flirting with me?" he jested.

"Indeed, I am," she said in a guiltless confession.

He always opened the door of her small white cottage, newly painted, as she continued to hold his arm. She invited him to come in and visit, which he politely declined, saying he had other nice ladies like herself to let off at their homes, and she knowingly nodded, letting him go, grabbing the edge of her door trying to find her way across the threshold.

"You will be here Wednesday, right?" she whispered.

"I wouldn't have it any other way, Mrs. Johnson."

It was enough.

There was still rich blood coursing through the veins beneath her thin flesh She could still desire. She still felt the same urges that any woman felt, given the moments to reflect and conspire. Yes, if only she were thirty years younger she might well have pushed herself on this young man, or another man, more attractive. But even then, she was willing to extend herself. She believed she still had a trick or two up her sleeve.

She gave me the hint of a smile, and then she turned toward the window.

Missy's husband, Charles, sat at an angle across from Mrs. Johnson He scrambled through the loose papers that lay beside him in the empty seat. They looked like drawings, schematics. He was agitated desperate. His suit was disheveled, torn from his body. His glasses dropped off his face and hit the floor.

"Damn it," he said. He looked defeated.

He shifted his body back and forth in his seat, knocking papers on the floor, trying to navigate his big frame to bend over, to find where is glasses had landed. He was heavier than I remembered. It made it difficult for him to move with any grace.

"Here, let me," I said.

I bent down and picked up the glasses, and I gathered the scattered papers. They were in my hand like a fan of playing cards. One of the papers looked like a divorce document.

"Thank you," he said. "My wife used to tell me that I was getting too old for this stuff. I'd like to retire, but I'm not sure what else I would do. I'm just a creature of habit. I tell myself I need to start slowing down, but it's hard. Do you know what I mean? Of course, you don't. I'm sorry. You're too young to think about stupid things like responsibilities. It would be so nice to be young again, maybe start a family. Responsibilities---it always comes back to responsibilities with me. Damn responsibilities."

"Are you an inventor?" I asked.

"What?"

"Do you invent things?"

"Why yes," he said, puzzled. "How did you know?"

"The drawings lying on your seat," I lied. I knew everything about him before I even saw the drawings. I created his fragile life. I lifted the papers in my hand. "I never met a real inventor. They look like important designs."

"Just doodles." He smiled, embarrassed. "Most of it is trash. I'm having a difficult time making anything work these days. My wife never thought much about what I did for a living. Take my advice; never marry a women better looking than you are. It hastens your life. It's just too much, especially if you have other responsibilities (hesitant chuckle). Oh well, pretty things take way too much time and money to maintain properly. Time was my problem. Who knows anymore how to choose just the right person for a life partner? It's a crap shoot at best. The smallest mistake can alter your life, terribly, forever. Look at me. Now, I'm scaring you."

"No," I said. I wanted to tell him I understood what he was feeling, let him know that everything would be okay in the end. But how would he be able to understand.

"I really thought we were good for each other. We both brought different things to the marriage: she her beauty coupled with her street

smarts, me my ability to provide. It seemed like a good match. H
chuckled again. What a curse, knowing your only redeeming quality i
your ability to provide---to be responsible, loyal. It seemed importan
enough when I was younger. I'm sorry. But I keep pushing the weigh
of my life onto you. It's not fair. It was very nice of you to help me
young man."

"I'm sure she will change her mind," I said.

"What?"

"Your wife," I said. "She'll come around. She probably just needs
little time to think things through."

"You think so?" he asked. I didn't expect him to take me so literall
I didn't really know. I wanted to make it so. But I couldn't. Ther
were certain responsibilities that went with the use of the imaginatior
like telling the truth. In the end, I was just being kind. But the
again, given the right circumstances, inspiration, anything coulc
happen. The right kind of thinking can change an awful lot.

"Of course she will."

His named was Charles Haden, and he was the high school math teache
in Mayetta, Kansas. Most of the time, he was consumed by his own thought
as he sketched equations on the chalkboard, scratching out numbers, and whe
the chalk didn't work right, he tapped it into the slate like he was trying to ge
ink out of a broken pen. Sometimes, he licked the tip. Then he turned aroun
looking over the heads of his students, leaning back against the chalk tray.

"What is C?" he asked.

There were no takers. They all looked at him, clueless, as he stood ther
tasting the chalk.

"If A squared is 36 and B squared is 16 then C squared is…52. It's th
Pythagorean theory, and it is something that you might use in your day-to-da
life once you get out of high school."

He turned back to write on the chalkboard and everyone laughed. A strea
of chalk dust brushed across the back of his gray polyester pants.

"What?" He turned and looked at his class. And like everything in his lif
he never got the joke, and no one ever told him.

He took the papers and placed them on the seat next to him. They lay there in no particular order, but he was careful to push the divorce papers under the schematics. He put his glasses on the tip of his nose and grabbed one of his drawings, looking up and down the page. Then he looked at me.

"Thank you," he said. And with that, he buried himself in the work in front of him.

I noticed the shadow of a woman against the light that swept through the dusty window of the bus, giving her face a sedate elucidation. The light above her was off. It was Maya, my first crush. A sharp pain wrestled with a bone in my chest. She was middle aged, in a tightly tailored suit. Her hair was cut short and teased, but I still recognized her eyes behind her dark glasses. She reached up with her index finger and her thumb and rearranged them on her face with conviction. She twitched her nose like it itched. She was still very beautiful. She sat in stoic consideration. Her skirt was pulled up above her knees, and I tried to see what I had wanted to see so many years before on that night at the Jackson County Fair.

I never saw her again after that night, and neither did Flip, but we did hear from Debbie that she had left school in Holton to finish her education on the reservation.

Her name was Maya Standingbear, and she suffered the ridicule of her peers, being one of the few Indians in her class, and she was quiet, so she buried herself in her books, and it paid off in the end. She went to Haskell Indian Nation University in Lawrence, Kansas, getting her law degree, and passing her bar after one testing. She wanted to do pro-bono work on the reservation, but instead, she found that she had a knack for contract law. Not the most romantic of practices, but she knew how to focus on detail. She jumped from law firm to law firm, looking for the perfect place to practice, a place where she could wield her skill without having one of the partners sexually pawing her, filling her with promises, incentives on which she placed no value from the beginning.

"You really are a cute thing, aren't you?"

"Excuse me, do you want to fuck me or do you want me to make money for this firm?"

"The problem with you, young lady, is your attitude. Success is all about

attitude."

She was always blunt. At first, it was to protect herself in a profession filled with vigilant junior associates. But later, it was out of pure conviction.

She considered most of the attorneys she knew as sophists, not so much concerned about truth as much as they were with the sound of their own rhetoric patching together the words necessary to get them to a measured end. Her primary flaw as an attorney was her altruism. Being a lawyer took a lot of self-deception, she believed, something she tried to perfect, telling herself that everyone needed a good defense, but it always caught up with her, giving her stomach pains. She had received a call from the Navajo Nation to work on some land issues. She couldn't get out of Topeka, Kansas fast enough.

She sat quietly in her seat; a notebook lay neatly across her lap. She looked entertained by her own thoughts, content to be left alone.

An older man coughed into his wrinkled handkerchief, his left hand raised to his brow. He massaged his temples, pushing his fingers into the top of his thinning head. The tie around his neck was a loosened noose, his shirt pulled away from his chest like he had been grabbing for air.

"Hey, young man," he said. He motioned with his soft fingers drawing me closer to him. "Come here. Let me show you something."

He fumbled through the pocket of his thin shirt and pulled out a grain of sand.

"See that?" he asked.

"The sand?"

"It's not sand, it's bone," he said, softy. "People always think it's a grain of sand. But they never look close enough. I got it from a dead man's skull in New Mexico."

"That's where I'm going," I said. "Albuquerque."

"I moved to New Mexico when I retired," the old man said. "I live near the golf course in the village of Cochiti."

"How did the man die?" I asked.

"He fell," the old man said. "He cracked the back of his head open on terracotta tile acting like a damned fool. There was blood everywhere."

"Are you sure it's the bone from his skull?"

The man smiled. He reached up to suppress a cough, and then he closed his left fingers around the grain in his hand, and he shook it softly.

"If I believe it is, then that's all that really matters, isn't it," he said. He grabbed my right wrist with his other hand. "Believing is a very powerful thing."

He waited for me to say something.

"I suppose," I said.

His grandfather liked to tell him the story about when he was a younger man and he sold the family farm. They moved to California because there wasn't much of a living to be made from the land in Kansas at that time. The farms were getting smaller and so were the towns. He said there just wasn't enough work for everyone.

"We didn't have farm subsidies back then," he said. "We were lucky if we could afford a used tractor. And markets? We didn't know anything about markets."

He packed his family into their sedan and made their way across the country, to Los Angeles, chugging across the cracked two lane highways in their 1949 Buick.

"There weren't interstates then like there are now," he stopped to let us know. "If you ask me, I'd say people complain too much today."

After moving to Los Angeles, he pounded the pavement looking for a job, day after day, but nothing transpired. He had spent his whole life on a farm, he said. What did he know about big city work?

"There were just suit jobs in the Los Angeles Tribune," he said. "Accountants and other paper pushers, I just didn't know much about that kind of work."

Finally, he stumbled into the Carnation Pasteurization Plant. The manager was nice enough to see him, but he could tell that he was more of a bother to the man than he was a prospect. But he pressed him all the same.

"I'm sorry, we're just not hiring," the manager said.

He begged the manager for a job, told him he had a wife and a family, and that he had sold everything he had, his farm and horses to move here, all the way from Burlingame, Kansas.

"We're still not hiring."

"Okay, I'll make you a deal," he said. "Let me work here for two weeks, no wages, and if you like me you can pay me, and if you don't, you can let me go,

and you won't owe me a thing. Just give me the chance."

The manager looked at him, stunned.

"You want to work for free?" the manager asked. He didn't know what to say. "It's just that I don't need anyone."

"Two weeks," he said. "How can it hurt? If you don't want me after two weeks, we are even, and you don't owe me a thing."

"Well, okay, I'll make room for you," the manager said. "But I can't promise you anything."

Neither one of them said a thing to each other when the two weeks had expired and he continued working there until the day he retired. At his retirement, he and his wife moved to New Mexico because he had always wanted to live in the desert. She died three months later. But he stayed.

The old man let my wrist go and shook his head.

"Yes, believing is a very powerful thing," he continued.

A woman wrestled with her anxious son, a pudgy blonde boy, not yet school age. The boy found it hard to stay in his seat for any length of time.

"It looks like you have a handful," I jested, pulling myself away from the old man.

She looked up at me, and I saw the Kristine I knew from years ago in her face. She was now much older than I, twice my age. She gave me an uneasy smile and grabbed the child's shirt, trying to pull him into submission. The boy gave me a blank look as he slithered through her arms and onto the floor. She was a fuller woman than I remembered, thick through her mid-section, but still firm. She tried to pick the child up, but she soon gave in, just letting him slip under the seat in front of her.

"No!" he screamed.

"Luke, hush!" She rolled her eyes. She was nervous. "Sorry. He has so much energy."

She was his childhood love, but he had never told her. The last time he saw her was at her family's new home. His parents had gone over to play pinochle

dle away the evening in small talk, and while they caught up on each other's lives, he and Kristine went swimming together. They were twelve, hopeful and anxious. No one else was in the pool, but her grandmother, who lived with them, strategically made her way to one of the lounges on the patio to chaperone. She ogled them, her eyes following their every move. She knew what young people were capable of, especially when their newly sprouted sexuality just waited to be tested. So Kristine pulled him to the lip of the pool in front of her grandmother, where she couldn't see, and told him to take a big breath and under the water they went. She tried to kiss him; it was all very awkward, but the fact that he tried made it wonderful to him. She grabbed his hand and put it on the nub of one of her breasts as they floated back up to the top for more air.

"Do you want to go back under again?"

"Yes," he said.

"I wish my grandmother wasn't here," she whispered. "Because then we could swim naked. Have you ever gone swimming naked?

"No."

"You would like it."

And he believed her.

I put them all in different pockets, every person I ever met, collateral for the future. I collected my memories selfishly, and I pulled them out when I was needy for a little truth, re-arranged their lives, gave them new names and meanings, like the toys I poured out on my bedroom floor when I was a child, using them for every purpose under the sun, mixing and matching. People can be anything you want them to be if you allow them.

I turned to the right side of the aisle, and I noticed a young woman sitting across from Kristine. Her head was pressed into a small pillow against the cold glass; a quilt was pulled up across her chest. The light above her head was off and she looked soft in the dark. I smiled, as I spied her eyes above the hem of the quilt. I remembered her walking down the hallway of her trailer, her wrinkled T-shirt hanging just below her thighs. She looked up at me and fixed her sleepy eyes as I drew closer.

"Sit down, Trace," she said.

"Thank you." I looked around the bus to see if Mundo or his mother were near. They weren't. Five naked men huddled in the dark, in the last couple of seats of the bus, next to the toilet. Their eyes looked surprised. We stared at each other as I put my duffle bag on the rack above the seat.

"What are you looking at?" one of the naked rednecks asked. Some things just never changed, no matter how hard I tried to arrange it.

"Nothing," I returned. I kept my eyes fixed on the men. "I'm sorry. You reminded me of some guys I met once in the mountains. They were naked, too."

"Oh," the redneck said.

"Did you say something?" Mundo's sister asked.

"I'm sorry," I said. "It's nothing."

"Let me move," she said. "This window is too cold for me."

She shifted toward the aisle seat and pulled her body up, allowing me to shuffle past her. She pulled her blanket closer to her chin.

"Let me get this thing out of your way."

"You're fine."

She smiled. I searched for the pink cheeks I remembered every time I went to her trailer, but all I could see was the ash of the night against her face.

By the time I got comfortable, stretched my legs under the seat in front of me, Pastor Flack was releasing the brake on the bus and we were moving forward, the fly wheel grinded as he started to work his way through the gears on the bus.

I looked out the window and noticed a woman in a loose robe, naked, in one of the lime-crusted windows of the gas station. She had her hand on the glass, her fingers making spots in the dust. She looked distant, waving at someone I couldn't see. The shoulder of her robe dropped and she pushed it back up. Her tear-streaked face looked confused. She seemed caged. People could see her, and I wondered if she stood there each night when the bus stopped in front of the gas station, looking out the window as people readied themselves for their trips, a hopeful goodbye. In all the time I had lived in Mayetta, I don't remember seeing her. I knew everyone in Mr. Humprey's family.

didn't remember her.

She looked like every person, in every small town, who dreamed about getting away, to anyplace but the place where they were. But like them, for some reason, she just couldn't leave. I wanted to put her in my pocket, but there wasn't room. I was sure she knew where every bus that stopped in Mayetta was heading, and I was certain that she waited for the day she could traverse those folding doors.

It was the last image I saw of Mayetta, Kansas, and she became the character that never quite transpired, an unfinished apparition. We moved, and I took the weight of my past and my future with me, past the city limits, to a new place, New Mexico. I breathed in the thickness of the cab; time and place was all mixed together, and I couldn't make out the distinctions between my younger life and my older years. I let out soft breaths of air and listened to my heart pound as I realized that I could never go back to Mayetta, and if I did nothing would ever be the same; so I filed the images away in my memory until they became important again, until they had a new meaning I needed to explore.

"Did you think she was pretty?" Mundo's sister asked.

"Who?"

"The lady in the window, I was looking at her, too. She looked very lonely."

"I think she wanted to come along."

Mundo's sister shrugged.

"This isn't her bus," she said flatly. She turned her head away, jealous. "If she belonged here, she would have bought a ticket. She's not like you and me. We have places we need to be."

"No one remembers me," I said.

"I do."

"Why?" I asked.

I thought I could see wetness around her eyes.

"Because, you're important to me," she said. "Are you okay? You seem somewhere else."

"I'm not sure my reasons are good enough for me to be here," I said.

"Don't you want to go to California?" she smiled.

I looked at Mundo's sister. I wasn't sure I knew what she meant. I was going to New Mexico. The ticket in my pocket clearly stated Albuquerque, New Mexico. I had been looking forward to this trip for months.

"I'm sorry," she said. "I didn't mean anything."

She drew herself up, sitting sideways in her seat. She pulled her blanket up around her neck and slid back down, closing her eyes. And though it was dark, I could see a satisfied smile curve across her face She looked content. I scanned the top of the seats in the bus. Dark heads moved in sleepy nervousness. Click. Click. Lights went off and on like Kansas fireflies on a humid night. And my memories lay back restful, without knowing where their journeys would end, finding their place for the night.

The big bus fought the road for miles, its massive engine, chugging pulling us along through the thick air. I didn't think it sounded very safe, the grinding of gears, the heaving of the engine, the weight of the bus's wheels scraping at the road. But it kept moving forward accumulating, always accumulating, and I believed, with Pastor Flack at the wheel, it would get me to where I was going. Moving forward was always the best thing, even if I didn't know for sure where I was ultimately going. It was always important to push ahead.

I looked out the window into the starry sky. It was wide, and the night cleared the further south we went on highway 75. The more the land flared out as we left Mayetta, the more I thought about New Mexico. I imagined crisp mornings that thinned as the day grew long. I thought about skies dabbed with cotton-white clouds, circling a line of low desert mountains. I believed the air to be fresher than any place I have ever been in Kansas. I wanted to live in a cabin in the mountains, in the middle of evergreens, a secret place to hide away.

There were scattered beads of light in the bus. There were people who just couldn't sleep, who were restless, reading magazines or working crossword puzzles. I saw the radiance of the green light on the bus's dashboard shine up into Pastor Flack's face, and he stared stoically at the road in front of him. He was entrusted with a cargo that he was determined to deliver. He always had that same certainty in his face. Confidence. It was a look that I had learned to believe in, to trust. The bus settled into a treaty with the road beneath its wheels. I listened to the hum of the diesel engine. I tried to sleep, but I didn't want to miss anything on the other side of the window, no matter how dark it became outside.

Nothing gave me a greater sense of being alone than being with a group of people huddled together in the night, especially when no one said a word, protected only by their fragile thoughts and the small spaces that separated each of us. It was the prayer that filled my head--- please don't let anyone hear what I am thinking. I listened to the sound of the wheels, like a Buddhist prayer wheel, and I reflected. Mundo's sister was right. All of us had places to be.

About an hour down the highway, the old man stumbled down the aisle of the bus toward the commode. Inside, I heard him coughing and spitting. His body slammed against the thin walls. Then there was silence. There was an uneasy shuffle in the seats at the back of the bus.

"Shit." I heard one of the naked rednecks whisper. There were a lot of sighs.

"Puke," one of the rednecks laughed. A light stench from the back of the bus tickled the air. People pushed their noses into their blankets and coats. Mundo's sister pulled her quilt up over her head without the slightest discomfort like this was nothing new to her, just a simple adjustment. She had spent her whole life making simple adjustments. I knew. It's the way she lived, the way her family always lived, moving from trailer to rented trailer, every day filled with new starts and new hopes. Her life had always been thick with human proximity. It stuck to her no matter how much she tried to clean it off her skin. She was raised with the idea that she needed to adapt, or disappear.

The old man floated back to his seat, bumping into the shoulders of passengers along the way, stopping to catch his balance and grabbing his chest. I heard apologies as he stopped along the aisle. He made it to his seat, but it took a long time, and he dropped himself on the cushions of empty seats along the way. Finally, pushing himself forward, he threw himself into his own seat with a soft grunt. He continued to suppress his coughing, embarrassed that he had wakened people from their sleeps.

Luke finally surrendered to the night, his head pushed comfortably into Kristine's lap. I imagined him floating amongst the stars, in the ever-expanding night, the touch of his mother's hand making his dreams dance. He looked content. Her head was thrown back on the back of the seat, her closed eyes pointing to the roof of the bus. She looked like she had finally exhausted the full volume of her energy. Her hand clenched the back of her son's shirt.

"Would you like to share my blanket?" Mundo's sister whispered. She reached over and touched the side of my face.

"You're cold," she said.

"I'm fine."

She pushed the blanket up across the front of my chest like she hadn't heard a thing I'd said. I reached up with my left hand and pulled the quilt behind my left shoulder. She leaned into my right shoulder, putting her right arm across my waist and fell back asleep. I lay there with my eyes wide open, looking out the window into a sky that was bigger than any sky I had ever seen, stars stretching into an endless stream of crystallized shards. It was a sky filled with infinite possibilities, stories, and I wondered how big it could get. Was there enough room for everyone who had ever lived to fit in my pocket? The lit night went on forever in front of us, making a trail, a way up and out. I smelled Mundo's sister's soft scent, and I felt something inside me swell.

"Are you awake?" I whispered as the sun broke over the flat horizon of the northern Texas panhandle. We had just entered the Amarillo city limits. There was a small scattering of sleepy cars on Interstate 40, dipping in and out of the frontage road.

"Hmm, is it morning?" Mundo's sister asked.

Her tousled hair snaked across the front of her face. She smelled damp with sweat. And after a brief recognition of the morning, she pulled the quilt back over the top of her head.

"Leave me alone," she mumbled. "I want to sleep."

We had stopped in every small town in Kansas and Oklahoma the previous night, and I had sat in my seat, listening to the idle of the big bus at each stop while people got off and new ones got on and Pastor Flack joked in the late night rime, smoking his pipe, the new passengers unpacking and putting bags on the bus. When he was ready to leave, I listened to him hit the lip of his pipe against a nearby pole.

cleaning out the loose embers, laughing, and then he pushed it back into his coat pocket. I let the whoosh of the closing and opening of the bus door lull me through the long night. It was like the background chatter of my childhood home, the muted laughter of my parents with friends, playing cards late into the night, while I tried to sleep. I always spied the line of light from the dining room coming up the hallway into my room. It made me feel safe.

"Amarillo!" a voice said. Pastor Flack was gone. I somehow missed the change of drivers under the cover of the night. It must have happened while I drifted in and out of sleep. I felt abandoned, and the journey was now less assured since he was gone. "We're going to be in Amarillo for about an hour if you'd like to get off the bus to stretch your legs and get a quick breakfast. There is a small café next to the bus stop."

"Hey," I said, shaking Mundo's sister. "Wake up. Let's get something to eat."

"No," she said.

"Come on, I want to buy you something to eat before we leave again. You need to eat something. We might not stop again until we reach Albuquerque."

She pulled herself reluctantly out from under the quilt. She looked like she had just come out of a blender. She rubbed her eyes. There was a shuffle of people at the front of the bus.

"Pastor Flack is gone," I said.

"Who?"

"Folks," the driver said. "We are going to be a little longer than we planned. We have an emergency situation that needs to be taken care of before we can leave again, so please leave your personal belongings on the bus. They'll be okay, and be prepared to depart in two hours, instead of one."

"Two hours?"

The bus filled with disappointed sighs.

Smokers hurried off the bus to light up cigarettes. They stood separated from each other, blowing smoke into the clean sky, looking in different directions, blinking through their morning yawns.

Mundo's sister stood, pulling herself up by the tops of the seats on each side of her. She let her quilt drop in a pile on her seat.

"There," she said.

I saw that she was pregnant, not full-termed, but showing enough to know, and she lumbered to get into the aisle of the bus. She pulled her shirt down over her stomach, putting her arms in front of her. She looked embarrassed. Her face was pale and rough. Her hair was a tangle of dirty blonde. She wore an oversized T-shirt over polyester stretch pants.

"Hey, buddy, fuck her, I did," one of the rednecks laughed. I turned around, and they were gone. The back seats of the bus were empty.

"Did you hear that?" I asked.

"What," she said. "It's too early for me to hear anything."

We walked up the aisle of the bus and the driver was standing in the row with the old man, waving people by. The old man lay slumped in his seat, his eyes closed, his neck bent against the side of the bus, his left hand clenched in a fist.

"The poor man," Mundo's sister said. She reached behind her and grabbed my hand. She squeezed it tight.

"Hold on to me," she said.

"Move along folks, please," the driver said.

Trace didn't believe it was fair. He had been asked to give the eulogy at his grandfather's funeral because he had thought about being a minister at one time in his life. His family was proud of him, but his grandfather had always said he didn't believe in religion. He never talked about God and he never allowed talk about God in his house.

"I don't know what I'm going to say," Trace said. "Grandpa wasn't a Christian."

"Is that what you believe?" his father asked.

"I don't know what I believe anymore."

His father hugged him and asked him if he wanted to pass on the eulogy. He told him it was okay if he did pass because it was a tough thing for anyone to do. He said everyone would understand.

"You don't have to do this."

"No," Trace said. "I want to. I think it is important that I stand up for my grandfather. I just have to figure out how."

"Good."

When he saw everyone gather around the grave, it made him nervous. His hands shook. His grandfather's casket sat on a frame just to the side of the freshly dug hole. There were big clusters of flowers huddled under the tarp near the podium. It was a sunny day, and everyone stood outside in hats and sunglasses.

"My grandfather was a very good man," Trace said. "He was responsible and knew how to take care of the people he loved, his family and his friends. He was the man I most respected in my life. He had what I'd like to call character and dignity. And make no mistake about it; he rests in the arms of God."

Trace's voice started to break apart, his arms shook, and it was difficult for him to pull his emotions together in order to finish the eulogy. He tried to push words out of his mouth, but it just didn't happen, and his father had to come up and help him to move away from the podium.

"No, wait, I want everyone to know," he said, holding to the edge of the podium. "Not only did my grandfather believe in God, he believed in a better God."

He looked out over the heads of everyone that had gathered. People took off their sunglasses and rubbed their eyes. Everything seemed much easier after that. All the things we think we believe, in the end, he thought, tend to disappear when we bury someone we love.

Maybe it was something I knew all along, but somehow, I didn't bother myself to say it the night before. No one asked the old man if he needed help or volunteered to walk him back up the aisle. No one told the driver that we needed to find the nearest hospital. The old man's coughing the night before was a death throe. We all knew it as we all listened, helpless conspirators, sharing the moment, hoping it would go away. The death of others is such an inconvenience. It's how we think, in our head, and it's a sin that is easily hidden, except in the deepest recesses of our conscious.

The bus line would wash his seat down for the next passenger. The grain of bone he held in his hand would fall when they pulled his fingers apart and disappear in the dust that built up on the floor. Bone, sand, it was all the same.

We stepped off the bus, and I saw nervous Andy handing out small handmade packets.

"Poems," he said, reaching his hand out to people as they exited the bus. He was wearing new jeans and a pressed T-shirt with a peace sign on the front. His hair was longer, and it was pulled back into a pony tail. He wore wire-rimmed glasses. He had a leather pouch that hung off his left shoulder filled with these packets. He handed me one: *Poems* by Andrew Swann. He pressed each person with a confidence I had never seen in him before. There was a small group of young men and women surrounding him, college kids, with signs that made comments about freedom.

Choose the right to be.

Freedom lost can never be regained.

Question Authority.

"Thank you," I said. I pushed the small book of poems in my back pocket. I would read them later when I was alone.

"What is it?"

"Poems," I said. "The man is just passing out poems."

"Why would someone pass out poems?"

"I don't know."

He was a painter, an artist, who bought a small house near the railroad tracks in Omaha, Nebraska. He gutted the house, took out all the walls that divided the house into rooms, and hung gypsum board along the remaining walls. The rest of the house was laid with treated oak flooring, and it shone like a sea of glass. He hung his art and the art of others on the walls. His house looked more like a museum than it did a home.

He preferred women, but he never liked to make distinctions in his sexual proclivities. He collected sexual experiences like he collected art; beauty always enflamed the passions of the beholder. He had parties at his house on the weekends, gathering every type of person he knew to see how the evening unfolded, and at some point, he'd always disappear into the only room in his house with walls, his bedroom, while the intensity of the evening escalated to its peak, then quickly diminished.

Andy met her on a warm summer night. He didn't remember inviting her, so she must have come with someone he knew. He noticed that she was lost, standing alone, looking at a painting of a little girl dressed in a red dress reaching and floating toward a yellowed moon. Bubbles filled the night. The little girl's face illuminated the room. The woman pushed a handkerchief up to her nose. She had red hair, and it fluffed down the back of her blouse.

"You're looking way too long. It's not that interesting," he said.

"It makes me think of my childhood, my dreams" she said. She looked distracted. "I'm sorry. My friend and I got separated. I feel a little lost."

"I like to see everyone having a good time at my parties."

"You're Andy Swann?"

"Sometimes," he said. "I'm not in trouble, I hope."

"No."

"Then come with me," he said. They walked out into the dusty night, across the scraped lot, straddling the rails, hopping from railroad tie to railroad tie. She laughed when her feet slid off the side of the glassy rail. And her hand went up to her mouth.

"I have lived here for five years, and I have always wanted to make love out here on these tracks under the lights," he said. She spit out a laugh.

"Surely not now?" She looked around and pushed her right hand up through her thick hair.

"Why not?"

"It's very light out here. It looks almost like daytime. And I don't even know you. You're being very presumptuous," she stammered, shooting out the reasons. "Someone could see us."

"Exciting, isn't it?"

"And what if someone sees us?" she asked. He took her continued questions as her way of looking for a reason to say yes.

"They will have something wonderful to talk about when their lives are too boring to talk about anything else. It might even save a marriage or two, give them a secret to protect. Or, they may hesitate and remember the whole thing as some prickly dream."

He gave a light tug at one of the loops on her jeans.

"There are always reasons to say yes," he said. "And there are always reasons to say no, in my estimation missed opportunities. But of course, I'm not being very fair. We are strangers. You don't even know me. We should go back up to the house, find your friend. You can finish looking at the rest of the art."

"No," she quickly offered, pulling him back.

"You don't like my art. I'm devastated."

"Please, no. It's not that," she assured him. "You will just leave me for someone more interesting once we get back, and I will be left alone, again."

"One should never have sex just because they're afraid to be left alone. I know people do it all the time. But ultimately, it's very destructive behavior."

"I'm not afraid."

They looked into each other's faces. Nothing else needed to be said. They pulled the clothes from each other's bodies, and then they lay along the cool rail naked, and created a memory they would never forget.

Mundo's sister ordered a bowl of dry cereal and a Pepsi. She fingered through her Lucky Charms, picking out the marshmallows. She plucked one into her mouth while looking up at me, taking sips of her Pepsi after each bite. I ordered eggs, sunny side up and runny, and coffee.

"It's a terrible thing to see a man dead on a bus," she said.

"Does that type of thing happen a lot?" I asked.

"What?"

"People dying on the bus," I said.

"I imagine it does," she said. "This is my first bus trip. Why?"

"I never seen a dead man in public before, only at funerals," I said. "I didn't know what I was supposed to think."

"I don't think you were supposed to think anything, Trace," she said. She looked concerned. "People die. And sometimes they go away, which is like a death. I think when people go away it hurts even more because you know they are alive and you will never see them again."

Mundo's sister looked into my face.

"Listen, you don't have to do this," she said.

I looked at my eggs torn apart on my plate. I put my fork in the middle of the leftover food, along with a used napkin.

"You think I'm embarrassed?" I said. "Well, I'm not. I don't let what others think make me feel one way or another."

"You don't owe me anything," she said. "It's not your baby."

"Please. I told you I was taking you as far as New Mexico."

"New Mexico?" she asked. "You're not going to California?"

"You don't know?"

She let out a frustrated sigh.

"Hey, it doesn't matter. You never promised me anything. I'm just glad you are here," she said. She looked drained. "Listen, I want to tell you something. I'm not even sure who the father is. Does that shock you?"

"I don't think about it."

"I can stay with my mother's sister in California. I'm not looking forward to it, but I have options. It's just that they already think I'm the biggest slut in the family."

"I don't think your family thinks that," I said.

"Thank you for being next to me last night, Trace," she said. "I needed that."

Everyone was gone: Mrs. Johnson and Charles, Kristine and Luke and Maya. The new faces who took their seats were people I didn't recognize, ordinary looking people, people I would forget the moment I stepped off the bus. They were people with whom I had no history.

Only a little girl captured my imagination. I had been afraid to talk to her the night before, and she was still on the bus, like she was waiting. She pushed her small body into the wall. She was by herself. Her long black hair tangled down the front of her torn dress that dusted up around her. She wore old soiled red shoes with broken buckles, and she clenched a bottle of bubbles that she pushed into the lap of her dress. I stopped in the aisle.

"Do I know you?" I asked her. Mundo's sister walked back to our seat without stopping. I heard her body drop with disappointment. She pulled the quilt back over the top of her head. I sat on the edge of the empty seat across from the little girl.

"I don't think so," she said. "I'm not supposed to talk to strangers, especially grown up strangers."

"I'm not so grown up," I said. "But I do have something I want to give you."

"I'm not supposed to take anything from people."

"You'll be able to take this."

I walked back to my seat, pulled my duffle bag down and dug through it for the box of chocolate-covered cherries, a present from my little sister for the trip.

'Don't eat them all the first night," she scolded. "They will make you sick."

Then I took the cherries back to where the little girl sat.

"Where are you going?" Mundo's sister asked.

"I'll be right back."

The little girl sat tucked into the back of her seat.

"Here, I got these for you. It's a box of chocolate-covered cherries."

"Daddy?" she whispered. "You're supposed to be dead. You were hit by a big truck."

"It's hard to explain, princess," I said. "But I promised you these chocolates."

It was crossing a line. It created a confusion that I knew would be impossible to reverse. I lay the box of chocolates on the seat next to her.

"But you're too young to be my daddy," she said. "Something's not right. You're fooling me."

"I know this seems strange."

She dropped her eyes, looking into the opened bottle of bubbles on her lap and smelled the liquid soap.

"Do you want to smell the bubbles?"

"I can smell them from here, princess," I said. "They smell wonderful."

"I love you, daddy," she said. "I want you to come home."

My heart sank.

"I can't, princess. I wished I could," I continued. She shrank into her thoughts, into her bubbles. "Where is your mother?"

"She's sick," the girl murmured. She scraped her shoes on the seat in front of her. She stared at the toes. "I'm going to see my auntie in Albuquerque."

"I'm going to Albuquerque, too," I said.

"Do you know my auntie?" she asked.

"No."

"Are you sure you are my daddy?" the little girl said. It was a revelation. She was confused. Nothing fit the way it was supposed to fit. "How could you know me, if you don't know my auntie?"

"I never met her," I said. "Maybe someday I will."

As we neared the New Mexico border, I began to see desert. It was the most beautiful span of land I had ever seen in my life. It was just like I imagined it. It was paradise, at least to me. It was like a huge empty canvas. It would be so easy to disappear into the vast spaces I saw out the window. There were sparse rolling hills, torched by the sun, and they were dotted by the ruins of adobe buildings and trailers, long in disrepair.

Mundo's sister turned around and lay on her back. She placed her head in my lap.

"I like you a lot, Trace," she smiled.

She reached up and pulled me down and kissed me. She put her tongue between my lips. It had a sweet stale taste of cereal.

"Is that okay?" She asked.

"It's okay," I said.

"I don't want to lose you."

I looked up and a man with long blond hair and a beard was sitting in his seat sideways, staring at us. He was taking up both seats in his row. He looked like he had a broken nose. His right arm rested on the back of the seat. In his right hand he had a crooked branch that looked like it had been ripped off a dead tree. He tapped it on the back of his seat. He gave me a friendly nod when he noticed I was looking at him.

Mundo's sister scooted up and put her small pillow against the side of the bus. She pulled the quilt over both of us, up to our necks. She grabbed my right hand and pushed it up her T-shirt and over her ripped bra.

The scruffy man smiled like he knew what was happening.

"It's okay," she said. I touched the top of her bra and then moved my hand to the side to feel the softness under the foam pad. It was a softness I had always wanted to touch when we were younger. We looked into each other's faces. "I want you not to be afraid to touch me, Trace."

"I don't want to hurt you," I said.

"Why would you hurt me?" she asked.

"I don't know," I said. "People always get hurt."

"Sometimes you think too much," she said. "You need to learn to just let a moment happen sometimes."

I pulled my hand out from under the quilt. I wasn't sure if she was real or just another one of the characters I tucked away in my pocket. I felt confused.

"Did I say something wrong?" she asked.

"No. It's just me. I think my arm is falling asleep."

I looked out the window and watched the landscape pass by without taking in the details. Glimpses of what looked like real things flashed past my eyes: old cars, metal sheds, rusted trailers, and signs. They were indications of the images I was already creating, fading in and then out. The world was all mixed up. Mundo's sister looked like she was about to cry.

"I can't make you like me," she said. Her words skipped in their enunciation.

"You don't have to."

She looked in my face for assurance. She didn't know what was going on.

"It's not you," I said. "It's something I'm going through. I have to work it out on my own. I can't trust my feelings. I think I need to talk to that little girl again. There's something I need to do, something unfinished. I just can't let it pass by me."

"What little girl?" Mundo's sister asked.

"The one we passed when we got back on the bus in Amarillo."

"I don't remember a little girl."

"You walked right past her. I stopped. Remember?"

"No, you walked me right to our seat," she said. "Trace, are you okay?"

I pulled myself up, moved past Mundo's sister, and ran up to where Kristi had been sitting, and she wasn't there. The box of chocolates lay open on the seat, and there was a half chewed piece lying in the gel in its fluted paper cup. It was a perfectly good cherry, unsoiled. I let her get away from me. She was right here, and I let her get away, again.

"She's gone, Trace," the scruffy-haired man said.

"That's impossible," I said. "We haven't had a stop since we left Amarillo."

"True." The man shrugged. He looked up to the front of the bus. The images of the desert poured through the tinted window, racing to the side of us. They were like an endless barrage of arrows in flight slicing through the air moving around us. "Then where is she?"

"I don't know."

"Have you noticed that all the people you know disappear or change?" the man said.

"Yes. What's going on?"

"I don't know," the man said. "It happens to me all the time, too."

"It's driving me crazy."

"I've been giving it a lot of thought, and I think maybe we are making room for new people."

"New people? That doesn't make any sense."

"I have learned that the truth never makes any sense," the man said. "You make room for new people, and when they have filled out in your head, done what they were intended to do, you move on to other people. I can't explain it any better than that. People are always coming and going."

"So maybe she was never there from the start."

"Oh, I think she was there. At least in your mind."

"I have these thoughts in my head," I said. "They never leave. They just expand, and they don't stop."

"And you don't get any rest until they come out in some way," the man said.

"Yes," I said. "Do you know who I am?"

The man shook his head.

"I know everything about you," he said. The two of them looked at each other. It was like repelling magnets pushing each other away. Clarity can be so uncomfortable.

"Are you me?" I asked.

The man was silent.

Tap, tap, tap, the murmurs in my chest ticked like a warning sign and all the reasons and all the excuses and all the meaning poured through me in one big revelation. All things converged.

"I'm afraid," I said. "I'm not sure what is going to happen next."

"Everything is going to happen next," the man said.

"I don't know what to do. It's all too much," I said. "I think I'm supposed to be that child's father. But I don't know if I can do it, I'll just walk away later."

"Why will you walk away?"

"I don't know. Maybe I don't know how to stay."

"It's something you can at least try."

"Try? I would make a terrible father. I mean, look at us."

The man wore a ripped overcoat. His jeans had frayed slices along the legs. His hair tangled in knots along the back of his neck. He hadn't shaved in months. Deep creases were etched across his face.

"So why do you want to walk away?" The man asked.

"Because, it will change everything, and I don't think I want any more changes. Things change enough already. My world is already too unstable."

"You are right---everything changes. And in spite of what you do, you will never be able to do anything about it," the man said. "Even if you hid away in the desert, by yourself, away from everything, in a cabin, things would still change. Look. You're constantly creating life. Even alone, you would still continue to create new life. It's something you do. I think it's something everyone does, without even knowing it. We people the world around us."

He pointed his stick at me and squinted one eye.

"We create life?" I asked.

"Yes, like God creates life, but differently," he paused. "It's not a good or bad thing. It's just what it is. It happens every time you think. You can't stop thinking."

"Why do you have a dead tree branch?" I asked.

"It's my tool. I use it to point at the moon when it is full. I stand out in the middle of an open space at night, and I aim the point of the stick right at the heart of the moon, and I create something," he said.

"That sounds pretty silly," I said.

"Yes it does, Trace," The man said. "It's a game I learned when I was kid. Do you remember? You point at the moon with a stick and cough, and then you take the stick and draw in the dirt. You draw the world the way you want it to be, and then you invite others to join you. I never understood the potential of this game until I got much older. Of course, I don't draw the moon in the dirt anymore. But I do draw it in my head."

"I remember," I said. "I always thought that was a stupid game."

"I don't think it is stupid anymore," the man said.

"I'm not looking forward to getting older."

"Why?"

"I don't feel like a very good person," I said. "I feel like I make all the wrong decisions. And I can't see it getting any better."

"I think that it takes a whole lot of living to figure out something like that," the man said. "Don't be so hard on yourself. So far, I'm very happy with the way we are turning out."

"What do you mean," I said. "Look at me---you."

"It will all make better sense later."

The bus screeched to a halt in front of the Albuquerque bus station.

"That was quick," the man laughed. "Who needs an airplane? Cross country buses are where the real people dwell. Don't forget it."

"I need to get my bag and say goodbye to the girl I'm with," I said.

"Her name is Linda Scott, Trace," the man said, soberly. "She is real. Go back to your seat and get to know her better."

"But Albuquerque?" I asked.

"This is where I get off," the man said. "Your life is in California."

"My ticket stub says New Mexico."

"Look at it."

"It's too messed up, I can't read it." I pulled the stub out of my pocket and all the smears were gone. The ticket was smooth, brand new. It said *Los Angeles, California.*

"Why do I need to go to California?" I asked.

"Because everyone ought to go to California at least once in their lifetime," he said. "There are things to see in California you will never see anywhere else, different kinds of people, lots of them, living desperate lives that need to be told. There are spaces to define in California. It's a good place to find out who you are. It is a good place to see where you are going."

The man stood and gave me a short wave.

"I wish I could touch you, Trace, shake your hand, hug you, but there are rules. You understand? It's those damned laws of physics. Sometimes the empirical world is just a little too rigid for me. But that's our job, isn't it, to loosen them up a little, give people different ways to think," he said. "So, just keep doing what you're doing."

He pointed his stick at the ceiling in the bus, closed one eye, winked, then laughed. "I wish I could tell you about all the wonderful things you are going to experience, but that wouldn't be fair to you. Well, I'd better move along. It's far from over for us, Trace. I'm glad we had a brief opportunity to see each other."

"Will I see you again?"

"It's a crazy world," he said. "One can never tell. Time is really getting mixed up out there. Things are accumulating thicker than ever before. History is compressing. I can almost touch it. It's really heavy with life. If you pay attention, you might see things that will surprise you, like now."

He walked slowly up the aisle of the bus. The bus driver smiled at him like they were friends, and he tipped his hat. He was already welcoming his new adventure.

"See you later, Johnny," he said to the bus driver.

"It's always a privilege, Trace," the driver said.

And as quickly as he blew into my life, fate swept him out onto the streets of Albuquerque, New Mexico. I couldn't wait to get there, but I knew I had to be patient. One day I would have the opportunity to be everywhere. I just needed to learn to be in the moment, like Linda said. It was hard.

I walked back to my seat where Linda waited for me. She had been crying. She tried to brush the tears from her face. She tried to be brave.

"I've decided to stay, Linda," I said. "I've always wanted to see California. I think I know a place there I can get a job, a milk plant. I will try to take care of us. But I can't promise anything."

"That's all I can ask."

"Don't tell me the moon is shining; show me the glint of light on broken glass." - Anton Chekhov

It starts with the clip-clap of a notion, conceivable only in the weaker moments of my predilections, when I cast caution into the windless sky and believe it will fly. It comes when I'm caught between an immoveable resolve that lingers in the humidity of my day and the places I fill for just the short periods of my impatience, and it carries me through to the ever-thinning warmth of a welcome.

Even the worst obstacles are ninety percent air, or so I'm told, and I count on it, blowing my life past them like smoke through a fluted net, allowing me to fabricate further inquiry. The lighter I live, the more it takes to push me down. It's an address I can accept in this flustering wind, being swept from a bus into a crisp New Mexico morning, rife with a thinning sky. There is the shuffle of busy people, frantic to find the places they fit, crowded in the random slices of the seconds they have. They wedge themselves between concrete bookends on the quickly disappearing ground. They look up to these tall buildings, these monoliths of ingenuity, which were designed from the beginning to be permanent storage. They are wide wallets to hide those who struggle for a calmer acquiescence.

And in the middle of it all a brown-bodied evangelist in his loin cloth rattles his reasons, shaking the glass between us and him, to crack open an indifferent misfortune. He preaches in public forums on saving your stool, the chicken soup of the soul, for days, for nights, in these convenient times when eclectic pursuits spin through the imagination like a disappearing fog. He knows how to mitigate the weight of his own sun.

I float better than I stay, and when the nervous weather around me bleeds on these misdirected streets, filled with coats that dwell too long for my liking, then I can do nothing but back it all up just a little with some unconventional lore. I stand under awnings that fit like heavy hats, and it's a doubtful comfort, but not enough to make me consider the costs and the strategies that trip past me in turns that take me down, to a damper bed, where men spray their faces with paint until they float, a demise I could never anticipate.

We live one wall away from a bed of dirt, and our desperation collects all the new ways we can gauge the greater distances needed to separate ourselves from the caves of our past, and we pile wood and gypsum so high we can hardly hear where we have been. Our walls grow thicker with each careful accounting of the gold and deferments we have squirreled away for a grayer day.

I have been pushed into the night on numerous occasions, wakened by fears I could never share, and my mind travels hundreds of light-years within the limited boundaries of my fingertips in order to elbow for a larger portion of this scattered surface, circling verities that never play their way to conclusion, and I never find the solid sand I was promised as a child. I leverage all my talents against a contrary wind. And I build castles in my head. They give clarity to the voices that carry me to deserts of considered temptation. Desperation always fills my gluttonous cup, and I learn to drink it alone.

Nothing is as hopeful as an Albuquerque sky settled in a bowl scooped out of the mountains and peppered with the colors of a paint tray on any particular October morning. It's a delightful diversion to get everyone to look up, higher than the blue in the clouds. There are only a chosen few who rise on these occasions, clenching their cash in white-knuckled hands and reluctantly letting it fall like spent confetti. They look from the heavens at the flecks of used landscape below, and their judgments spill over each gondola like the virga on a somewhat rainy day.

Given the minutes I have been allotted to spend on my reflections, I choose hills that never quite rise high enough to be seen for what they pretend to be, rounded shards of a promise, diluted by a lack of information. It's easy to drown in the spittle of an eternal moment, a neo-Platonist circle, dense with experience, but ignored. It excludes all those who are unwilling to wait in line for their own calculated enlightenment. I stack layers of discarded attentiveness on the idea that I will one day finger the nub of this flustering thing before me, a nervous clitoris waiting for a tickle that never comes. Each decision I make is leveraged against a greater cross that overwhelms me. I save my hours for more important endeavors, and I always find myself wanting more.

I collect slivers of chance that I put into my pockets like loose change gathered from a broken couch and spent on long shots that rain back on me like a thousand budding assurances, each with its own grand story. I beat out the same old tired pavements, morning after chimerical morning. It is better to spend my precious illusions on what is never meant to be than to dwell on what persists. How do *you litigate the terms of a reality that persecutes your every willful inclination?*

Some things I just can't hide from; they are unbending, and they diminish my dubious stature, illuminating my weaker sides. I find ways to give the gods their industry, assure their misguided directions, but I always blacken my face at the most inopportune times. It's essential to my survival, to find ways to make eager my chances, and to mitigate my odd variances. They solicit greater advantages on the most normal of days, and it is hard to keep them at bay; I supplicate for the preservation of my smallest breathing moment, playing to the confused attention surrounding me. I'm very good at finding a little slack in my own noose.

We all have our inside jokes; they are many, and they gain us little satisfaction, but like a solid truth they endure.

I follow the aristocracy to the top of ladders I will never see, but not without an infrequent reward, a deserved coin I flip at my closest indulgence. I never did trust a slippery handshake on a sunny afternoon.

I wake each morning filling my glasses with eyes that see days ahead, past signs that bring on the advent of a world without end, and the means to accomplish it. I keep my heart with all diligence and find it lacking.

Keep the change, I demand. It's the only charity I can afford, and I tell anyone who will listen that I can find my own miracles, thank you, through these cryptic voices that rise out of a latter-day fire and spark the beginning of the real new world that has been hidden in stoic hesitation for centuries, just waiting to have its vicarious way. Hard hands feign lust to escape the joyous harps of Moses song, and there isn't a humbled one among the throng, save a lamb mixing mercy in the dust, and he was sheared.

If Hades could breathe sweet rebukes, then wouldn't the air be fresher than we ever believed? The devil's promises are a great buzz in the midnight rime, and there were times I believed him. If the tears of my misfortunes could whisper a nuance, there would be kisses blown at all these desolate vessels that rise to any contrived occasion, lined single file in their own diminishing horizon. I want to see them chance a row of sixes between their ears, just for luck. They have earned their reward through committed enterprise.

I have been lured too easily in my past, in these hardened times, with promises made out of the dust I breathe. I hear angels falling into holes they will never escape. Their screams are muted and forgotten, their wings seared decades ago.

I have swum through the soot of this glass sea, this city, cut by a fallen flame, shards all, and reasoned that it is better to temper familiar whims in times when the sacred seas seem so small.

My will is as tight as a string being pulled into the darkened sky by a paper kite. I can only wait for the rip of that paper, the snap of that string, but it is stronger than I can ever relate to my own efforts. The circumstances built around me are made to endure.

A man scoops me out of the downtown mission to help him move furniture and I bathe in the salvation. I knew if I waited long enough, the wheel of progress would eventually rake me out of the side streets and into a more desperate condition.

I'm eating alphabet soup, and I count each letter to make sure I am getting a fair shake. He asks me what I think of the flashes of opportunity that come my way. I tell him it is enough for me to just cling to the shifting sand I am given, hands firmly burrowed into the terra, waiting for a wisp of wind to carry my name. Twenty-four hours a day is just too fast to live a daily life, contention he accepts as the perfect condition to include me in the surface of his successes. He hands me the set of weighted keys to his box truck and asks me to meet him in a distant place I can only briefly remember. Forgotten plans can always be revisited in the desperation of a ticking crisis. It's important to be fast on your feet in these relentless times.

It's funny how the worst of circumstances can shift in the twinkle of an eye and rise without notice. They are always rapturous and diminish in the thinning air.

After he leaves, I dangle the keys in front of a woman I notice curled in the corner of the mission kitchen. She succumbs to imaginary enemies that court her like an itch between her ears, and she says she admires the way I wield my many indiscretions like a brutal imperative. She obliges me her long forgotten world, and I ask her if she wants to come along for the interim. I am always weakened to shell out a reward I can never afford. She casts her caution into a windless sky and hopes it will fly. What could go wrong? We are only going to deliver a truck filled with dubious cargo. We will be back in plenty of time to forget we were ever needed.

We drive up Interstate 25 like a pair of loaded dice, and we tumble through the flecks of pinon trees that slumber like lazy green sheep on each side of the road and across the rolling hills. We finally come to an abandoned parking lot, in an abandoned mall, nestled in the lower mountains, suspended between the two great promises of New Mexico.

I tell her she is going to have to hide once we get there, that this is a singular effort. There are spies, hiding, looking for my considerable stumbles of incompetence. I have to protect my precarious circumstances, for sure. She's not having any of it. This was her time to rise above the lack of confidence usually accorded to her delicate situation. I hear the egg crack. She slaps the dashboard of the truck and challenges my resolve. There were promises made, she demands, and it becomes obvious to me that she starts to see through all my indiscretions and lies. We mingled assurances, she maintains, dipped promises in our own blood. She screams so loud that the world is convinced that I have done her wrong. She looks for my conscience to leak, to drip with shame, and it does.

It doesn't matter to her that with every promise comes a condition and the smaller the promise the larger the condition. I make her get out of the truck, and I point to a huddle of bushes on the other side of the parking lot. There are greater problems at hand, and hesitant assurances had to be confirmed before we could feast on our deferred inclinations: there will be plenty of time to gather the spoils of our diminishing dreams, filled to the top with broken chips that dust up with the lightest touch.

She starts to swear, spitting out all the reasons she never trusted my circumstances from the very beginning. Men, she accuses, never change, no matter what universe they inhabit.

This is just one in a long series of her known devastations. She can never quite keep her disasters together long enough to fall apart with dignity. Emotions have their own language. And she is fluent in hers. I am embarrassed for her many scattered ways. How can anyone ever tunnel themselves out of this pile of expectations?

I miss those vulnerable moments of my past when I used to embrace almost everything newly formed like the innocence of a newly born pup. It was nothing in those days to touch a flame, burn a finger or two, scorch a toe, and not take it personally. But smaller flames become blazing torches that ash the world around me. And so, I collect the fortitude necessary to walk away, far away, daily. I know how to level my expectations in these relaxed days.

I tell her I will be right back, maybe second thoughts away, and at an appropriate time I will collect her from behind the bushes and whisk her away to our already collapsing dalliance. Her sharpened fingers already pierce my better intentions.

I can't be an earshot away from her many thundered curses before she sneaks back into the truck, turns the key, grinding the gears with all her disappointments, and in one big burn of rubber, scratches out of the parking lot with all the dubious cargo. The back latch on the truck snaps like a dry twig, and the back doors slap open, a perky wave, furniture slipping out onto the asphalt like the tumble of dirt clods, falling apart before my eyes.

I watch the owner of the box truck pull into the parking lot, passing the crooked line of broken furniture. There is black smoke behind him. My future starts to melt like wet sand under my feet, and I can see my nuts in his eyes.

The next day I sit at a table in the downtown mission eating alphabet soup, and I count each letter to make sure I am getting a fair shake. Each day I linger, and I find that there are missing noodles that used to spell my name. My options thin with each frightening performance. It's difficult to accept that I could disappear so quickly.

I spend too much time on my knees and not enough time on my toes, looking over to other places where the air clears the spaces my thoughts used to occupy, hoping this time I have enough sense to pay for the crimes I commit against myself, and they are numerous. My feet never fit into the shoes handed to me the way they were intended. I always have to squeeze them between the narrow truths I have never embraced. Our gods are fed to us with miniscule confidences.

Days later, I meet a man selling paper cups filled with their own wax on the street for one dollar. I marvel at his ocular successes, and he flirts with the passing women, who remind him with every rejection that careless girls always slip free from the touch of a corpulent hand. He carries this knowledge high above him, a bag full of bullets, waving it like a broken promise, and everyone laughs as he staggers across the cracks of his own thinking, drunk. I pray for the dulled attention of everyone walking by us, and he ruminates through his dissipating thoughts like a tight balloon rolling across a bed of pins. This man could kill someone, and it is difficult to watch him bleed dry tears to capture the last threads of his own dignity. But at the end of the day, he manages to collect a pocketful of change, mend his bruised emotions, and promises to show me the city while it is still relevant. He takes me to the places he used to work, like the small butcher shop on the corner of a smaller place where he washed floors and stacked boxes. The people in the neighborhood soon remember him and his cringing ways, and they tell me stories about how he tickled a tit or two in his time, in the early morning clime between his multiple distractions.

When we get back to the mission, he tucks his daily Bible under his arm to use as insulation in the night, and when he is bored, he pinches through the pages for an odd job that he soon forgets. He sleeps with a contentment that *evaporates into dreams.*

The sidewalks grow sticky with people I will never loosen from my thoughts, but I try.

My first contacts are always the most important in this new real world, but they quickly disappear the moment they loom larger than what I can believe. So I try to walk away, like I did in the past. Sooner sunsets are always a welcome relief.

And finally, this is the moon, a circle in an ever expanding sky to point a stick at and cough. And it illuminates everything that bursts out of the ground to make itself known.   It comforts the places I stay, cupped by landscapes that blossom in alchemical wonder under the unsteadied hands that draw them.   It smiles on the foolish victories I claim in my life that fall from my brow like drips of unnoticed sweat, and it rewards each protected lie I tell with slices of hope that pour out into small glints of stardust that explode like rays of speckled light. It engulfs everything that the night can never offer.

I want to share in the secret of these limited successes I see surrounding me. They have the hook of a promise, even though I know they diminish with each stepping moment. I desire a substance that will take me to the final place, to my quiet moment.

Words are like paint that splash color in the cracks of my life.   Bleeding doesn't have to be such a bad thing in the end.   Release can be everything I ever hoped it would be.

Selah.